I0770488

Baker Lake

ᖃᒪᓂᑦᑐᐊᖅ

By

Gray Taylor

0

4500 B.C.

Nuna Sila ᓄᓇ ᓯᓚ **Island of the Souls**

Qamani'tuaq ᖃᒪᓂᑦᑐᐊᖅ **Where the River widens**

Sanavik ᓴᓇᕕᒃ **Nunavut**

The full moon made things clear as the ten males and seven females completed the circle around the image of Sednamaroq. The ancient talisman stood slightly higher than the naked figures surrounding it. Carved from a material that the Homo sapiens believed to be the bone of a large animal, the three-dimensional image portrayed a creature that modern humans would see as a mermaid with the head of a wolf. An offensive bastard of Sedna, who protected the deep waters around them, and Amaroq, the great wolf that hunted alone and protected them from anything wandering around in the night. The statue of Sednamaroq had always existed in this location.

The people, who would one day be called Inuit, held a duty to protect the image of Sednamaroq.

The seventeen beings surrounding the totem were the only ones of their people who knew the location of this sacred object. The people had always known that the image could heal. And that it could kill. It must be respected and not abused. Using the powers it contained was reserved only for those who now stood in a circle around it. They were called Qaujimajatuqangit'sila, the council of the souls.

At the base of the statue, the body of a young female had been arranged in a tight circle. She was covered in the white fur of the great bear. The white of the fur was streaked with red as her life fluid left her fragile body. Her hands were loosely tied to her feet so that her body appeared to create an altar between the ground and the upturned fish tail of Sednamaroq. The young female was the daughter of the leader of the people, and her eventual offspring would be crucial to their survival. The unfortunate attack by an unknown animal had left her close to death, and the council knew that Sednamaroq would save her.

Each member of the council lifted their right foot and placed it down firmly to make a sound on the earth. They each repeated the action with the other foot. This action was continued, right foot, left foot, right foot, left foot. The circle started to turn counterclockwise as the rhythm continued and increased in frequency. The sound that resembled the beat of a skin drum developed to a single pulsing sound as their feet moved faster and the circle turned.

With a slight stirring at the base of the statue, the circle stopped. The motion of the feet started again slowly as the movement reversed, picking up speed quickly. The body of the young female started to rise from the ground, turning in the opposite direction of the movement of the council. When her body reached the mouth of the great wolf, it ceased turning, and the council stopped turning with it. The world was silent as the moon illuminated Sednamaroq, which glowed softly with a blue light that emanated from the space between the being and the body of the young female. The light grew stronger until the brightness blinded those in the circle. Then the light disappeared. The body of the young female had returned to the ground and was writhing, trying to escape the bonds that connected her hands and feet.

One of the council members, a female, rushed forward and removed the strips of hide that had been used to bind her. The others moved forward, closing the circle into a tight knot around the girl. They pulled back the white hides of the great bear, and the young female's eyes were looking up at them with fear. She struggled to move from under the weight of the remaining hides and reached out her arms to the female who had loosened her bonds. The adult female held the younger one in her arms, moving away from the circle that was gradually dispersing. As they moved the young female into the moonlight, they carefully examined her body. The marks and deep gashes from the animal were gone. Her skin was pristine. There was no evidence that anything had happened to her. Satisfied with the actions of Sednamaroq, they returned to the mainland and to the rest of their people.

1

1916

Nuna Sila ᓄᓇ ᓯᓚ Island of the Souls

Qamani'tuaq ᖃᒪᓂᒃᑐᐊᖅ Where the River widens

Sanavik ᓴᓇᕕᒃ Nunavut

John Seagram had been tasked with establishing a trading post on the shores of the large lake. The natives called the lake Qamani'tuaq, which, his interpreter had said, means "where the river widens." This made sense to John, since the lake incorporated access to rivers at both ends. This feature is why he was here. Establishing a trading post on the lake would allow the movement of the furs to a wider area for trade and distribution. The Hudson Bay Company was focused on expanding their reach in Canada's far north, and he was one of a small group of men chosen to take the company in this new direction. His success in this venture would determine the overall success of the company, and he was driven to make himself invaluable.

John, along with his assistant William and their guide Akiak, had made the decision to explore an island just off the shore. According to Akiak, the island was called Nuna Sila, which he translated as 'island of the souls', and his people are forbidden to go there. With great difficulty, John and William had convinced Akiak to go with them to the island, providing a rationale that he would honor his people and their purpose by being present to protect any Inuit artifacts from desecration by the white men. Ariak agreed, thinking to himself that he would rather be present to protect any sacred items from being taken by John and William than allow them unescorted access. They were explorers, and he knew they had a strong sense of curiosity. His job was not only to help them communicate, but also to guide them in the ways of the Inuit.

The three men boarded the canoe that William had obtained through a complicated barter and pushed off from the shore. They could see the island ahead of them, and the journey would be short. The surface of the lake was like glass, slick and fluid as it moved silently beneath the boat. The sound of William's oar in the water was enhanced by the noise of birds in the distance and the slight wind that blew at their backs.

The landing on the island was easy as John jumped out of the front of the canoe, almost causing it to capsize in his excitement to explore. William and Akiak followed, pulling the boat fully onto the rough shore and then carrying it above them to the line of trees where it would be safe until they needed to return to the mainland. John led the way, pushing through the underbrush to see what treasures the island might hold. He was hoping to find a new animal whose hide he could trade to the French. Something not previously seen would make him rich beyond his wildest dreams. The French were always looking for something new. Last year, he had killed a bear with an anomaly of beige splotches on its fur. The hide had earned him enough wealth to fund this current expedition without having to barter for supplies. A new animal altogether would be the highlight of this expedition. Nevertheless, any abundance of animals whose hides he could trade would be beneficial.

By the time William and Akiak had joined John, they had spotted several minks and foxes, the furs of which were more valuable than the abundance of beavers and hares. John could see that this island would be profitable for him and the company. In a short time, William had killed a mink and had taken it back to the canoe. They would skin it and preserve the hide when they returned to the camp. John would use the hide to show potential buyers what he could deliver, without letting them know where he got it, of course.

William took the lead and pushed through a particularly difficult section of plant growth. He stopped suddenly, and John almost fell onto him. John looked past him to see a black bear with two small cubs. This was not good. While the black bears were usually not aggressive, a mother bear with cubs could be particularly dangerous. John motioned for Akiak to remain still.

The mother bear looked up, noticing the three men. She quickly moved in front of the cubs and raised on her hind legs. William backed up slowly but tripped over John, who was standing directly behind him. The mother took the commotion as aggression and rushed towards them. John scrambled to the right, standing to his feet and waving his arms to distract the bear. The mother was not deterred. She fell on William with a passion for protecting her offspring. Her inch-long incisors clamped onto William's left shoulder, holding tight while her razor-sharp four-inch claws tore ferociously at his torso.

William screamed. It was unlike anything that John had ever heard. The pitch of the sound was high and gurgled with the blood that poured from his mouth. Chunks of William's chest flew to each side as the bear shredded him, finally releasing the grip on his shoulder and taking new purchase on his throat. The bear pulled back, ripping the entire front of his jaw away from his body and dropping it to the side when she realized that he was no longer a threat.

Akiak stood motionless, frozen with fear. The mother bear stood and advanced on him. He turned to run, but it was too late. By the time the mother clawed his back, her thirst for the blood that would protect her cubs was insatiable. A single swipe down Akiak's back separated his spine from his ribs, leaving him paralyzed and helpless. He fell forward, his face buried in the soft dirt as the bear finished him. As he died, Akiak knew that this was his punishment for setting foot on Nuna Sila and for willfully bringing others with him. Giving in to his fate, he allowed himself to reunite with the earth.

John watched in horror as the mother bear brutally killed the two men. He turned to run. In his confusion, he ran in the direction that they were initially headed. He ran towards the cubs. As he passed the young bears who playfully looked on as their mother protected them, the mother perceived his direction as an additional threat.

She took chase after John and caught up to him within seconds.

Before the bear caught him, John emerged in a clearing. He kept running towards an object that he did not understand. Even without his fear, he would not have been able to comprehend what stood before him. A pristine white statue stood in the center of the clearing. As the bear attacked him from behind, she pushed John closer to the object. Pain coursed through his body with each slash of her claws and bite of her teeth as he focused on the statue. It had the tail and body of a fish, but the head of a wolf. It looked as if it were carved from bone, but what bone would be large enough to accommodate such artistry?

The blood pouring from John's mouth coursed down his chest and splattered up into his face, making it difficult to focus on the statue. His pain subsided as his vision blackened. The mother bear was almost done with him. One final swipe of her massive paw pushed John into the object. His body collapsed, one hand attempting in futility to grip the tail of the fish. His brief contact with the tail caused his body to shift. As he fell, he landed in a fetal position with the statue against his belly.

John died with the peace of one who had found a treasure, knowing that no one else will know about it. His last breath caused his body to spasm, his hand extending forcibly out and landing on his knees as he died. His body formed a perfect circle around the base of Sednamaroq.

2

1916

Nuna Sila ᓄᓇ ᓯᓚ Island of the Souls

John Seagram opened his eyes and quickly closed them again. He brought his hands to his face to defend himself against the mother bear, even though he knew that she would take his life. He braced himself for further swipes of her powerful and sharp claws, which never came. He opened his eyes once more, squinting at the bright sun that prevented him from seeing more than a blinding white directly in front of his face. The tension in his body released as he realized that the bear must have thought him dead and continued her journey with her cubs.

He moved his head from side to side to see if he could adjust his eyes to the sunlight that continued to blind him. As he turned his head to the left, he saw a glimpse of trees and sky. It was then that John knew the blinding light was not coming from the sun itself, but rather from the reflection of the sunlight on the white object an inch from his face. He pushed himself back in panic, scrambling away from the grotesque image of the fish with the head of a wolf. He called for William. There was no answer. He called for Akiak. There was no answer. Then he remembered their fate. Conflicting emotions flooded him as he stood to his feet, steady and sure. He did not know how he had survived the attack. For that, he was grateful. Overshadowing his own well-being was his immense sadness in the brutal death of the two men who had trusted him to lead them.

He was alone.

He looked down at his clothes. His wool tunic had been torn to shreds and barely remained on his body. His leather belt and cross-strapped harness hung to one side; the thick leather having been severed in twain by the bear's claws. The furs that he had been using for warmth were scattered in pieces on the ground around him. His muslin undergarments remained intact except for large rips and tears. Everything was tinged with the rust color of dried blood.

Frantically, John ran his hands along his body, searching for the wounds that had caused the blood. He found none. Not one scratch could he find. As confusion settled into realization, he walked over to the statue. Tentatively, he reached a trembling hand towards the face of the wolf. As his fingers made contact, a strange sensation ran tentatively down his arm and through his body, dissipating into the ground beneath him. He withdrew his hand in shock and then carefully placed it on the tail of the fish. The same sensation pulsed within him.

He pulled his hand back and stepped slowly away from the object, keeping his eyes firmly on the eyes of the wolf that seemed to stare at him, while saying, "You know what has happened."

John knew what had happened.

He had been healed by the statue.

Whatever magical power existed in it had helped him. He recalled Akiak's frantic pleas to avoid the island. The uncertainty in his eyes as he agreed to guide them here. Akiak had mentioned sacred places and dangerous power. He had begged William to convince John to forget this place. But in the end, he had conceded. Now John knew that Akiak had intended to protect this place from their knowledge. It was a place that must never be seen by anyone other than him. He walked back to the canoe and threw the dead mink in the water, mindful that the mother bear might still be nearby. When he was back at the camp, he developed a plan to make sure that only he would have access to the island.

He worked tirelessly over the next weeks to mark the shoreline of the island as a place that was dangerous. The markers and signs he left told anyone approaching that the island was infected with polio from native settlers. He wrote the signs in English and French and made symbols that would be understood by any other person. John further protected the statue by setting traps and barriers around the paths that might take anyone towards the cleaning. He carefully noted the location of the island on his maps and made private notes so that he would be able to find it on other maps.

John moved on to other areas to scout as he made his way home to Winnipeg. When there, he tried to negotiate with the company to deed the island, surrounding islands, and a portion of the shoreline to him, telling them that it was a place that had no value except in his heart and that he could see himself settling there when his job was done. The company said no to his frantic request, perceiving that there might be value to the land that John was hiding from them. They dispatched other trappers to the large lake, instructing them to report back on anything of value that might be hiding in the remote area.

The other explorers found nothing other than overhunted wildlife. Presumably, John's attempts at deterrence were successful. Nevertheless, the company delayed giving him the land, offering excuses that the paperwork involved was extensive and was not a priority. John focused his efforts on building his wealth. He purchased whatever land was available and that he could afford. He feared drawing too much attention to the land, concerned that the company would change its mind. So, he let it play out. After three years had passed and seeing no value in land that would not produce fur, the company complied, even though, in the end, the land was not theirs to give.

The letter that John wrote to his heirs described his encounter on the island and gave specific instructions to keep the information secret. He included any information that he could gather, including the locations and nature of the traps. During his future travels, John listened closely when the Inuit told stories of their myths. Only once did he hear a reference to a deity that combined a fish and a wolf. The reference was made by a drunk man and said the name Sednamaroq. When John approached the man, he denied saying the word and punched John in the face before passing out. John included this information in his death-bed letter with specific instruction that more information was needed on the Inuit mythology and practice involving the statue.

3

1954

Winnipeg, Manitoba, Canada

At the age of 62, John had settled into his retirement on the large family estate in the Tuxedo area of Winnipeg. He had married a local girl and produced a son, James, who became his reason for living. John had shielded his wife from the complicated and political life of the family business, choosing instead to shower her with the bounty that his diverse investments had returned. From an early age, James was taught that he had two goals in life – to make sure his mother was able to live the life of luxury John had given her, and to protect the family interests.

The years had not been kind to John, and his life of exploration had taken a costly toll on his body. Before succumbing to an early death, he privately confided in his son James about the island, handing him a sealed envelope with the letter of confession outlining the events that had occurred many years earlier on the sacred island. James was 27 years old when his father died. The almost unbearable weight of being the sole heir to the Seagram fortune was tempered by his resolve to investigate the island in Baker Lake.

James developed the land on the shore of Baker Lake, making agreements and concessions with the Inuit people that benefited them both. He built a home for himself in the clearing. The home concealed the statue but was never occupied. Concerned that the legacy would be lost, James passed the information to his son Jacob well before his own death. He needed companionship within the secret and wanted Jacob's advice on how to further protect the artifact. When Jacob's daughter, Beverly, was born with a rare disease that would slowly kill her, James knew that fate had called his father to the island that day in 1916. The best doctors that Seagram's money could buy provided consistent advice for James and Jacob: enjoy the short time they had with the child.

James and Jacob took little Beverly to Baker Lake and the island now known as Rio. They would allow Beverly to play around the statue, where she would fall asleep at the base. When she woke, she would be free from symptoms of her illness for a few weeks. The power of the statue never healed her, but it did allow her life to continue. As long as she had occasional contact with it, she would live a life of only intermittent pain, rather than death. They knew this was not a viable long-term solution.

One evening, as little Beverly played around the statue, James looked at his precious granddaughter with sadness as he thought about the limits that would be imposed on her. His life's focus was to provide for his family in a way that would leave them wanting for nothing. He was determined to give Beverly a life that would be limitless. He confided in his son about the ideas that consumed him. How could they best provide for Beverly's future?

Together, they developed a plan.

The family had invested heavily in Canada's burgeoning extractive industry, concentrating on mining with side ventures into oil, drilling, and forestry. The financial returns had been staggering and promised to increase. Wise investing and land ownership had given the Seagram family a wide reach over Canada and America. Money was no concern when it came to providing for Beverly's future.

During a long conversation in the house on Rio Island, James and Jacob decided to build a private research facility around the statue. The island provided the perfect amount of discretion for a venture that, to them, was a private family matter. In the course of their discussions, they continued to refer to the new facility as Rio House, seeing it as a new iteration of the house that currently occupied the island. They would build the facility with the latest technology and hire scientists who were experts in their field. The apprehension, according to Jacob, was how to ensure secrecy concerning Sednamaroq. The argument that continued ended with a shared decision – anyone working at Rio House would never be allowed to leave.

The year that followed this momentous discussion involved a flurry of architects and designers working long days to create plans for a research facility that they were told would be developing advanced vaccines for some of the world's deadliest diseases. James and Jacob constructed a small town on the shores of the big lake to house the workers who would build the facility. They used their extensive network of resources to recruit the most capable team of people needed for the two-year project. The result was the emergence of a cohesive village working towards a common goal. A goal that they believed would benefit the human race through cutting-edge medical research. Only James and Jacob knew the true nature of the new facility.

James and Jacob had constructed a tight wooden structure around the statue. The workers were told that there were Inuit artifacts on the island that must be respected, and no one questioned what appeared to be a sizeable wood shipping crate sitting in the middle of the active construction site as they seamlessly built the large, modern building. As with any project of this nature, rumors circulated that threatened to expose the true nature of the building and the secrets of the island. Jacob curated a small team of operatives that lived and worked among the others in the village, their sole purpose being to dispel any disruptive rumors and manage the flow of information concerning the project.

Two hectic years after the land was cleared for the building, construction was finally complete. James and Jacob stood on the shore of the lake, each holding a hand of seven-year-old Beverly in the dim evening light. They admired the concrete and glass structure that contrasted starkly with the Rio Island forest as an immense sense of hope washed over them, and the sun set behind the Seagram Institute for Scientific Research.

4

Present Day

Seagram Institute for Scientific Research (SISR) – Rio House

Rio Island

Baker Lake, Nunavut, Canada

A sharp chemical smell pierced Jake's nostrils. What was that? Disinfectant? Burnt plastic? Blood? The smell was accompanied by a sound that he did not recognize. Sharp. Metallic. Echoing. Gunfire, he thought. It had to be gunfire. Pop–Pop–Pop! It was close. Too close. Jake cowered in the corner of the dark room, shielded by the table that he had overturned to protect himself. A tray of small sandwiches and a ceramic mug of some unknown liquid had scattered across the floor when he had upended the table. The tile floor was cold beneath him. He did not know who had been shooting at him, nor did he know

WHY they were shooting at him. He looked around the dimly lit space, his eyes wide with fear. The ceiling above him was smooth and white, as were the walls. There was a distinct clinical look to the space. The small room was dimly illuminated by light that was coming from outside the room.

The room he found himself in appeared to be a small conference room. A floor-to-ceiling glass wall separated him from a large room with equipment that Jake did not recognize. He could surmise that it might be a lab of sorts, but he wasn't entirely sure. He ducked down behind the table as shadows moved in the larger space. Then, another pop. A panel of the glass wall shattered. A ricochet as something whizzed past his ear. He rolled to the side, his instinct surprising him as his shoulder slammed into the wall. Dust showered over him as the wall exploded mere inches from his head. He gasped, not from pain but from the sudden and paralyzing clarity. Someone was trying to kill him. And he had no idea why.

Jake rolled back behind the overturned table to take cover. He heard footsteps, fast and heavy, boots on tile. The shadow of two figures ran past what remained of the glass wall that separated him from the commotion. A voice shouted – deep, male, accented. It was too muffled to understand, then another. Orders, maybe? His instinct said they were hunting him. As the sound of the men's boots hitting the ground diminished, the silence became deafening. No gunshots. No footsteps. No sounds of movement. No hum of equipment. He was safe for now.

He leaned back against the wall and checked his position. He adjusted the makeshift barrier to make sure he was completely hidden from view. Jake checked his clothes – tan hiking pants, dark blue hoodie, hiking boots. He reached for the cargo pocket on his left leg, suddenly remembering putting his phone there after taking a selfie with Tanner on the trail before they had stopped for dinner at their favorite restaurant. No phone. He touched his right wrist. No smart watch.

He tried to remember where he was and how he got here. Where was Tanner? Jake took a deep breath, held it for a few seconds, and released it slowly through tight lips. His back pressed into the wall as he forced himself to relax. He repeated the slow breathing, his eyes closed, and his body remaining as still as possible while he centered his mind on his current predicament. He remembered hiking with Tanner on the east side of the Sandia Mountains east of Albuquerque. They had decided to stop for dinner on the drive back to the house. Dinner had been good. He remembered Tanner pulling the car in the garage, then he woke up here. Someone or something must have attacked them, and he had lost consciousness.

Jake looked around the small room. No windows to the outside. One partially open door led to the strange lab area. He could not see beyond that. He would not be able to stay here forever. Now might be the time to make a run for it, but run to where? He had no idea where he was or where he would go.

Should he just stay where he was until they found him? No. He had to try to get out of this building. Maybe then things would be clear. Jake moved with fast, quiet clumsiness. He reached the larger room where a red emergency light pulsed at intervals like a heartbeat. – thump... thump... thump – illuminating fragments of the chaos in flashes: overturned chairs, machines toppled to the floor from their tabletop perches, blood smears on the tile, and bloody handprints on glass.

Another burst of gunfire in the distance broke the silence. He darted to the far side of the room and dove through an open doorway into a small storage room, slamming the door behind him. He quickly turned the lock and slid a heavy bucket in front of the door. He backed away, scanning the room. Metal shelves lined three walls, all neatly arranged with glass vials, square plastic containers, and trays of individually wrapped sterile lab equipment. The vials and square containers were labelled, but only with numbers. B-43, HN-5, S24764i2, S-1, S-2, S-4, X-4-L1.... there were hundreds of them. Jake had no idea what these meant. He turned back to the door. A map was on the back of the door. It showed what he assumed was the floor he was on. A comforting red dot indicated his location. The rooms were not labeled, but Jake could discern that the entire floor consisted of the large laboratory with smaller rooms around the entire perimeter. Stairwells at all four corners and an elevator adjacent to one set of stairs. The closest stairwell was only two rooms away from him. He developed a plan. He would quietly open the door, drop to his hands and knees, and crawl along the wall to the stairs. The map indicated he was on the third floor. He would re-assess the situation once he got to the first floor.

The heavy bucket moved begrudgingly away from the door with pressure from Jake's legs. He turned the lock and firmly gripped the paddle-style handle. Applying gentle pressure, Jake eased the door open. Pop—Pop—Pop... the gunfire returned, closer than before. Jake slowly closed the door, unable to prevent the loud click as the latch caught. He quickly locked the door. He held his breath. The gunfire had stopped. Then steps just outside the door. Jake stepped back a few feet. The door handle moved, then stopped when the person on the other side realized it was locked. Silence.

The door shook with the force of someone kicking it from the other side. They had found him. Jake stumbled backwards, crashing into the shelves. Vials tumbled to the floor as the sound of shattering glass deafened him. He remained still, hoping they would go away. The next kick tore the door from its frame, shattering the wood as it fell towards Jake and slightly to the right. Jake could not make out the details of the man who stood in the doorway. The light from the lab showed him only as a dark silhouette, the clear image of an automatic rifle extending to his side.

Final thoughts whispered in his mind. Where was he, and where was Tanner? What was happening? Why did these men want him? Then, just before he lost consciousness, the world became chaos once again.

5

6 Months earlier

Jake and Tanner

Jake West woke up at 6 a.m. just like he did every morning. The rising Albuquerque sun created shadows on the corners of his older adobe home. He liked his morning runs along the canals leading to the trail that ran through the Bosque and along the river. The soft morning light created a magical environment that enhanced the natural energy that he had always had in the morning. There were days when he felt obligated to take a different route, but today he would take his favorite. Half a mile along the drainage canal, crossing over Rio Grande Blvd, and onto the paved path that led to another canal, eventually joining up with the Bosque trail. He found the mix of running on the dirt, gravel, and paved paths invigorating. And since this particular route alternated between all three surfaces, it had quickly become his favorite. He moved into his house three years earlier, and it had taken him several months of trying different runs to find the perfect 5 km loop.

Jake never paid attention to the cluster of park benches just past the entrance to the trail. He could not remember anyone using them and never had a need to use them himself. Today, however, he could not help but notice a man sleeping on one of the benches. More specifically, it wasn't the man that he noticed; it was the expensive road bike chained to the bench. The lock that held the bike also secured a backpack, which was placed carefully under the bench that supported the man in the sleeping bag. Jake ran past this spectacle without slowing, his mind churning with possible scenarios that would result in a person being homeless yet maintaining possession of a bike that cost more than some small cars. By the time his loop circled him back to the benches, the man, his bike, and the backpack were gone.

Two days later, Jake woke at the usual time, rolled out of bed, peed, and ran a damp washcloth over his shaved head and face, running his hands over his trimmed dark beard as he glanced at himself in the mirror. He looked good for a man in his early forties. He had always taken care of his skin and, with the exception of a few gray hairs here and there, had been told that his trim, hairy body rivaled that of men in their twenties. Jake pulled on his running shorts, a fitted t-shirt, his socks, and zero-drop running shoes, all while nibbling on an energy waffle. He grabbed his bone-conducting headset and started the music on his smart watch before putting it on his wrist. As soon as he stepped out his front door, he started the tracking app on his watch and took off at a good pace, his feet hitting the ground with energy and purpose.

As he approached the set of benches, he noticed the man was back. This time, he was standing beside the bench, carefully folding his sleeping bag. The man's tan skin and dark, well-groomed hair told of New Mexican heritage. He looked to be roughly in his thirties; his appearance aligned with the sleek, expensive bike that rested against his left hip. It was a peculiar sight, one that caused Jake confusion in its context. It also intrigued him.

Jake considered the guy might be a dedicated athlete who had fallen on hard times. His bike could be a testament to his commitment to the sport, its carbon frame and aerodynamic designs showcasing a level of passion and investment that was undeniable. Jake imagined that his dreams and aspirations had collided with the harsh reality of life on the streets. His curiosity got the best of him, and he slowed to a walk as he approached.

The guy looked up as Jake approached, his eyes cautious.

"Hey, I'm Jake." He said, extending his hand in greeting.

"Tanner." The guy said. "What do you want?"

"Uh, I just wanted to say hi. I like your bike." Jake struggled with where to take the conversation.

"Thanks. Anything else?" Tanner asked.

"No," Jake said, slightly annoyed at the short exchange. "I always see you here when I go for a run and just wanted to say hi."

"Enjoy your run," Tanner said as he turned and continued to pack up his things.

Jake stared at Tanner for a few seconds before continuing his run. That was odd, he thought to himself. The run passed quickly, his mind occupied with the possible scenarios that would create the situation of a well-groomed man, with an expensive bike, homeless, and living on apark bench. At the end of the loop, Tanner was gone.

Curiosity often got Jake into trouble, and he could not resist changing his workout schedule to go for a run the next morning. His timing was perfect. Tanner was packing up his things as Jake approached. He looked up and smiled as Jake approached, giving a slight wave of his hand.

"Good morning," Jake said.

"Mornin'." Tanner replied.

"Hey, I don't know your schedule, but any chance you want to get a cup of coffee?" Jake asked hesitantly.

"I have to get to work. Maybe another day." Tanner said.

"Got it," Jake responded.

"Listen," Tanner started, "I don't need charity. So, if this is your way of trying to do a good deed for the day, let's get that settled up front. Okay?"

"Okay. But who are you to assume that this is charity? I didn't offer to pay for coffee. I really am just curious. I mean, you're an attractive guy, with a very expensive bike, living on a park bench. I see you every time I run, so it seems natural to me that, at some point, I might introduce myself." Jake rambled.

"Fair enough," Tanner said. "I'd love to have a coffee with you. Since tomorrow is Saturday, let's meet at La Luz on Griegos. 8 a.m. good?"

"Sounds good. See you there." Jake said and jogged back in the direction of his house, deciding to forego the run.

The next morning, Jake woke at his normal time and pulled on jeans, a plain black t-shirt, and a dark gray hoodie. He wandered around the house in his bare feet, trying to kill time before heading out to the coffee shop. He eventually decided to take the chance on being very early to the agreed meeting time, put on his socks and a pair of his favorite cowboy boots and started on the mile walk to the coffee shop. He liked to walk and enjoyed the leisurely stroll along the canals before joining up with the street. He approached the coffee shop from the rear of the small building and noticed Tanner's unmistakable bike secured to the bike rack. Jake experienced a flutter of nervousness at meeting Tanner like this. He knew nothing about this man except that his situation seemed bizarre. Curiosity overtook his nervousness as he opened the large wood door to the coffee shop.

Tanner was seated against the far wall, his legs crossed, looking at his phone. His backpack sat on the floor at his feet. He was dressed in jeans and a light tan hoodie, with a brown knit cap covering his dark hair. The look was casual and attractive. It was the look of someone who has money and likes spending their mornings casually at a coffee shop. No one would ever guess this guy was homeless. The scene caused confusion in Jake's mind, as his curiosity grew. Tanner looked up and waved Jake over, motioning for him to take a seat.

"Good morning!" He spoke. "What'll you have? It's on me."

"Black coffee," Jake said, thinking it better not to argue after the exchange the day prior.

"Be right back," Tanner said.

Jake waited patiently, noticing that Tanner paid with cash when he ordered the two coffees. Tanner returned, carefully set the large ceramic mugs on the table and walked back to the counter, returning a few moments later with two breakfast burritos wrapped in foil. He reacquired his seat in the chair facing Jake and pushed one of the foil-wrapped rolls towards Jake.

"Potato, egg, cheese, and green chile," Tanner said.

"My favorite." Jake smiled as he picked up the burrito, tore off the foil from one end and took a big bite.

Tanner picked up his mug by wrapping his hand around it rather than using the handle. He took a sip of coffee and looked directly at Jake for a few seconds before speaking.

"So, Jake." He started. "Tell me about yourself." He picked up his burrito, carefully unwrapped one end and took a small bite, chewing slowly as he continued looking at Jake.

"Uh, well, I've lived here in Albuquerque for just over three years. I grew up in Nebraska. Went to school there, worked there for a while and moved here for work. You?"

Jake was anxious to hear Tanner's story but knew that there would need to be a sharing of information.

"Grew up here. Went to school here. UNM. Travelled around for work. Ended up back here recently." Tanner said. "What do you do for work, Jake?"

"I'm a systems engineer for a tech research company. I mostly work from home. I go into the office one or two days a week." Jake said. "You?"

"I work at a home improvement store," Tanner said. "Listen, Jake, I know you are wondering about my situation. I'll tell you some of it, but I really don't know you well enough to tell you all the details. Maybe in time. Just don't push. Okay?"

"Okay. That's fair. So just tell me what you want, and we will go from there." Jake responded. "I'm going to ask questions. If you don't want to answer, just say so and I'll be okay with it."

"Deal." Tanner agreed. "The short of the story is that I had a successful career as an accountant. Some things happened that ended that, and now I'm working at getting back on my feet. I didn't sell the bike because I use it to get around. And it's the one possession from my previous life that I just couldn't part with."

"Two questions." Jake continued. "First, how long do you plan on living this way before you can get back on your feet? And second, where do you shower? You're clearly clean and well-groomed."

Tanner laughed. "Those are understandable questions. I've been unhoused for about two months, and I'm planning on another four to be able to get a place to live.

I just want to have enough saved to make it work without living paycheck to paycheck." Tanner paused, taking a sip of coffee before continuing. "As for the shower question, I belong to a gym nearby. It's 24/7, and I talked with the owner about my situation. I pay the monthly fee, have a place to work out, and use their bathroom and showers to take care of my personal hygiene."

"You're full of surprises, Tanner," Jake said softly. "I've never met anyone so resilient."

"Thanks, Jake. That means a lot. Some days are harder than others. But most of the time I'm just really focused on getting back to a normal life."

They finished their coffees and burritos, tossed the foil and napkins in the trash, and placed the mugs on a tray near the service counter. Tanner led the way out the door, dispensing a pump of hand sanitizer into his hand from the unit by the door and turning left toward the bike rack where his bike was locked securely to the metal poles. He set his pack down carefully at his feet as he unlocked the bike. He unclipped a helmet that was attached to his pack and held it loosely in his hand as they talked.

"This was nice. Thanks for saying hi. I'm sorry about my initial response. I get a lot of people who want to buy the bike or just want to start trouble." Tanner confided.

"Yes, this was nice." Jake agreed. "Tanner, come over for dinner one night. To my place. I smoke a mean brisket." Jake chuckled.

"Uh, okay. Are you sure?" Tanner asked. "What night is good?"

"Thursday?" Jake offered. "6 p.m.?"

"Sure," Tanner replied. "Text me your address. Here, give me your phone and I'll enter my contact info."

Jake unlocked his phone and navigated to the contacts, created a new contact and handed the phone to Tanner. Tanner typed quickly and handed the phone back to Jake. The entry read Tanner Kingman with an area code that Jake did not recognize. He shared his contact info with Tanner, including his address.

Tanner placed the helmet on his head and buckled the strap under his chin.

"See you Thursday at 6. "He said as he put his pack on his back, mounted the bike, and rode off.

Jake smiled, excited to see where this would go.

Thursday morning arrived quickly. Jake took the brisket out of the fridge, cut open the vacuum-sealed bag and placed the meat on the small electric smoker that he used. He had prepared the piece of meat two days earlier, letting it sit in the vacuum-sealed wrap in the fridge for a few days to marinate in the dry rub. He turned on the smoker, set the timer, and went back in the house to shower and dress before going to the office. The smoker would do its thing while he was at work. It was an easy meal that was his go-to for dinner parties. He would roast potatoes and have a salad to go with the meal. Easy.

The workday went by quickly. He kept his mind occupied with the complexities of a new project to avoid thinking about Tanner. When he got home, he worked quickly to get the potatoes cooking and prepared the salad, placing it in the fridge until they were ready to eat. He took the brisket off the smoker, wrapping it in butcher paper to rest on a cutting board in the kitchen. Tanner arrived a few minutes before the agreed time.

"Wine?" Jake offered.

"Sure," Tanner said. "I prefer red, but I'm good with anything."

"Same," Jake said, opening a bottle that he had placed on the counter. He poured the wine into two glasses, handing one to Tanner and tilting his forward for a toast. Tanner reciprocated as the glasses clinked together.

"To new friends," Jake said.

Tanner smiled and took a sip of the wine. "This is good. New Mexico?" Tanner examined the bottle.

"Yep. There's a lot of really bad wine here and a small number of good ones." Jake said. "This is from a local winery."

"Not bad," Tanner said, taking a seat on the sofa where Jake joined him.

They talked for a few minutes before Jake moved them to the kitchen to get dinner together. He sliced the brisket, gathered pickled jalapeños, sliced raw onion, dill pickles, and a few bottles of barbecue sauce from the fridge, along with the salad. He removed the potatoes from the oven and placed everything on the counter.

"I thought we might just serve ourselves and sit at the table to eat," Jake said.

"Perfect. It smells delicious." Tanner said.

They loaded up their plates and moved the table nearby, where Jake had moved their wine glasses and the bottle of wine.

They ate in silence, enjoying the food and the companionship. Jake told Tanner about his childhood, growing up in western Nebraska, coming out in high school, and finding his groove as an adult. He talked about failed relationships, his career, hobbies, and anything else to fill the time. Tanner disclosed a few more details about his situation. He told Jake about growing up as an out gay kid in rural New Mexico on the reservation. His boring journey towards getting his degree and career. Jake learned that Tanner had been in a long-term relationship that ended badly. His partner had been an alcoholic and had evidently ruined them financially, as well as destroyed Tanner's career in the process. According to Tanner, he found himself unexpectedly homeless and broke, having lost his license to work as an accountant, with his reputation irretrievably tarnished.

The story did not make complete sense to Jake, and he realized that Tanner might be withholding crucial details because they were too painful to talk about. Jake had also not considered that Tanner might be gay, and this presented a new dimension of his growing attachment to the guy. Jake had a habit of making bad decisions with relationships and considered that the direction he was headed with this one would be no different.

When they had finished dessert - fruit tarts that Jake had picked up at the grocery store bakery, they settled on the sofa to talk. Tanner asked if he could open another bottle of wine and did so with Jake's approval. Halfway through the second bottle of wine, Jake made the decision to make a bold suggestion.

"Tanner, I've really enjoyed tonight. I have a proposal." Jake started.

"Okay... Should I be scared?" Tanner laughed. "I've also enjoyed tonight, Jake."

"Why don't you move in here until you get back on your feet?" Jake paused, waiting for a reaction. Tanner simply stared at him and waited for him to continue. "No strings. No expectations. Just help with the housework. No rent, no cost to you. Maybe you could cook or buy food like you normally would."

"And why would you do that for me?" Tanner asked.

"Because I like your company," Jake said, slightly insulted by Tanner's response, but quickly realizing that the guy really did not know him, either.

"It's kind of you to offer. I like my independence, and I don't want there to be any pretext or expectations. We would need to have firm rules about personal space. And an agreement that I would pay you rent when I can." Tanner continued.

"Agree. All those things." Jake said, getting excited that he might have someone to talk to in the evening.

"Let me think about it. Let's have dinner this weekend, my treat. I'll have an answer for you then." Tanner offered. "And Jake, thank you. It's refreshing to meet someone like you."

"Sounds good, my new friend. Would you be up for a hike on Sunday? And dinner after?" Jake asked.

"I like that idea. Meet you at my place at 2 p.m.?" Tanner asked, laughing at the reference to the park bench where they met.

"Deal," Jake said, finishing his wine.

Tanner downed the last of the wine in his glass and gathered his things to leave. Before walking out the door, he gave Jake a hug that felt like more than friends. They met on Sunday and had a pleasant hike, followed by dinner – Tanner's treat – at a local restaurant that served down-home New Mexican food. Tanner moved in, and it only took a few weeks for them to realize that there might be something more than friendship. Their weekends were spent hiking and exploring. They cooked together most evenings. Tanner remained reserved about his past, revealing small tidbits of information that reinforced what Jake was thinking - there was more to the story than what he was being told.

6

Mateo

It was still dark outside when Mateo Trujillo López arrived at the Chemical and Biological Engineering Lab at the University of New Mexico campus in Albuquerque, NM. The cool morning air moved lazily around him as he locked his bike to the rack near the side entrance of the building and paused for a moment as daylight began to appear. This was his favorite part of the day. He loved the magical moment when the New Mexico sun illuminated the brown and pink hues of the buildings. The accent of turquoise paint on a structure nearby and the green of piñon pines provided the perfect complement to the dawn light. The past year had been tumultuous for Mateo. He was close to finishing his PhD, and the resistance to his research had been stronger than he had anticipated.

He had expected controversy — but had not expected to be marginalized to the extent that he was.

One final deep breath and a glance up at the slowly brightening sky calmed him before he slung his backpack over his right shoulder and tapped his identification badge on the pad by the door. He paused briefly at the click of the lock disengaging before pulling on the handle and stepping into the stairwell. He took slow, deliberate steps up to the third floor, opened the door to the main hallway, and silently walked the ten feet to the door that led to the suite of labs where he had been given a small space in a dark corner. He flicked the switch to turn on the lights and walked through the maze of lab benches, equipment racks, and oddly placed succulents to his dedicated space.

The University had been enthusiastic about his research proposal when he first applied. He had been accepted into the synthetic biology program with the caveat that finding a mentor and gaining funding would be necessary towards the eventual completion of the degree. The combination of engineering, genetics, and biology was still an emerging field, and he had presented his ideas to several professors, who were unclear as to what he was trying to do. He finally found one that simply needed a research assistant to bolster her own work. She had been very clear with him — Mateo was to work on her research first and use whatever free time he might have to work on his own. It wasn't the ideal situation, but given the lack of interest from other faculty, he had no other choice. So, his life for the past five years had been accommodating the lack of balance between the two. As his mentor's research neared publication, she told Mateo directly that she would allow him to finish his degree, but not to expect any assistance. The next day, he was told that his workspace would be moved to a shared lab.

Mateo placed his bag on the floor next to his workbench and settled into the bar-height chair that wobbled when he moved in it. He looked at his surroundings. His cozy, tiny corner of the shared lab was tucked away from the rest of the large room. He had no window and could not see a window from where he sat. Nor could he see another person. He would guess that most people in the room didn't even know of his existence. He turned on a small speaker that he kept on his bench and picked up his phone to play some music. He chose a playlist that contained his favorite songs – a mix of everything from pop to country to EDM – and started getting his work organized.

He planned to publish his research within the next few months and spent most of his days making connections with potential employers, proofing his work, and reminiscing about his journey to this point in his life. His idea for using an alternate base for organic nanobots had occurred to him in a microbiology class during his undergraduate studies. The current and accepted construction used cells from the African clawed frog to grow the xenobots. It worked but had limits to the functions that were inherent in the frogs themselves, like movements and basic interactions. Mateo knew there must be a better base that would allow for unlimited programming of the micromachines.

After graduating with a Bachelor of Science in molecular biology, he worked for a lab in Albuquerque that performed research under a government contract. The research involved heavy use of a variety of algae for medical applications. The algae were so versatile, and he was constantly amazed at the behavior that he could elicit from their growth. During one particularly successful lab procedure, he had an epiphany – could algae be used as a base for the bio-nanobots rather than frog cells? The idea consumed him. He could not find any scholarly articles, nor any anecdotal mention of the idea. He told his ideas to a few colleagues who laughed at him and made comments that let him know they thought he was purposefully trying to interject some humor into the conversation.

Mateo started keeping a journal of his ideas. He would call them *phycobots*, building on the term *xeonbot* (which pulled from *xeonpus larvis*), the name for the current frog-based organic nanobots, and substituting *phyco*, the root word for algae. He imagined the unlimited uses of an algae-based nanobot. It would be infinitely programmable, undetectable by most methods, and easy to grow. He also surmised that the algae base would allow them to self-replicate. The idea consumed him. One day, during lunch with a work friend, Mateo mentioned his ideas. The response was encouraging in a way that a parent encourages a child to explore a new idea, knowing that the failure will be a learning experience for them. But the comments gave him an idea. What if he could get into a doctoral program that would provide him with the resources to develop the idea? So, he applied to UNM, got accepted, continued to be ridiculed for his radical ideas, and begged for funding that came from sources where the money needed to be spent on tax-deductible research without any serious interest in the topic of the research itself.

His research had produced results, but not in the way he had hoped. The theory was solid, and the implications significant. But growing the algae-based machines required equipment and supplies that his funding did not support. Without the ability to produce a prototype, his work remained theoretical. His only option was to publish what he had, hope the university would confer the degree, and resume working while he tried to get a lab to fund further research.

And that's where he found himself this morning. Contemplating his future, listening to music, and trying not to think about the absence of a social life. He missed dating and having the money to go to dinner with friends, and generally just having a life outside the lab. Regardless of how this all turned out, he would find his way.

He heard commotion in the lab, someone moving around. It was too early for anyone else to be there. The one thing he had learned about this lab was the "daytime" schedule of the other researchers. No one ever arrived before 10 a.m. and rarely stayed past late afternoon. So, the idea that someone would be here with him piqued his curiosity. Mateo paused the music and slid out of his seat, quietly moving into the main area of the large space. As he rounded the corner from his sequestered niche, he came face to face with a woman whom he did not recognize. She was shorter than his own five foot ten, brunette, shoulder-length hair cut in a simple and elegant style that seemed easy to maintain, and a face that told of a person who cared for her skin with no concern for the cost. She was dressed in simple dark brown pants, a cream-colored silk blouse, and colorful purple running shoes. A simple crystal pendant hung from a silver chain around her neck.

"Mateo Trujillo?" She spoke. "I'm Beverly Seagram. Do you have a minute to speak with me about your research?"

7

Beverly

The malformed big toes of the baby were the first sign that something might be wrong. The competent obstetrician immediately launched down a path of further investigation. Six months later, when baby Beverly Lynn Seagram was having trouble flexing her jaw to nurse, x-ray images confirmed what the medical team had feared. Jacob and Betsy Seagram's new baby girl was diagnosed with Münchmeyer Disease. Formally known as Fibrodysplasia Ossificans Progressiva, a horrifying disease which the doctors kept calling 'FOP' and was more commonly called Stone Man Syndrome.

The doctor patiently explained the disease to Jacob and Betsy – and the prognosis.

Young Beverly would suffer. Her connective tissues – muscle, tendons, ligaments – would slowly turn to bone. It would be severe and disabling.

And there was no cure.

The disease was rare, with fewer than 500 cases worldwide. Treatment options centered around managing pain and surgical removal of the newly formed bone, which encouraged new, healthy bone growth. Treatment would be painful, but not as painful as the progression of the disease itself.

The doctor described, in detail, what they could reasonably expect. A fall on the playground that might cause any other child a simple bruise on the shoulder would have very different consequences for Beverly. The area of impact would swell painfully over the days following the simple fall. The muscles and other connective tissues would harden, never to soften again. Random lumps would appear on her body. Biopsies and surgeries would be out of the question, only triggering more bone growth. By the age of ten, they could expect her neck to be completely fused, preventing her from turning her head. Each injury, every muscle strain, every fever could instigate new bone growth. He described a teenage girl, frozen in place, entombed in living bone.

Jacob and Betsy cried. They held each other tightly as the doctor detailed the horror that Beverly would endure. Betsy held the baby close to her chest on the drive home.

Both she and Jacob knew what must be done. No family member had ever tested the powers of that thing on Rio Island. But now, it was time. They arrived at the family house in the wealthy Winnipeg area of Tuxedo and packed the things they would need for the complicated trip to Baker Lake. Jacob called the staff together and barked orders, arranging for a private seaplane to take them from Lake Winnipeg to Baker Lake. It was the costliest way to get there, and the quickest. The Seagram family could afford it.

The trip to Baker Lake was hard on them. Beverly cried during the entire journey, and Betsy cried along with her. Jacob remained stone-faced, a futile effort to be strong for his family. The female nanny and two male assistants remained silent during the journey. The Seagram's had not shared with them the details of the trip, and their loyalty was being tested. They arrived at the lake, and Jacob's assistants made Rio House as livable as possible on such short notice.

The fire in the large fireplace did little to heat a building that was never intended to host occupants. Betsy and Jacob cared little about the comforts of life at this moment. Their concern was for their daughter and her future. Within minutes of being settled in the house, Jacob pulled down the cloth shroud that surrounded the statue of Sednamaroq. He gently and hesitantly placed the baby at the base of the alabaster column, remembering at the last minute his grandfather's note on the placement of the body. But how could this tiny baby encircle the base? Panic set in as Jacob paced back and forth, glancing occasionally at Beverly, who had become silent next to the white column. Could it be that she would receive some benefit just by proximity to the thing? Yes, he would wait. She was quiet for the first time in many hours. What could it hurt? So, he waited.

Betsy fell asleep in Jacob's arms, her head on his chest as they looked patiently towards baby Beverly. Jacob soon followed Betsy into the sleep that only comes from exhaustion. As they slept, they failed to notice the very faint blue light that filled the space between Beverly and the object.

Betsy woke with the panic of a mother who hears her baby's cries, knowing that the baby is not with her. Beverly's tiny arms flailed above her as the cries became more frantic. Betsy recognized them as only a nursing mother would – she was hungry. Betsy extricated herself from Jacob's embrace and crawled across the floor to her child. She retrieved the baby and backed away carefully, unsure what it might mean if she remained too close to the statue. She had read John's letter and had talked at length with James about the purported powers - and she did not want to tempt the thing. She scuttled back to where Jacob remained asleep on the mattress on the floor against the wall. Beverly searched for nourishment before Betsy could expose her milk-swollen breast. When Beverly attached, it was as if the child had never been fed. Her muscles of mastication flexed normally as she suckled.

Betsy gently stroked her baby as she nursed, running her hand along Beverly's head and down to her tiny arm that ended in a hand that rested lovingly against the plump flesh of Beverly's breast. Betsy pulled back the cloth that wound its way around the baby's body and ran her hand down the child's torso and along her chubby baby thighs. It was then that Betsy noticed it. Beverly's toe was no longer malformed. The single joint that had been missing had miraculously returned. Frantic, Betsy pulled back the rest of the cloth to reveal the other foot. Yes, the other toe was normal. Did this mean that she was healed?

Jacob woke with the urgent shaking of Betsy's hand on his shoulder.

"Jacob! Jacob! Look!" Betsy exclaimed.

"What, Betsy? What are you talking about?" Jacob was still half asleep, his exhaustion still not fully recovered.

"Look at her toes!" Betsy said, cupping her hand under Beverly's feet and pulling them up for Jacob to see.

"What does this mean?" Jacob asked. "Is she healed?"

"I don't know, Jacob. I simply do not know." Betsy replied. "Maybe? Could it be that quick? Your grandfather's letter said that he was healed when he woke, but we don't know how long he was asleep."

"I don't think we will know the answer. I don't think we will ever know the answer. Let's just take it for what it is. We will go back to Winnipeg, and if we need to come back here, we will. Agreed?" Jacob looked into Betsy's eyes with the love that is only seen by a man looking at his wife who is holding his child.

"Yes, my love. For now, she is healthy and safe." Betsy said the words with confidence, carefully controlling her voice to avoid betraying her doubt.

They returned to Winnipeg the next day. Beverly rarely cried and seemed happy for the next few weeks, then Betsy noticed the baby making unusual sounds when she moved her arms. Beverly's discomfort increased over the next two days, and Jacob and Betsy made the trip up north to the lake without discussion or hesitation. Two days of little Beverly playing around the statue brought her back to normal. Over the following year, they determined that three weeks between visits to the statue was the perfect interval.

James frequently accompanied Jacob and Betsy to Rio House. Beverly was seven years old when James and Jacob realized the completion of their vision.

55

8

On her twenty-ninth birthday, Beverly Lynn Seagram reflected on her life of privilege. She had always had everything that a person could want or need. The regular trips to Rio House had been such a normal part of her childhood that she could not imagine a life where she did not go there. He parents had made every attempt to help her fit in with other children her age, but traditional school had been a failure. The teachers had told Jacob and Betsy that Beverly was overly sensitive and sometimes aggressive to other students. By the time she was eleven, Beverly had been in and out of two public and five private schools.

Home schooling with private tutors was the only thing that worked. Jacob had hired a special project manager to coordinate the rotating group of highly qualified teachers who consistently quit. The primary complaint was that no amount of money was worth tolerating Beverly's mood swings, depression, and severe impulsive behavior. Betsy herself had noticed that Beverly seemed terrified of being abandoned. She clung to anyone who would give her attention as if they were her best friend, only to vilify them as her worst enemy when attention from another person was noticed.

It was only when Beverly was in her early teens that Betsy suggested they take their daughter to see a psychiatrist. Up to that point, they had excused her behaviors as the symptoms of a wealthy child with too much privilege. The fourteen-year-old Beverly had admitted to the doctor that she could not control her emotions and frequently felt like she was empty inside. She occasionally had suicidal thoughts but quickly pushed them aside when she considered the amount of money that her family had at its disposal. For her, the wealth made suicide seem like an act that would only further alienate her from society.

Beverly enjoyed her meetings with the psychiatrist, which made Betsy and Jacob happy. They were finally seeing stability with her behavior, and her current set of teachers had been in place for several months. The doctor had settled on a diagnosis of borderline personality disorder and worked diligently with Beverly to teach her the coping mechanisms necessary to fit in with society. Beverly took to the doctor's instructions with a vigor that surprised her parents, making new friends and participating in the ongoing efforts to recruit scientists to work at Rio House.

The push to cure her illness had always been a part of Beverly's life. There was a brief period at the age of ten when she resisted a trip to the Baker Lake facility. The petulant Beverly had thrown a tantrum that frightened Betsy and Jacob to a degree that they decided to allow her to see what would happen if she did not go. The result was traumatic, both for Beverly and her parents. During a particularly strong argument, Beverly had swept her arm across a credenza, causing a variety of heavy decorative objects to fly through the air with the force of her anger. The impact of her arm with the objects started a reaction in her muscles and ligaments that began to ossify within days. The pain and reduced mobility were so severe that Jacob became unsure if they would make it to the statue in time for her to survive. They stayed at Rio House for two weeks while the scientists and doctors managed her pain amidst her sessions near Sednamaroq.

Over the following five years, the research made promising advancements that always ended in disappointment. Nevertheless, Beverly remained resolved to find the right scientist to curate the best treatment. Her trips to Rio House became more frequent and her stays there longer. By the time she had turned eighteen, she was spending more time at Baker Lake than in Winnipeg. She listened to the scientists and participated in efforts to uncover new treatments. Things were going well, and her moods remained stable for longer periods. Then her world fell apart.

It was the week after her eighteenth birthday. Her parents had travelled to Rio House to celebrate with her there, at her request. Their private chef and other staff had pulled out all the stops for a birthday dinner that would rival any high-society soiree back in Winnipeg.

Beverly had come to think of the scientists and staff at Rio House as her family, and celebrating this milestone birthday with them seemed appropriate, so she decided to stay for another week after Jacob and Betsy left for Winnipeg. When she received the news that there had been an accident, she didn't immediately understand. She had just spoken to her parents mere hours ago. She had hugged them both and told them that she loved them. She had told them how happy she was that they had given her a good life. They had told her that she meant more to them than anything in the entire world. Her world had been complete. And in a moment, they were gone.

The investigation revealed that an unusual combination of limited visibility due to the shifting weather, a microburst, and unfortunate rudder failure had resulted in a situation that would have been irrecoverable by any pilot, regardless of experience. There most likely had been a brief moment of terror followed by a quick death as the plane hit the water. The force of the impact with the choppy waves would have been enough to render the plane's occupant's unconscious as they drowned in the icy waters of Lake Winnipeg.

She felt alone, abandoned, and isolated — her worst fears realized at last. The following weeks in Winnipeg were a blur, interrupted only by frequent sessions with her psychiatrist and short trips back to Rio House for treatment. The family attorney was brief and direct with Beverly — she was the sole heir to the entire Seagram empire. The diverse portfolio of businesses, land, investments, and life insurance provided more wealth than any single person would ever be able to exhaust. In the midst of her grief, she moved permanently to Rio House, selling off as much of the family estate in Winnipeg as she could. The only reminder she wanted of her parents was their true legacy to her — a research facility with the single goal of finding a cure for her disease.

Beverly continued to see her psychiatrist, tolerating phone sessions when she was at the facility. During one particularly distressing week, she had coerced the doctor to visit Rio House for a series of sessions. Beverly had attempted to make the stay attractive enough to entice the doctor to move there permanently. Sensing the dysfunctional nature of the request, as well as Beverly's growing obsession with the research, the psychiatrist had refused, instead offering to be on call for Beverly. The doctor had also added a new diagnosis of monomania to her ever-growing list of ailments. Beverly was growing to hate the abomination that kept her alive and dreamed of a day when she could never see the white statue again.

She had a small house built near the institute, a place where she could comfortably live and still maintain occasional separation from her obsession, rather than living in the apartment that had been incorporated into the main building. Most mornings, she would summon the small collection of researchers to her home for updates, rather than walking the short distance to the glass and concrete building. These meetings ended in disappointment, and her wrath towards the scientists was often severe.

Some of the scientists and staff tried to quit, threatening to leave each time Beverly's retaliation became too much to handle. Their threats were swiftly met with odd accidents, and they were replaced within days. The atmosphere that resulted was one of complete and utter fear for the employees of Rio House. Escape seemed impossible as Beverly's loyal security team kept constant and watchful eyes on everyone on the island. The only respite was the days that Beverly would leave the island to scout for new talent. She would always return with a promising new scientist, none of whom knew what they had done by agreeing to work at the institute.

Beverly herself spent countless hours scouring the internet, research journals, and fringe medicine groups looking for obscure paths to follow towards her goal. And one day, she uncovered something that sparked a level of hope in her soul that she had not felt in many years. A very brief blurb in the journal *Nature Nanotechnology* mentioned a PhD student at the University of New Mexico who had proposed an algae-based organic nanobot to treat disease. The three-sentence side note at the bottom left of the second-to-last page in the journal said that PhD candidate Mateo Trujillo would soon be granted his degree with the controversial and peer-rejected focus of phyconanobots. To Beverly, he seemed like the perfect candidate for Rio House.

Immediately following her next 'treatment' around Sednamaroq, she left the institute for Albuquerque. Her excitement started to build on the two-hour boat ride to the west shore of Bake Lake, where her private jet lived on an airstrip that her grandfather had constructed years before. Shortly after her parents' death, Beverly had paved the packed gravel airstrip and built a series of buildings to house her aircraft, as well as a few others, as well as overnight accommodations. Since her parents' accident, Beverly had avoided seaplanes, even though they provided a more direct access to the island. She had come to enjoy the boat ride and used the time to allow her mind to wander. On this day, her mind churned with the possibilities of this new marginalized technology. It might be just what she needed for a breakthrough. Her passion was fueled by the disgust that she felt at her regular visits to the statue. Even now, she could feel the disconcerting energy of the thing coursing through her body. A lifetime of exposure to it had rooted within her a complicated mix of need and hate.

As she settled into the plush leather seats of the Pilatus PC-12 that had been fitted to accommodate her frequent travel across the vast Canadian North, she thought of how she would approach Mateo Trujillo. She would first test him to see if he would respond to money. That was the approach that worked most of the time. Everyone, it seemed, was motivated by money. If that failed, she would offer unfettered ability to conduct his research. Considering his status among the research community, that might be what worked. Regardless, she would get what she wanted – she always did.

9

BarsTech Industries

Barstow, California

When Jacob Seagram invested in the small start-up ten years earlier, he had no idea the true level of success the research would attain. Jacob had seen promise in the young researcher who had presented the idea. And with a name like Chuck Morozov, Jacob felt a tinge of sympathy for the guy. Chuck's ideas were interesting, and he was asking for such a small amount to get his research off the ground. So, Jacob gave him a check on the spot and had his attorney draw up a simple partnership agreement. It was one of many similar ventures that he supported that year, and as with other investments over the years, some turned profitable, and others were a complete loss. Such was the nature of the tax-deductible donations of the wealthy class.

Chuck's idea of growing organic nanobots to help produce a more sustainable food supply was interesting, and Jacob thought that it had a 50/50 chance of becoming anything useful. Two years passed with no word from Chuck, and Jacob had forgotten about the small investment. Then Chuck showed up at his office in Winnipeg one day without warning. Curious about the unexpected visit and about his investment, Jacob rescheduled an appointment to take the meeting.

Chuck settled into the fabric sofa as Jacob himself took a seat in a leather side chair. A large desk dominated the corner office on the 31st floor of the Seagram Industries glass skyscraper, sitting at the corner of Portage and Main Streets, and the comfortable sitting area to the side of the desk provided a nice area to have conversations. He thanked Jacob for seeing him, speaking frantically about the failures of his attempts to create a viable organic nanobot with a cyanobacteria base. Jacob started to realize that the meeting was a plea for more funding. Jacob listened patiently for a few minutes while Chuck rambled about the African clawed frog, adaptive cellular memory, and new directions for the research. None of it made sense to Jacob, and he finally had to stop Chuck's diatribe.

"Chuck, stop talking," Jacob said forcefully. Chuck continued rambling.

"Chuck! Chuck! Be quiet!" Jacob yelled.

"Sorry, Mr. Seagram. I just get so excited." Jacob replied, sitting silently, his hands held tightly together in his lap.

"Let me ask a few questions, and please just answer yes or no. Agreed?" Jacob demanded.

"Yes, yes, please ask." Chuck wrung his hands together nervously.

"Your research using cyanobacteria as a base to create organic nanobots has failed? Jacob asked.

"Yes," Chuck answered, starting to speak as Jacob held up a finger to stop him.

"And you're here to ask for more money?" Jacob asked.

"Yes, but..." Chuck started to explain as Jacob held up a finger again to stop him.

"Tell me, very simply, why you need more money," Jacob said firmly.

"Because it worked," Chuck said.

"What worked?" Jacob asked. "You just told me it failed."

"Yes, the cyanobacteria base failed. But the frog cells worked." Chuck said excitedly, clearly wanting to say more.

"Okay, Chuck. Now, in simple terms that a non-scientist will understand, tell me what worked and specifically why you need more money." The conversation was trying Jacob's patience.

Chuck took a deep breath, "When the cyanobacteria failed, I looked at other options and started using frog cells. The results are amazing. I mean, the bots are limited to the inherent cellular memory of the frog, but they work. And the possibilities are significant. Defense applications, medical applications. I mean, it's still years out, but they work. And they could make us both a lot of money." Chuck stopped talking and stared at Jacob.

Jacob stood from the chair and walked to the door. He opened it and poked his head out to speak with his secretary, Janet. "Cancel my day, get Mr. Morozov a nice room at the Fort Garry. And arrange transport for him to my home this evening for dinner around 6 p.m."

Jacob returned to the chair, sitting on the edge of the seat, his forearms resting on his knees and his hands clasped together. "Here's what we're going to do, Chuck. I have a room at a nice hotel, and my driver will take you there. The driver will also pick you up at 5:45 p.m. and will deliver you to my home for dinner and a very frank conversation. In the few hours between now and then, I want you to come up with a comprehensive number that will allow you to pursue this research. Please prepare a very simple list of what that money would accomplish. There is no need for a formal presentation; just notes on scraps of paper will do. I want us to have a gentlemanly conversation about it this evening. Okay?"

"Okay. Thank you, Mr. Seagram. You won't regret this." Chuck said.

"Chuck, make that number realistic. Don't short yourself. And please call me Jacob. If we're going to do this, we need to dispose of the formalities." Jacob requested.

"Thanks, Jacob. This research will change things. For humanity." Chuck's voice had calmed, and his look indicated that he truly believed this statement.

Jacob escorted him to the door and closed it after him. He picked up the phone and called his wife. He told her about the visit and how his intuition told him that this might be beneficial to the research at Rio House. It might take a few years, but it was more promising than anything else that existed. He gathered his things and told his secretary to have his driver retrieve him after dropping Chuck off at the hotel, which was only a few blocks away. Jacob arrived home and excitedly rambled on to Betsy about Chuck's research, as Betsy herself communicated to the staff about dinner preparations. When Chuck arrived at the house, Jacob could barely make it through dinner without getting fully involved in the discussion about the investment. Betsy mitigated his excitement by asking Chuck about his life in Barstow, his childhood, and other social pleasantries.

When they had finished the meal, Jacob, Betsy, and Chuck retired to the sitting room adjacent to the formal dining room. The room was furnished with formal but comfortable furniture. Two matching brocade easy chairs complemented a long blue leather sofa. A surprising number of gilded side tables dotted the room, providing ample space for guests to rest their drinks, or anything else that would impede social interactions in a crowded room. Side chairs, various pieces of antique furniture handed down through generations, a mahogany Steinway grand piano, and valuable artwork completed the look of a room that might only exist in the home of a family of extreme wealth. Chuck settled in a chair while Jacob and Betsy sat next to each other at one end of the long sofa.

Jacob did not waste any time getting to the business at hand. "So, Chuck, give me the figure first, then read me the list I asked you to prepare. We can discuss details after that."

"Okay, Jacob, the amount is two million American dollars. With that, I will build a state-of-the-art factory and research facility in Barstow. I will hire scientists, as well as someone to help me develop the business and gain clients. I will not pay you back the two million, but I will sign an agreement giving you forty percent ownership and the accompanying profit. Thoughts?" Chuck read from his notes, which had been scribbled on a notepad provided in the hotel room.

"Thanks, Chuck. That was simple enough. Let's come to an agreement on the profit first, then I have many questions. I'm going to counter your offer. I'll give you a scientific research grant of one million and a business loan for the second million. That loan will need to be paid back. I'm good with the sixty-forty split. The loan will be paid back from any total profit, and any remaining profit will come to me at forty percent. How does that sound?" Jacob leaned back and crossed his left leg over the right; his fingers were tented in front of his chest. Betsy's hand rested lightly on his leg. He stared at Chuck, waiting for a reaction.

Chuck released the breath he had been holding, his body collapsing into the chair. "Yes, I can do that. Does that mean you're going to give me the money?"

"Yes. I'm going to have my attorney draw up the contract tonight. I'll come to the hotel tomorrow, and we can review and sign. If everything goes well, the money will be in your account in two days." Jacob was matter of fact with his response. "Now, we have so many questions."

Betsy started by asking about the broad details of organic nanobots. Jacob interjected with questions of his own. Chuck answered their questions late into the night. The next afternoon, Jacob met Chuck at the hotel, and they sat in a small conference room to review and sign the contract. Chuck flew back to California two days later, the two million dollars securely in his account. Jacob and Betsy left Winnipeg the same day as Chuck to fly to Beverly's birthday party at the Baker Lake facility. They would never see Chuck again, and they would never realize the impact their decision would have on their daughter's future.

10

The driver informed Beverly that it was a fifteen-minute drive to BarsTech Industries from the small Barstow airport. She had rediscovered her parents' investment in the company a few months ago when her accountant had mentioned the significant success and associated profit of the holding. At the time, she had put it aside to look at later. It was on the same day that she learned of Mateo Trujillo that she had looked at the work being done by BarsTech. The two things could not be that much of a coincidence – it had to be fate. She immediately called her assistant in the U.S. and told him to make an appointment to meet with the person in charge at BarsTech. Her assistant, Stephen, called her back within minutes. She would be welcome at the Barstow facility at any time. The gentleman who had originally solicited the investment from her father, Chuck Morozov, was still in charge and would be happy to see her.

The driver pulled up to the security gate at BarsTech Industries and rolled down the window. Beverly lowered her window as well, holding her identification out to the female guard who was dressed like a mercenary, complete with two firearms and a well-stocked tactical utility belt. The guard smiled as she matched the identification with her records.

"Welcome to BarsTech, Ms. Seagram. We are excited about your visit." The guard said.

"Thank you," Beverly responded before raising her window.

The guard activated the large gate, which opened towards the car. The driver drove through the gate and proceeded down a long, paved drive. The road continued in front of him with no buildings in sight. After a mile or so, the road started a gradual downward slope, and the actual campus of the company appeared in a clearly man-made depression.

The compound was comprised of three rectangular buildings, side by side, with the short end of each building facing the approach. The tan colored buildings matched the color of the dirt around them and were separated by a space of about twenty feet with no noticeable connection between them. There did not seem to be any doors or windows in the two buildings to the left. The building on the right had a single very large roll-up door almost to the edge of the right side of the building. To the left of that door, a regular door sat almost unnoticeable and unassuming. The approach road curved slightly to the right and ended at the roll-up door. There was a small parking lot to the left, with a walkway leading to the smaller of the doors. Solar panels provided shelter for the vehicles parked there.

The driver parked the car under the shelter of the solar panels and quickly exited the car to open the door for Beverly. Beverly swung her legs out of the back seat and planted her feet firmly on the pavement before standing. She adjusted her sunglasses and ran a finger through her hair on the left side to tuck it neatly behind her ear. She stared at the building, unsure how to proceed. At that moment, the smaller of the doors opened, and a gentleman stepped out. He was slightly taller than Beverly, mid-50s, balding, and dressed in khakis, a button-up shirt, a light argyle sweater vest, and what Beverly would call old man shoes. His glasses and his thin frame made him look older than he probably was. He wasn't unattractive but seemed to Beverly to be the type that spent way too much time at work and not enough time having fun.

He waved at Beverly, his smile widening as he walked briskly towards her. Beverly started walking so that she could meet him. As they neared each other, the guy extended a hand, which Beverly accepted.

"I'm Chuck. We are so happy to have you visit us." The man said.

"Hi Chuck. Beverly Seagram, which I'm sure you already know. I'm also excited to see what you're doing here." Beverly reciprocated.

"Let's go inside. We have a place where your driver can wait, but I would rather him not see the production, if that's okay." Chuck asked kindly.

"Of course. Lead the way." Beverly motioned forward as they walked.

Chuck opened the door and ushered them into a large room that resembled a warehouse. The garage door they had noticed outside and a matching door at the far end seemed to be the only entrances and exits to the space, other than the smaller door they had used. To their left, about halfway down the long space, a regular door and another roll-up door were all that occupied the entire left wall. This roll-up door was smaller than the ones at either end, looking more like a traditional garage door. To their right, four 20-foot containers sat on their chassis, with a bright green forklift that was used to move the containers. Each of the four pairs of wheels under each container had been placed on a low platform with some sort of ball bearing system that allowed the container to be moved easily in position, presumably behind a truck for transporting them. The entire space was a bright white. Everything looked sterile and new, the only contrast being the containers and their moving systems.

Beverly and her driver followed Chuck through the smaller door to the left, which led into a room that was clearly designed for casual meetings and waiting. The room was comfortable and had the appearance of a living room in a high-end home. There were two leather sofas, facing each other, with a low table between them. Each sofa had two end tables, with expensive-looking lamps positioned in the center of each one. At the end of the two sofas, two cloth club chairs were angled slightly towards one another, with a small round table between them. A wet bar to the side of the conference table looked well stocked with a variety of snacks and non-alcoholic beverages in a small, glass-front fridge. A single door on the far wall was the only indication that there might be more to this room than it appeared.

"There are snacks, drinks, and a rather complicated coffee machine for your comfort while you wait." Chuck addressed the driver. "Ms. Seagram, if you will please follow me."

"Please call me Beverly." Beverly requested of Chuck as she followed him through the door at the far end of the room. She glanced back and noticed her driver settling into one of the plush fabric chairs with a cup of coffee.

The door opened into a long, white, sterile hallway that was devoid of any visual interest. It ran perpendicular to the long side of the building, and Beverly could not see the end. There were several doors along the course of the hallway, and other than the one they had exited, all were on the left side of the passageway. Chuck walked to the second door and paused.

"You're going to have a lot of questions," Chuck stated. "I'll explain as much as I can along the way. When I'm done showing you the overview, I have a comfortable place we can sit and talk."

"I'll hold my questions," Beverly responded flatly.

"Thank you." Chuck sighed. "It's a lot for most people to assimilate."

"I'm not most people, Chuck." Beverly smiled, her expression betraying mixed messages of seriousness and joviality.

"Okay then, here goes..." Chuck opened the door and revealed a small room that was large enough for no more than four people. The walls were glass, and Beverly immediately recognized that it must be an elevator. He held his hand out, palm up, indicating that Beverly should enter first. She complied, and Chuck stepped in after her, firmly closing the hallway door behind them. The glass cube started to rise into the center of a larger room with benches and chairs placed irregularly throughout. The simple and modern furniture presented muted tones of grays, beiges, and dusty blues with natural wood accents, creating a calming contrast to the stark white of the walls. Opposite the elevator door, a floor-to-ceiling wall of windows looked out over a landscape that Beverly could not comprehend.

The space that extended out in Beverly's field of vision was one of organized chaos. Mobile cubes moved around the large floor space, seemingly on their own. They connected with each other, then separated, only to connect with others. There were people walking amongst them, supervising but not interacting. The cubes themselves had light bars around the top edges. Some were glowing a soft, steady blue, some green, others white, and one cube had a red light that pulsed. The cube with the red light was being attended by two technicians. Beverly assumed the red light meant that it had malfunctioned.

"What am I looking at here?" Beverly asked.

"This is the beauty and grace of a completely AI-driven automated production facility," Chuck answered. "The pods, as we call them, are each completing tasks that culminate in the growth of a crop of organic nanobots."

Beverly nodded in understanding. "This is one building. Is the same thing happening in the other two?"

"Yes," Chuck answered. "The second building is identical in production to this one. The third building is for research and development. We're always working on new projects."

"I want to know what kind of projects, then I want a more detailed description of how the AI process works." Beverly was curious how Chuck would react to introducing a new R&D project that wasn't his idea.

Chuck answered quickly. "Well, an example of a new project is a small fusion reactor that charges electric cars. The engine is too small to power a car itself, but it will be able to charge an electric vehicle's battery to 80% in a few minutes. It's not intended to be regularly charged the vehicle, even though that might eventually happen. The intent is to be an emergency power source. With current technology, if you run out of battery and you are not near a charging station, you're pretty much fucked. It's not like a gas-fueled vehicle where someone can simply bring you some gas and get you back on the road. It might even eventually allow electric vehicles to have unlimited range."

"Or would allow them to go to places where charging might not be convenient, or possible," Beverly added. "I'm sure you have other projects but tell me about the process I'm looking at here."

"It's surprisingly simple," Chuck admitted. "We supply a cube with cultivated cells from the African clawed frog and the reagents and other ingredients needed to start the process. The AI in the cubes grows the cells, filters them, transfers them to other cubes for programming, and preserves them in sealed containers for our customers. The initial programming is done by a computer for each cube based on the needs of what has been ordered.”

“Thanks, Chuck, I appreciate you stating that as simply as you did,” Beverly said. “Now, let’s sit down and talk. I have a proposition for you.”

Chuck motioned to a cluster of blue and tan chairs near the glass wall that overlooked the production facility. “We have privacy here. If this will work?” Chuck offered.

“Of course,” Beverly said as she took a seat. Chuck sat in a chair perpendicular to hers; his legs crossed in Beverly’s direction. “I have hired a scientist who is going to grow organic nanobots from a different base.” Beverly paused, letting the simple piece of information sink in.

“I tried that.” Chuck responded quickly and with a tinge of anger.” It didn’t work. For many reasons.”

“You tried with cyanobacteria. He’s using algae.” Beverly again paused.

Chuck was silent for several minutes, and Beverly allowed him the time to turn the idea over in his mind. “That might work. If he’s already doing it, why do you need me?”

“I need you for production. He’s going to perfect the process in my lab, then share the information with you. I will need you to produce them in large quantities.” Beverly paused, but only briefly. “Chuck, you and I both know the versatility of using algae. The limits that your current product has would be eliminated.”

"Yes, Beverly. That would be a significant breakthrough. I wish I had thought about it." This time, Chuck paused before continuing. "Nevertheless, I want to be a part of it. What do you need from me?"

"Nothing right now. Just sit tight. I'll personally funnel the info your way when I have it. It might be a few months. He's just getting started." Beverly said.

"Can you tell me his name?" Chuck asked.

"Mateo Trujillo." Beverly replied immediately.

"Never heard of him," Chuck said as he stood and motioned for Beverly to follow him back to the glass elevator.

11

Mateo stared at the woman standing in front of him. Few people outside the lab knew anything about this building. For a person not involved with the University's research to simply wander in was unusual. But his curiosity was piqued, and he was also trapped, since she stood between him and any possible exit. Therefore, he decided to tolerate the potential verbal attacks that usually accompanied someone wanting to discuss his research.

"Who are you and how do you know about my research?" Mateo asked brusquely.

"Well, Mateo, those are two very complicated questions, with even more complicated answers," Beverly answered comically, smiling and laughing slightly. Her eyes twinkled as she spoke, almost as if she were talking to a child who did not understand what they were asking.

Beverly continued, "We should go somewhere to talk in comfort; this is going to take a while."

"Let's start with your name, then we can go from there," Mateo said, his curiosity growing stronger after her cryptic comments.

"My name, Mateo, is Beverly Seagram, as I said previously," she said matter-of-factly.

"Why does your name sound familiar?" Mateo mumbled, half in question to Beverly and partially to himself. He turned his back to Beverly and reached over to his workbench to grab his phone. He quickly opened the browser and typed in her name. His facial expression varied from awe to concern, then back to curiosity as he read the Wikipedia page on the Seagram family.

"Satisfied that I'm not going to abduct you?" Beverly said, again laughing as she spoke. "I'm here by myself. I just want to talk. I find your research fascinating. And potentially useful."

"Then you're the only one," Mateo responded.

"That's unfortunate." Beverly continued. "I have a feeling that it is largely misunderstood. And grossly underestimated. Is that enough for you to sit down for a conversation?"

"Yes," Mateo said, allowing himself a moment to enjoy the warm and fuzzy feelings flowing through him with the compliment, rather than being called a disgrace to the synthetic biology community. "I'm still skeptical, but I'm also curious. Do you prefer where we might have this conversation?"

"Let's meet where I'm staying. Los Poblanos, in North Valley. Do you know it?" Beverly said casually.

"Of course. Everyone knows the lavender farm there. And their restaurant, which I've heard is very expensive. I've never been." Mateo admitted.

"It's a nice place. Comfortable." Beverly said, almost as if to herself. "Meet me in the restaurant at five. Dinner is on me. And we'll talk."

"Okay," Mateo said. "I'll see you there."

Beverly nodded, turned, and walked out of the lab. Mateo walked back to his workspace and continued organizing his tasks. He worked for another four hours before realizing that his focus was limited. As he gathered his things, his thoughts turned to the upcoming conversation. What did she want from him? And why was she interested in his research? What he found online had been vague. There was a lot of information about the companies owned by the Seagram Family. And an obscure article about a daughter who had a rare childhood disease. As well as information about the death of her parents when she was only eighteen. The woman he had met in the lab was definitely not disabled. So, what was it then?

These thoughts became more urgent as he walked to his bike. He removed the lock from the bike, threw it in his backpack, and raised his leg to get in the bike seat. He pushed off and started the ten-minute ride to the house, which he shared with five other people. Once in his room, he realized that he would need to clean up for this meeting. And that the thirty-minute bike ride to the expensive hotel might leave him unpresentable. He decided that he would splurge and take a car service. He rarely spent money on those kinds of luxuries, but tonight his instinct told him it was the right decision.

Mateo undressed in his room and turned on the shower in the small, shared bathroom. He looked in the mirror as he moved a towel from the hook on the back of the door to drape it over the shower curtain rod. His faced looked tired, but his body was fit. Taking his bike everywhere and eating a diet that fit with his limited resources kept him trim. His tousled dark mane, short dark beard, and hairy chest only accentuated his toned physique. He showered, letting the conditioner sit in his hair for longer than usual. When he had adequately rinsed the conditioner out of his hair, he turned off the water and grabbed the towel to dry himself. He started with his hair, giving his head a vigorous rub before drying his body. He stepped out of the shower and used a black plastic comb to detangle his hair, letting it fall down his forehead to partially cover his eyes. He let his hair hang this way while he applied a cheap drugstore facial moisturizer, followed by anti-perspirant to his armpits. He wrapped the towel around his waist and opened the bathroom door.

As he walked back to the bedroom, he ran his hands through his hair, pushing the bangs back and to the left. The result was a look that seemed like he had taken no effort to look like he could model loungewear for a high-end outdoor clothing company. And truthfully, he put only a small amount of effort into anything about his appearance. He trimmed his beard once a week with clippers that he bought on sale at a discount store and used personal care products that were cheap and usually also on sale. Regardless, he always looked good, no matter what he wore or how much lack of effort he put into it.

The slacks he chose to wear were one of two pairs that he owned. Between the black and the olive green, he chose the green. He threaded his brown belt through the belt loops and tossed the pants on his unmade bed before retrieving a clean pair of black boxer briefs and matching boot socks from the second-hand dresser on the wall by the bathroom door. The top of the dresser supported a small television, and Mateo paused briefly to try to remember the last time he had turned it on. He pulled on the underwear and sat on the bed to put on the socks, pulling them up over the well-defined calf muscles of each leg. The slacks, paired with a black t-shirt and a dark gray long-sleeved button-up, left unbuttoned and untucked, looked casually elegant. He slipped on a pair of tan ostrich cowboy boots, a splurge as a treat for himself when he matriculated to the doctoral program, and which he only wore on special occasions.

The ride-share app said the car would arrive in fifteen minutes. The longer wait time was the price he paid for choosing the cheapest option. It was all good; he would still arrive a few minutes early. The car arrived, and Mateo opened the door, climbing into the back seat and buckling his seatbelt before the driver could place the transmission in drive.

"How's your day going?" Mateo asked the driver, whose name he remembered from the app, to be Tony.

"Good. Busy." Tony replied. "Got a date? Most people don't take a car to Los Poblanos in the evening for a casual dinner."

"Yes. Sort of." Mateo said. "I'm not really sure what it is."

"You buyin'?" Tony asked.

"No. It's her treat." Mateo answered.

"I see what you mean. You should enjoy it. I've heard it's pretty good." Tony suggested.

"I plan to," Mateo said, as they finished the remaining two minutes of the drive in silence.

"Have a good evening," Tony said, pulling up to the double silos at the end of the small parking lot that marked the entrance to the resort. A sign indicated the restaurant was to the right of the silos.

"Thanks," Mateo responded as he exited the car and firmly closed the door. He waited for Tony to drive off before turning and walking towards the restaurant. He glanced at his watch. He was right on time.

Mateo bypassed the host stand and stepped through the door that led to the bar area. He could see the restaurant dining area to the right. The décor was what he would consider farmhouse elegant. Shiplap wood on the walls, elegant, antiqued fixtures, and comfortable seating was accented by heavy velvet curtains separating the rooms.

This place looked expensive, Mateo thought. He turned his head towards the bar and saw Beverly sitting at the far end of the bar, a classic martini in front of her. Her hand rested lightly at the base of the stemmed glass, her second and third fingers bisecting the stem of the drink. She looked up and noticed him as his gaze turned towards her. She raised her hand in acknowledgement and smiled as she stood from the wooden barstool.

12

Beverly noticed Mateo as soon as he entered the bar, and before he noticed her. She looked down at her drink, waiting until he had a chance to look around before she acknowledged him. She looked up just in time for his glance to meet her eyes. She waved at him and walked briskly towards him, signaling to a restaurant employee as she approached the entrance to the dining room. The employee, the restaurant manager, smiled at Mateo as she walked towards them.

"Right this way, Ms. Seagram." The manager said, motioning with her open hand towards the dining room. The manager walked to the side and just ahead of Beverly and Mateo. They wound their way through the main room and into the open kitchen, walking past the busy staff preparing meals for other guests. They exited the kitchen at the other end and entered a short hallway. The manager opened a door to the right and ushered them into a small, private dining room with walls painted a deep navy blue. The room contained rustic credenzas on each side framing a table and two chairs in the center. The table was set with a white cloth, simple silverware, soft burlap napkins, and a single tealight candle in a holder that looked like the bottom of a discarded wine bottle. The light from a dimmed crystal chandelier soft illuminated the room to not distracting from the view. The floor-to-ceiling window provided a portrait of the lavender fields. The brilliant evening sun highlighted the Sandia mountains in the background with hues of bright whites, tans, and pinks as the light began to pick up the feldspar deposits in the rock. The look of the room was the epitome of rustic elegance.

Beverly motioned for Mateo to sit as she herself took a seat. The server, a young girl with her blonde hair pulled back in a tight ponytail, entered and walked to the credenza on the left to get water glasses and a pitcher of water. After pouring water into short highball glasses, she walked to the opposite credenza and opened a bottle of wine, placing two very tall wine glasses on the table before pouring a small amount of deep red liquid into Beverly's glass. Beverly swirled the wine and lifted the glass to her lips, allowing the wine to sit for a moment before taking in a slight breath through pursed lips. She nodded to the server, who poured an ample amount into Mateo's glass before pouring a similar amount into Beverly's glass.

The server held out menus to each of them, cream-colored paper and narrow in shape, with a simple list of five entrees. The menu had no prices, and the entrees had no descriptions, only a list of proteins: Steak, Chicken, Fish, Shrimp, and Lamb. It seemed more of a formality than an actual menu. Beverly did not look at her menu, choosing instead to place it on the table as she observed Mateo trying to decipher the list. Bread was set on the table with whipped and seasoned lard, a concept that Mateo found funny. High-end restaurants often took ingredients used by poor people and reimagined them to become a luxury condiment. Nevertheless, he took a piece of bread and smeared it with the lard. The taste was amazing – rich and decadent. So different than the lard his grandmother had incorporated into daily cooking.

"What would you like for your entrée?" The server asked Mateo.

"Uh, Beef. Please." Mateo said nervously.

The menus were removed, and the server left the room.

Beverly raised her wine glass, tilting it towards Matteo. "Here's to the potential of something life changing." Mateo lifted his glass and clinked it against Beverly's, quickly taking a sip.

"I don't know much about wine, but this is delicious. I've never had anything like it." Mateo said, taking another long sip.

"1982 Château Margaux." Beverly said. "It's a pedantic choice, but still one of my favorites. And at $1500 a bottle, still a deal over other wines of lower quality."

Mateo was silent, not sure what to say.

"I'm guessing you haven't had this wine before?" Beverly asked, knowing the answer and feeling a need to establish facts about her wealth.

"No. Nothing close to it." Mateo said. "Ms. Seagram."

"Please call me Beverly."

"Beverly... I don't know where this is going or what I'm doing here. Can we get to the conversation that you requested in my lab? It will make dinner more pleasant for both of us." Mateo adopted the direct approach to help manage his growing anxiety.

"Very well. That's a fair request." Beverly began. "I'll start with a compact version of my reason for being here. Then we can talk about your possible involvement. Will that do?"

"Yes, that will do." Mateo agreed.

Beverly continued, "I was born with a rare and incurable disease. My family has a lot of money. My father and grandfather built a private research institute to find a cure. My symptoms are managed, but the method is... well, let's just say the method is not convenient. But it keeps me relatively symptom-free for short periods. It's not a long-term solution. I'm twenty-nine years old, not much younger than you. I think your research might hold the key to making progress on the work that my team of scientists has already achieved." Beverly paused, allowing Mateo time to process the vague information.

"I see," Mateo said. "And what do you know about phyconanobots?"

"Honestly, Mateo, I know very little about your research. I read a short blurb in a research journal that said you had proposed an alternate base to organic nanobots. And that you imagined they would help treat or cure a disease. It also indicated that your peers did not appreciate your ideas." Beverly spoke honestly, looking directly at Mateo.

The door opened, and the server entered with two identical plates of food. Each plate contained a ribeye steak, cooked medium, a baked potato topped with what Mateo later learned was house-made butter, and grilled asparagus. The butter on the potato was dotted with small black crystals, which Beverly excitedly identified as Icelandic lava salt. Mateo delayed his response to Beverly's diatribe as he cut into the juicy steak and placed it in his mouth. It was literally the best steak he had ever had. He followed the bite of beef with a generous fork full of potato, butter, and salt. The flavor was more complex than he had expected, and he ignored the vegetable as he cut once more into the steak.

"It's good, right?" Beverly smiled as she slowly enjoyed her steak.

"Amazing!" Mateo said. "I've never had food like this."

"I'm glad you like it. Now tell me about your research as we eat. "Beverly moved the conversation back to the topic at hand.

"Okay," Mateo said. "Here's my idea in a nutshell. Currently, organic nanobots use the cells from the African clawed frog as a base. This limits the programming of the bots to behaviors that are inherent to the frog itself. Things like direction and locomotion, behavioral constraints, and sensory perception are all they can be programmed to do, so telling them what to do is limited. There are also problems with temperature, pH levels, and immune response. If we use a different base, we could make the nanobots limitless. My research focuses on using algae based. Algae are much more versatile. The bots would be self-replicating, infinitely programmable, and relatively undetectable. I call them 'phyconanobots' and sometimes just 'phychobots' because the root word for algae is phyco."

Beverly listened quietly. She took deep, slow breaths to avoid betraying her excitement at what this might mean to the efforts at Rio House. It was important to approach the negotiation with Mateo carefully. She did not want to scare him off with her enthusiasm, and she knew that it was crucial that it be his own decision to join her team. So, she asked questions that would allow Mateo to remember the excitement he must have experienced when he first thought of this idea. Then she would make him an offer he would not be able to refuse.

"How would this technology be applied to a situation like mine? Once it is fully developed, of course. Give me an example." Beverly asked, feigning skepticism.

"Well, let me think," Mateo responded, clearly becoming more excited at being asked to provide more detail. "In the case of muscle that calcifies with trauma, the phycobots would be programmed to do one of two things, or maybe both. "Mateo paused and stared off to the side, clearly thinking it through before responding. "We could program them to alter the ACVR1 gene itself, but I think that would be a long-term solution. And by that, I mean, over time, it would prevent future occurrences. The other option would be to program the bots to counter the heterotopic ossification as it occurs. Since the mechanism of that is specifically not known... or at least I don't think it is, then we would have to learn that first. There might be other ways, but that would take more thought on the way the specific disease manifests. Sorry, I'm rambling and thinking out loud. It feels good to think like this. It's been a while."

Beverly took a sip of wine. Mateo mirrored her motions. The server arrived and cleared the diner plates, refilling both wine glasses. She walked over to the credenza on the left and lifted an antiqued silver dome to reveal a plate of bite-sized pastries and sweets. She moved these to the cleared table and asked if they wanted coffee, which they both declined. They sat in silence as Beverly pondered what Mateo had told her. She had specifically omitted information about Sednamaroq, which might turn him off from joining the team. He would learn about it soon enough when he got to Rio House.

"That sounds very exciting," Beverly said, picking up a small petit four and placing it in her mouth, waiting to finish the sweet before continuing. "You keep mentioning that these... what do you call them... phycobots, are programmed. What do you mean by that? Are they controlled by a computer?

"No, no. No computer once they are grown. They are organic, so it's basically like creating designer DNA. The DNA in the phycobots is specific to the purpose. It does what it was made to do once it is introduced into the host. Does that make sense?" Mateo tried to avoid using big words and concepts.

"Yes, to a degree," Beverly said. "I guess what I really want to know is how they get to that point. Can you walk me through the process, what equipment would be used, and how many staff?"

"Of course. I see what you mean. "Mateo took a deep breath so that he could speak more slowly. "First, I would use a PCR machine to amplify the DNA. I've always called these machines thermocyclers, but my current lab calls them PCR machines, which stands for polymerase chain reaction. Please stop me if you know this stuff already." Mateo paused.

"I don't. Please continue." Beverly encouraged.

"Okay. So, after the DNA is amplified and sequences are available for analyzing, I would use an electrophoresis system for separating fragments. This equipment would need to be more customized. Then the CRISPR gene editor would do the rest. I've thought that maybe a TALEN would be more effective since it makes more precise modifications to the DNA itself, but I've never been able to test it with the bots. I've actually never been able to create the bots. Just not enough funding to make them. So, all theoretical. But I'm pretty certain that it would work."

"So, your lab has never created a single bot?" Beverly asked.

"No," Mateo said, realizing that this was most likely the end of the discussion.

"So, here's the big question, Mateo. What would the funding look like to test this?" Beverly leaned forward across the table, her hands extending, palms down, towards Mateo. She looked him in the eyes, waiting for a response.

Mateo met her gaze with difficulty. He wanted to give her a truthful answer but knew from experience that it scared off potential investors. He usually cut the number in half, thinking that he could get acceptable results to warrant asking for more. With Beverly, however, he decided to go for it. What did he have to lose at this point? "Minimum five mil. That would buy all the equipment, pay for a lab, and staff, including a salary for myself, which I haven't had in a long time."

Beverly stared at him. "Five million dollars to get viable phycobots?"

"Yes," Mateo replied, remaining silent and waiting for the denial.

"Let me think on it. I might be interested in investing." Beverly said cryptically as she reached into her pocket and pulled out a hotel key card. She placed it flat on the table and pushed it towards Mateo. "I got you a room for the night. No strings. Just thought you might need a break. Get some rest, enjoy the amenities, and meet me back here for breakfast at 9 a.m."

Beverly's offer wasn't a request. Mateo took the key card and picked it up. A small sticky note had a room number written on it and was attached to the card. He didn't expect this and was unsure how to react. "Uh, thank you. I don't know what to say."

"Nothing to say. Just get a good night's rest and meet me here for breakfast. It's that simple, Mateo. I'm either going to invest or not. If nothing else, you'll have a pleasant night in a hotel that you would not otherwise be able to afford. Sorry to be blunt, but it's how I prefer to operate. I don't like unnecessary pretense, and I've enjoyed this diner with you. I'm going to get some rest. Please stay here as long as you want; you can even order more food if you want. "Beverly stood and placed her napkin on the table before walking to the door. "I'll see you tomorrow, yes?"

"Yes. Thank you." Mateo replied.

Beverly exited, and the server returned. Mateo ordered coffee to enjoy with the small desserts. He remained in the room for an hour after Beverly left. Could this be the break he needed? He had gotten his hopes up in the past, only to be severely disappointed. Two cups of coffee and all the sweets later, he left the room and asked for directions to his room. The room faced the back of the property and consisted of a king bed, a small sitting area, a kiva fireplace, and a private covered patio. The furnishings were simple and luxurious, tones of beige, brown, and white accented with soft colors from the original artwork hanging on the walls. Having only his phone with him, he turned on the television and selected a reality show that he remembered enjoying in the past but had not watched in a long time. As he curled up under the soft duvet, he remembered what it was like to relax. He had not been this calm in a long time. He drifted off to sleep quickly, resting deeply and peacefully.

Mateo woke at 7 a.m., realizing that he had not set an alarm. He had a moment of panic before looking at the clock. He stretched as he stood up from the bed. He walked to the patio door and stood there in his underwear, considering that this was how the wealthy must live. If Beverly funded his research, he was going to get his own apartment, or even a house, where he could create this kind of peace for himself. He turned and walked to the bathroom, starting the water in the shower and peeing down the drain while it warmed up.

He opened the lavender scented bath products and sniffed each – body wash, shampoo, conditioner. They all smelled the same and reminded him of his only trip to a day spa. It had been a gift from a friend for his birthday. The gift had included a massage and sugar scrub. The experience had been relaxing, and the scent of the scrub was like what he was smelling now. Mateo stood under the hot water and wet his hair and beard, lathering it up with the shampoo. He rinsed his face, hair, and bread and applied the conditioner liberally, allowing it to sit while he washed the rest of his body with the shower gel, rinsed everything and turned off the water. He toweled himself off and used the provided comb to groom his hair and beard, looking at himself in the mirror and thinking that this might be a turning point for him.

He dressed in the clothes from the night before, which he had folded neatly and placed on the chair in the sitting area. He wanted to take what was left of the toiletries but had not brought his backpack with him and could not find a suitable substitute that would look like he wasn't pilfering residual hotel shower gel. If Beverly funded his research, he would come back to the store at the lavender farm and buy a bottle of it. He looked around the room, not having brought anything to leave behind except his phone and wallet, which were both in his pocket. As the door closed behind him, he slid the room key in his pocket and walked to the restaurant where Beverly was sitting in a chair on the patio.

She smiled when she saw him. She stood quickly and walked to meet him at the host stand, which had been moved to the outside and near the door to the dining room. The host, a local young man in his twenties, nervously escorted them to a private area on the patio. The table for two was set with white linen that matched the curtains that separated them from the other diners. The curtains that faced the mountains had been pulled back for them to enjoy the view. A server arrived with fresh coffee, a basket of breakfast breads, and silverware rolled in white cloth napkins. She asked how they liked their eggs – scrambled with cheese for Beverly and over easy with hot sauce on the side for Mateo.

"How was your night?" Beverly asked.

"It was nice. I slept the best I have in years." Mateo admitted.

"That's good to hear," Beverly added cream and sugar to her coffee, stirred it well, and took a sip. "Let's eat, then I have a proposal for you."

"Okay, I'm nervous about whether or not you're going to give me funding. Can you just give me a yes or no? It's too much pressure to enjoy my food otherwise." Mateo was honest about his intentions.

"Fair enough. Yes, I'm going to fund your research. The extent of that funding is what I want to talk about after we eat. But I need more coffee first." Beverly said with a smile and lifted her coffee cup to her lips.

The server arrived soon after with two plates of food, which he described as eggs, with green chile turkey sausage, and roasted baby potatoes. A small cup of cut fruit accompanied each plate. Mateo and Beverly ate in silence, enjoying the morning breeze and the stunning view of the mountains. After finishing their food, the server removed the plates, refilled their coffee cups, and placed a wooden tray on the table next to Beverly. The tray contained a set of stapled papers that looked to be about ten pages.

"This is an agreement to fund your research. I'm going to give it to you after we have talked. You can take it with you and look it over, have a friend or colleague, or even an attorney, review it before giving me a decision. I will, however, need a decision before I return home in four days."

"What's the catch?" Mateo asked.

"No catch, per se. Just the details." Beverly said. "I'm willing to support your research with unlimited funding. There is no amount that you could spend on it that would be a problem."

Mateo stared at her. "That doesn't make sense."

"Really? Do you have your phone?" Beverly asked.

"Yes. Why?" Mateo was confused.

"Search for the phrase *Beverly Lynn Seagram net worth*. You will see a number that is inaccurate. It's actually much higher than reported."

Mateo pulled his phone from his pocket and searched. The results were consistent that Beverly Lynn Seagram's net worth was approximately four hundred billion Canadian dollars. Mateo was shocked. He looked from his phone to Beverly and back to his phone.

"You see, Mateo, when my parents died, I became the sole heir to the Seagram family fortune. My great-grandfather, grandfather, and father had invested in many businesses, including mining operations, land ownership, and technology research. And those don't even touch the surface of my portfolio. Considering the way my money is invested, it would be literally impossible for me to exhaust my fortune. So, yes, I want to fund your research in an unlimited manner." Beverly was matter of fact with her statement.

"There must be a catch," Mateo said.

"The single condition of my offer is that you must move to the research facility and live there. You will be provided with full room and board. And a salary. And unlimited resources. The only thing you will sacrifice, Mateo, is a normal social life. The extent of your social circle will be the other scientists and me. No outside contact is allowed while actively conducting research. Depending on how long it takes for a breakthrough, you could retire at an early age and be very wealthy. Two years with me, and you could build a new lab at the university with your name on it. Imagine the legacy. Imagine the credibility. Mateo... imagine the feeling your colleagues will experience when your research is published in every major journal as legitimate and successful." Beverly's speech cadence increased as she talked, causing Mateo to place high value on her offer.

"To clarify," Mateo asked, "I leave my life here and move to your research facility, get paid a salary, and have unlimited funds and resources. The only catch is that I can't have contact with the world outside the facility while I'm there. Is that correct?"

"Yes," Beverly said simply.

"Where is your facility?" Mateo asked.

"Rio Island, Baker Lake, Nunavut. Do you know where that is?" Beverly asked.

"No, but I'm going to look it up while we talk." Mateo picked his phone up from the table and opened the map, typing in the location. "Wow! That's way up there. I didn't know people lived that far north."

"Not many people do. But there is a reason the lab is there. That will become clear when you are there. If you take the offer, of course." Beverly was careful not to reveal too much about the location. "You have four days to decide, Mateo." Beverly pushed the papers over to Mateo. He glanced at them quickly and noticed the salary was more than any researcher could expect in their career.

"I'll read through this and get back to you. Can you send me your contact info?" Mateo's pulse raced with the thought of this opportunity. Was it too good to be true?

"Of course." Beverly navigated to her contact card and texted it to him. She seemed to already know his number, which did not surprise Mateo. "Text me when you decide. If your answer is yes, then I'll provide further instructions. If your answer is no, then we will have no further contact. Understood?"

"Yes, of course." Mateo was still browsing the agreement. His mind swirled with excitement and confusion.

"I look forward to hearing from you, Mateo. My driver will take you home. Whenever you are ready." Beverly offered.

"Thanks. I think I'm ready to go now. I have a lot to think about." Mateo said.

Over the next two days, Mateo read the agreement over and over. It was very simple and very clear. He would receive the stated salary and a very attractive benefits package; he would be required to relocate to Rio House, which evidently was the name of the research facility, and he would have unlimited resources to conduct his research. He was shocked; it actually said 'unlimited resources' in the agreement. It was surreal and bizarre. The final two pages were a standard non-disclosure agreement. To be safe, he called an acquaintance who was a professor at the law school. He had met Stan two years earlier at a faculty function, and they had dated briefly. It had not worked out, but they had remained friends. Stan looked over the agreement and agreed that it was solid in Mateo's favor. He also mentioned that it must be a joke because no one ever offered unlimited resources. His professional guess was that the agreement would never be countersigned, and the offeror would never follow through with initiating the job.

Mateo woke at 2 a.m. on the third day after his meeting with Beverly. He was going to do it. What did he have to lose? Even if he didn't like the environment, he could tough it out for a couple of months and have enough saved to live on until he could find other options. He texted Beverly before he fell back asleep.

I'm in.

What next?

When he woke at 6 a.m. to go for a run, Beverly had responded.

Let's meet at your lab this afternoon.3 p.m. I'll give you details then.

Mateo's run was full of energy, and he completed the three-mile route in record time. He felt lighter, like his life had purpose again. In the early afternoon, he rode his bike to his lab, parked and locked it as usual, and tapped his access card on the pad by the door to get himself into the building. He walked up the stairs and to the lab more quickly than usual, taking the steps two at a time. The lab was busy with other scientists, and no one paid him any attention as he walked briskly to his corner. He dropped his bag on the floor by his bench and looked over his crowded but neatly arranged workspace. His mind raced with a list of tasks that he needed to get done to complete the submission for his degree. As he attempted in futility to organize his thoughts, the phone on his bench rang.

That's odd, he thought. He had never used the phone and didn't even know it worked. His communication with his advisor was by text, email, or in person, and considering the dead-end that his research had taken lately, there was no one else who would contact him.

"Hello?" Mateo answered the phone with an interrogatory.

"Good afternoon, Mateo." Clara DiViccio responded.

Mateo tried to think of the last time he had actually spoken to his doctoral advisor, Clara. He was sure it was when she had told him that she would continue to be his advisor and not to expect any assistance from her.

"Hey. Long time." Mateo said.

"Yes, well, this will probably be the last time," Clara responded. "I've signed off on the last draft of your dissertation research article. The university has decided to confer your doctorate without publication. Congratulations." Her tone was flat, with a touch of condescension.

"Uh, okay. I'm not sure what that means." Mateo admitted.

"What it means, Mateo, is that you now have a PhD in synthetic biology. I'm sending a courier to your lab with the documents you need to sign. It's up to you if you want to attend the graduation ceremony this year." Her tone continued to sound like she was reading from a script while trying to suppress her anger and sarcasm. "My advice to you, Mateo, is to take the degree and get on with your life."

"Okay. Thanks for the advice." Mateo said flatly, matching her speech.

"Oh, and if you can have your bench cleared by the end of the day, that would be great. We have other people doing real research that could use it." Clara could not help herself with this final dig before she disconnected the call.

Mateo held the phone to his ear as the line went silent. His anger towards the situation with Clara and the university faded as he thought about the opportunity with Beverly Seagram. He placed the phone back on its base and grabbed his backpack from the floor. He threw things in it, starting with items that he thought most important – the backup drive with his notes, a small stack of notebooks with his handwritten notes, charging cables, and his favorite coffee mug. Some items on his desk were simply not important, and he walked to the other side of the lab to get a few trash bags from the shared supply closet.

When Mateo returned to his isolated corner, a short young woman in bicycle shorts, a university logo t-shirt, and a bike helmet was waiting for him. She extended a large white envelope imprinted with the university logo in the upper left corner to him as she spoke. "Mateo Trujillo?"

"Yes," Mateo replied simply.

"I was told to wait while you signed these. There are three copies. Sign all three and keep one for yourself." She pushed the envelope further towards him. He could see that his name was hastily written on the front.

Mateo took the envelope and ran his finger under the seal, tearing the envelop in the process. "Sorry." He spoke.

"It doesn't matter to me. I was just told to bring the signed copies back." She stated.

"I have an extra envelope somewhere here," Mateo said as he searched in a drawer, finally pulling out a similar large white envelope.

He placed the new envelope on the desk surface and sat in his tall chair before removing the documents entirely from the torn envelope. "You might as well pull up a seat. I'm going to read this before I sign them." Mateo suggested. The courier found a nearby low desk chair and plopped into it, pulling out her phone and opening a social media app.

Mateo started reading the document. It was very straightforward. The university had determined that his time in the lab and the work that he had completed were sufficient to be awarded the degree. There were no promises of any future funding, nor was there an offer to continue in the lab, which was counter to the standard offer made to PhD graduates in the sciences. Instead, there was a brief statement that he was to remove all personal belongings from the workspace the university had provided to him by a date that was thirty days out. He thought briefly about making things difficult for Clara by keeping things here for the next thirty days but realized that he simply did not care. He wanted out of here as much as she wanted him out.

He signed the three documents, shoved one copy roughly in his backpack, where it crumpled on contact with the other items he had tossed in there and neatly placed the two remaining copies in the fresh envelope. He wrote the name 'Dr. DiViccio' on the front and handed it back to the courier. She took the envelope from him and quickly placed it in her courier bag, and removed another heavier cardboard envelope, which she handed him. She adeptly slung the bag crossways over her torso and adjusted it to rest against her lower back.

"Thanks." She said as she turned and walked away from him.

He waited until she was out of his sight and pulled the tab to open the envelope. Inside was his certificate of graduation, elaborate with the silver seal at the bottom center. He felt a sense of surreal pride holding it in his fingers. He took more care placing it in his backpack, settling it against his computer in the special protective pocket.

The number of discardable things in his space shocked Mateo. How had he managed to accumulate so much junk? He filled two trash bags and walked them to the trash chute in the hallway, listening as they fell the short distance to some mysterious space below. When he returned to his bench, Beverly was waiting for him. Her smile widened when she saw him.

"Mateo!" She exclaimed as she stepped forward and hugged him. "I'm so excited about this. I see you are working on emptying your desk."

"Thanks, Beverly, I'm excited too. And a bit nervous. Things are happening so quickly." Mateo said quietly.

"It's going to be a fantastic journey for both of us," Beverly said. "Did you settle things with the university?"

"Uh, yes. I just returned the paperwork. Assuming you had something to do with that?" He laughed nervously.

"Maybe." She smiled and laughed. "Money can make things happen, Mateo. In this case, I used it for something that was long overdue and in our mutual interest."

"Thank you, Beverly. You could have just hired me and let me worry about this on my own. I appreciate this little touch of consideration." Mateo said gratefully.

"One thing you will learn about me, Mateo, is that I take care of my people," Beverly responded, a slight tone of possessiveness underlying the statement.

"Well, I appreciate it. I just have a few things left to go through here. I can take a break, and we can talk. Are you okay talking here?" Mateo asked.

"Yes. But this won't take long." Beverly answered. She extended two copies of the agreement to him; her signature was already on both. "Sign these, please. I'm going to assign an assistant to help you with the move. His name is Stephen, and he will meet you at your residence later this evening. Stephen will arrange for anything that you want shipped to Rio House. Any requests that you have, just tell him and he will take care of it. I'd like you up there within the week. Is that doable?" Beverly was speaking quickly.

"Uh, yes, I think so. I do want some of that shower gel from the hotel." Mateo said, immediately realizing that she might be talking about lab equipment, as he signed the two copies and handed one copy back to her. The other copy he placed neatly in his backpack.

Beverly laughed. "Of course. That stuff smells amazing. I'll take care of that myself. But sit down over the next day or two and make a list of equipment and supplies. Stephen will know if we already have things or if we need to get them. And Mateo..." Beverly paused, making sure that she had his attention, "don't hold back. Literally anything you need, just tell him. Understand?"

Mateo nodded. "Yes. I understand. It's a bit overwhelming, having such carte blanche on a lab. I didn't even know that was a thing. Most research scientists have to fight for every small thing."

"This is a special situation, and you are a very special person. Get used to it," She smiled at him. "Now, let's get this started. You have my number if you have any questions. Otherwise, I will see you week after next." Beverly hugged him again, smiled, and left.

The emotions that coursed through Mateo were satisfying and somewhat confusing. For the first time in a long while, he felt needed and wanted. And he felt validated. He could see a friendship in the collaboration with Beverly Seagram. Yet there was something in the background that nagged at him. He could not clearly identify it, but something about the arrangement gave him a slightly uneasy feeling. Fortunately, this feeling was overshadowed by the excitement of having the resources to properly conduct his research.

13

When Mateo arrived at his shared house that evening, Stephen was waiting for him. "Hi Mateo, I'm Stephen Cook. I'm Beverly's personal assistant in the U.S. I take care of things for her when she's here." Stephen extended a hand in greeting.

"Good to see you," Mateo said, shaking Stephen's hand. Stephen was taller than Mateo, of African American heritage, with close-cropped hair and a trimmed beard. He was fit and had the greenest eyes that Mateo had ever seen. He was dressed in a light blue golf shirt that accented his physique. His jeans were clean and well-worn, perfectly complemented by new hiking boots.

"Do you want to grab a bite to eat while we talk?" Stephen suggested.

"Sure. Let me put my things in my room. Do you have a place in mind?" Mateo asked as he unlocked the door and motioned for Stephen to follow him into the house. He stowed his bike in the garage and walked to his bedroom, which was near the front door. Stephen waited patiently in the foyer for Mateo to place his things in the bedroom.

"I live in Denver, and this is my first time in Albuquerque, so I don't know what to suggest. Is there anything we might walk to? Maybe a favorite place of yours?" Stephen asked.

"Yeah, there's a place two blocks away that has good New Mexican food. Are you familiar with the local cuisine?" Mateo asked.

"No, but I'd like to try it. I arrived this morning and had fast food for lunch. Although I did notice that everything seems to have green chiles on it." Stephen said.

Mateo laughed. "Yeah, it's a way of life here. Outsiders either love it or hate it. Let's see where you fall with that."

Stephen laughed. "Can't wait."

They walked the two blocks to the local eatery, and Mateo ordered for both of them, suggesting that Stephen could try two things. Stephen tucked into the green chile chicken stacked enchiladas with a fried egg on top and could barely contain his enjoyment.

"I guess you're a fan." Mateo chuckled.

"Hell yes, I could eat this all day," Stephen said.

Mateo pushed his own plate towards Stephen. "Try the adovada."

Stephen took a bite of the tender pork in red chile, and his eyes rolled back. "That's amazing. And spicy! I love it." He pushed the plate back to Mateo and continued working on his enchiladas. When the server delivered fresh, hot sopapillas with a squeeze bottle of honey, Stephen found another level of enjoyment.

"You're very fortunate to live in a place that has food like this. The chef at Rio House might be able to replicate it, but you will need to provide guidance." Stephen said.

"Speaking of that, how do we approach the list of equipment that Beverly mentioned?" Mateo asked.

"You just tell me what you want. I keep a list in my phone. And I'll make it happen. It doesn't have to be equipment. Anything you might want, just tell me." Stephen said, Honey from the sopapilla dripping from his fingers.

"The lab list is complicated. It might be better if I text it. Here, enter your contact info." Mateo suggested, passing his phone across the table, the contacts app opened.

Stephen wiped his hands with his napkin, then dipped his fingers into his water glass to clean them further before taking the phone. He entered his contact and handed the phone back to Mateo. Mateo shared his own contact with Stephen.

"I'm going to start a text now with a few things, and I'll just add to it. Sound good?" Mateo said, starting a text message.

"Yep. That'll work." I might have questions that are more specific. I'm going to suggest that we meet each day until you leave. I'll make the travel arrangements, and we can go over those tomorrow." Stephen said.

"I like that," Mateo said distractedly as his fingers quickly typed and corrected the list on his phone. "Sorry, I'm making a list in my notes and copying it to the text so that I can track what I've sent you."

"It's all good, Mateo. I have nothing to do but take care of these things for you." Stephen said, winking at Mateo. "It doesn't have to all be about business as well. If you want to do social things, I can help with that. You're going to be sequestered at Rio House for a while, so you should do things that you might miss while you are there."

"Good idea. I'll think of some things." Mateo said as Stephen paid the bill for dinner.

"Good. Let's walk back to your place. When would you like to meet tomorrow?" Stephen asked.

"Let's do lunch. I want to go for a run in the morning. Do you know if there is a place where I can run or ride my bike at Rio House?" Mateo inquired

"I think so, but I've never been. The weather in winter will prevent outside activity, but there is a well-equipped gym, so you should be okay." Stephen answered cryptically.

"You've never been?" Mateo seemed shocked.

"No. No reason. Beverly keeps tight control over the flow of information there. I know only what I need to know to do my job. And I like it that way." Stephen said confidently.

They arrived back at Mateo's house, and Stephen drove off in his rental car. Mateo went inside, undressed, showered and brushed his teeth, and settled into his bed. He propped himself up on pillows to go through his initial list:

- x4 Roche real-time PCR machine (most current model)

- x4 Cole-Parmer gel electrophoresis device (most current model)

- x4 CRISPR-CAS9 system (or newer prototype model, if available)

- x4 Thermo Fisher Scientific CRISPR and TALEN gene editing toolkits

- All manufacturer-recommended peripheral and accessory equipment for each device above (they publish a list of supplies)

- Assuming the lab had most other standard lab equipment, or can get it if identified when I get up there.

- x20 Algae culture complete growing kit from A1 Science Supply Company

- x10 each algae cultures: R. subcapitata, Chlorella, Spirulina, Nannochloropsis, and A. platensis. (I will cultivate custom variants from these and possibly any local sources, if they exist up there)

- Los Poblanos lavender shower gel

Mateo laughed at the last item on the list as he copied the items into a text message to Stephen. He knew Beverly would follow through on her promise, but he wanted to make sure.

14

The sunrise over Barstow was not spectacular. The hues of purple and blue, tinged with dull yellow, slowly changed to a brighter yellow and muted orange as the dull and unassuming landscape failed to compete with the colors produced by the desert heat and the rising sun. Knox Creed stood in his living room, looking out the large window of his small house, admiring the contrasts that living in the California desert offered. He sipped at his hot coffee and allowed a sense of satisfaction to wash over him.

His joy was not rooted in the surreal sunrise, nor in the taste of the satisfying coffee. His joy this morning came from what sat in his driveway - a Volvo VNR Electric 6x4 tractor in Dark Gray Metallic. In small script on each side, the name *Cyber Wolf* was etched in a shade of gray slightly lighter than the color of the truck itself. The name he had chosen reflected the nature of the truck's electric motors and his self-designated status of being a lone wolf on the road. He had purchased the new truck eight months ago, after years of saving for the substantial down payment on the expensive vehicle. Shortly after purchasing the truck, he obtained a contract with BarsTech, a local defense contractor, to transport sensitive materials across the country.

The truck itself was designed for regional distribution, but the unique requirement of his current contract made it a perfect fit. It was an opportunity that came along rarely for long-haul truck drivers. It was also an opportunity that changed Knox's life for the better. With the exceptional pay from the company and the lower operating costs of the electric truck, he would be debt-free in less than two years rather than the seven years he had planned.

Knox liked living simply and efficiently. He didn't spend his money on things he didn't need. There were a few exceptions to this, the first being good coffee. It was a vice that he enjoyed, and he had invested in several high-end coffee systems to enhance this mild addiction. His favorite was his siphon system with its halogen torch base. It took time to make, but it produced an exceptional cup of coffee. For his everyday cup, he had spent $1500 on a Gaggia Academia, which he cherished. His second vice was art. Occasionally, Knox would come across a painting or sculpture that made him feel happy. He often joked that his art was worth more than his house. It was not a true statement, of course, but it reminded him of the value of surrounding himself with things that made him smile.

And then there was Ryder. Knox turned and looked across the small living room and through the open door to the bedroom. Ryder Garcia was asleep in the bed that he and Knox had shared for the past eight months. The emotions that consumed him when he looked at the man asleep in the bed were things that were once foreign to him. He had met Ryder in Amarillo on a cross-country trip delivering cargo for BarsTech. An admitted player, Knox had never expected to find love, and yet here it was. And he could not imagine a life without Ryder. His truck, his art, and his coffee — all things that he would gladly abandon for Ryder Garcia.

As he looked at the truck, he admitted to himself that he considered his truck a piece of art. It was not only beautiful to look at but also served as an investment in his future. The all-electric truck had a base range of 275 miles, which extended to 350 miles with the regenerative braking and solar options that his employer had attached to the top of the short, 20-foot containers he usually hauled. The truck would charge to 80 percent in 90 minutes, just enough time for a bathroom break or a quick meal. He had opted for all the options with the truck, deciding that if he was going to make the investment, he would enjoy it. All the bells and whistles included a sleeper cab that would rival the finest Japanese pod hotel, with state-of-the-art entertainment systems, a mini fridge, microwave, and the most comfortable bed of any truck on the market.

Knox's typical run consisted of month-long hauls across the country to the East Coast and back. He rarely drove more than 300 miles a day, delivering small pieces of equipment along the way, all along the I-40 corridor. He didn't know much about what he delivered, only knowing that it was expensive, and BarsTech insisted on extensive legal paperwork to go along with the locked trailers that he hauled. When he arrived at each of his delivery destinations, he would wait patiently while the truck was unlocked, unloaded, and relocked. His evenings were spent in truck stop overnight lots. He loved the life this type of work provided. He loved the freedom and independence, as well as the absence of personal accountability to another person. Some might call him a lone wolf. He preferred to think of himself as self-aware until Ryder. When Ryder moved in, he made the decision to abandon his life of complete independence and seek a balance with him by his side.

Chuck, his primary point of contact at BarsTech, had recently offered Knox an incredible offer. Rather than his typical multi-stop runs across the country, there was an opportunity to complete a single delivery. The challenge was the route. According to Chuck, Knox would drive to Thompson, Manitoba, for the delivery, then return home at his leisure. The route was long, and the roads were often treacherous. The bigger problem was finding charging stations for the truck along the way. As usual, Chuck had a solution to the most difficult challenges. BarsTech had been developing a small thorium salt generator that would be installed behind the cab of Cyber Wolf. The generator would charge the truck in the absence of a traditional charging station.

So, Knox had signed the contract. The fee they were paying him was enough to pay off the truck and live comfortably for at least a year before his next contract. Alternately, he could bank the money for retirement and continue working for BarsTech. He had asked Ryder to come along with him on the drive, and it had resulted in their first fight. Ryder could not accept being away from Knox for such a long period, particularly in the infancy of the long-term commitment to which they had both agreed. The solution was for him to ride along, and Knox could not understand why Ryder did not see this as the most viable solution. Ryder had significant responsibilities managing his family's ranch in Texas and abandoning that for several months was something that he did not consider viable. In the end, Ryder had made it work, and they were scheduled to leave in two weeks.

When Ryder had told Knox that he would join him, Knox cried and hugged him. Telling him he would not regret it. That contentment still flowed through him as he looked out at the truck in the driveway. For the first time in his life, he felt that he had everything that he could possibly ever want or need.

15

The journey to Rio House was, to say the least, interesting for Mateo. Following two weeks of coordination and a lot of help from Stephen, he found himself on Beverly's private plane to Baker Lake. What few belongings he had been allowed to take with him would be waiting for him at the Baker Lake facility. Everything else had been placed in a storage unit, courtesy of The Seagram Institute for Scientific Research — or SISR for short. That was the name on the contract that he signed, and, according to Stephen, was how his paycheck would be labeled when the money was directly deposited into his bank account each month. He had spent every evening of the past two weeks with Stephen, ensuring that all details for his absence from society were adequately handled.

During the six-hour flight on one of Beverly's private planes, Mateo had a lot of time to reflect on his life, as well as his situation. The attendant on the plane, a nice young man named Kevin, made sure that Mateo was comfortable and had everything he wanted. The only frustration sat with Kevin refusing to engage in conversation. Mateo was certain this was a result of Beverly's tight control over her employees and the need to keep information compartmentalized. Nevertheless, it resulted in the flight being rather lonely.

After a few glasses of an exceptional red wine and a rather heavy meal of roasted chicken, potatoes, asparagus, and warm sourdough bread, Mateo became drowsy and sank into the wide seat to try to sleep. The soft leather wrapped itself around him, but he could not quite get there. He drifted close to slumber but always hovered in the space just in front of it. His mind took him to a state of introspection, which was not always productive for him. He recalled the confusing feelings that dominated his mind as a teen. Realizing his attraction to other boys and trying to explain this to his catholic mother and father. His father had demanded that he never feel that way again. His mother told him that she would pray for him and that God would fix it for him. Neither of those things happened.

From the age of 13 until he was well into his early twenties, he came out to his parents every week. And every week it was the same discussion. His mother would pray for him, and his father would demand that he 'Stop this nonsense and be a real man. ' In the end, God either did not hear his mother's prayers or simply decided that Mateo needed to stay as he was created. Mateo chose to believe the latter. And further, he did not follow his father's advice. In contrast, he embraced his 'gayness' and lived open and proud. However, out of respect, he never brought guys home to meet his parents.

His mother was diagnosed with breast cancer when Mateo was a senior in high school, and she did not make it to see him graduate. His father told him that she would be proud of him for graduating, not knowing that he would receive a similar diagnosis a few weeks later, albeit with his prostate. Mateo made it through his first semester at the University of New Mexico before his father passed away. Finding himself alone and with an inheritance that barely paid off his parents' debt, Mateo allowed his studies to consume him. He dated occasionally but never found anyone with whom he felt he could form a real connection. His standard was also set at finding someone that his parents, if they were alive, would accept. And therefore, accept him.

Mateo did not consider his life empty, but it was unfulfilled. That was until the moment that Beverly Seagram showed an interest in his work. Having a wealthy heiress offer to give him unlimited money to do what he loved gave him a new sense of purpose.

The small but luxurious jet landed at Baker Lake airfield on the western shores of the large lake. It only took a few minutes for the plane to taxi to the hangar and park inside. Once the hangar doors had closed, the attendant opened the door and lowered the steps to allow Mateo to exit the plane. Beverly was waiting for him.

"Mateo! So good to see you. How was the flight?" Beverly seemed genuinely happy to see him.

"Hi, Beverly. It was nice. I've never been in a private jet before." Mateo said demurely. "It was very comfortable, and I appreciate all the snacks, food, and beverages. You really know how to treat your guests."

"I've learned to use the resources provided to me, and to extend those to the ones I care about. That's all it is, Mateo." Beverly smiled at the understanding that her wealth was something that she was given and did not earn. "Now, we're going to take a boat to the island, which sits at the eastern end of the lake. It's a two-hour ride, so we can get to know one another better."

The boat was not like any boat that Mateo had seen. The extra-wide, forty-foot pontoon craft had been fitted to resemble a houseboat in style and function, appearing more like a giant floating cube than a watercraft. He assumed that it would only be welcome in harbors with other luxury watercraft. Of the two levels, the first was divided into two staterooms for sleeping, each with an ensuite bath. A galley and a small suite of rooms for the staff fit into one end of the space. The second level was a single open lounge area, interrupted only by the helm station at the front of the vessel, which was sequestered by a glass wall.

Mateo followed Beverly up a set of wide steps to the second level, where they settled into each end of a large leather sofa, which was flanked by two overstuffed chairs and a variety of tables. The remainder of the space was occupied by a dining table with six chairs and various other, more intimate seating areas. The attendant, a woman named Sandra who looked to be in her fifties with a trim frame and dark hair pulled back severely into a ponytail, approached Beverly. Sandra was dressed elegantly in black slacks and a white blouse. White deck shoes contrasted with her look and must be necessary for other tasks that she might be required to complete on the boat.

"May I get you anything before we push off?" Sandra said.

"Yes, thank you, Sandra. I'll have a tomato juice, no ice, slice of lime. Mateo?" Beverly and Sandra both turned to look at Mateo.

"Uh, I'll have the same. Thank you." Mateo responded.

"Right away," Sandra said as she turned and quickly descended the stairs to the lower level.

"Beverly," Mateo started, "Why not take a seaplane to the island? This is nice, of course, but it seems a plane would be faster."

"I don't use seaplanes," Beverly said flatly. "My parents died in one, and I have not been on one since."

"I'm sorry," Mateo said. "I didn't know."

"Of course not. But it was a fair question. It was a week after my eighteenth birthday. They were returning to Winnipeg from my party on the island. It was traumatic, and I was not prepared to manage the family fortune. Thankfully, my parents had people who worked for them who were trustworthy and respected them, so I was surrounded by people who guided me. "Besides, the boat is nice and gives us time to talk before we get to Rio House," Beverly said kindly.

"It sounds like you've been through a lot. I'm sorry you had to endure that on your own." Mateo offered genuine empathy.

"Thank you, Mateo. Tell me about your childhood. From what I know, you were not immune to strife."

For the remainder of the trip, they talked about Mateo's childhood and his parents' deaths. He was surprised that he had not previously recognized the similarities between their two stories. It gave him a stronger resolve to find a cure for Beverly's disease.

16

Seagram Institute for Scientific Research (SISR)

The boat docked at the shore near Rio House. The dock had been purpose-built for both Beverly's transport vessel and the cargo barges that transported supplies and equipment from the Baker Lake airfield to the institute. The reinforced composite dock is connected to a walkway made from the same material. Beverly escorted Mateo off the boat and casually strolled along the walkway towards the glass and steel structure fifty yards away. Beverly explained that the July weather was the warmest they would see as the temperature hovered in the mid-sixties. A soft breeze swirled around them as they walked. Beverly was quiet for the first half of the walk. Then she spoke with a seriousness that frightened Mateo.

"I need to tell you something about the island that I did not disclose when we first met. I don't think it will change your mind about being here. It will, if nothing else, enhance your research." Beverly was cautious in approaching the subject of the statue with Mateo.

"That sounds ominous. Should I be worried? Scared? Both?" Mateo replied with a nervous humor in an attempt to hide his concern.

"No, none of those," Beverly said calmly. "I'm going to tell you a story as we walk. You will have questions. I will answer those, and then I will show you to your lab and your apartment."

For the following twenty minutes, Beverly told Mateo the story of her great-grandfather, John, and his initial encounter with Sednamaroq. She kept the tale as brief as possible, spending more time on the efforts of James and Jacob to find a cure for her ailment. She detailed the building of SISR, the containment of the statue within the building, and the types of research that had been attempted over the years. All of this sounded bizarre to Mateo. He did not fully believe that there were supernatural forces at work on the island, but Beverly believed it, and that made it important to him, so he would play along. The only thing that truly concerned him was the expectation that he would be the one to find the cure. That was a lot of pressure to place on a single scientist with an unproven theory.

"The obvious question," Mateo asked, "Is why the statue can't heal you completely?"

"Yes, that question consumed me for several years. The short answer is that we don't know. I've tried mimicking my great-grandfather's posture around the statue. I even slept there one entire night with my hands bound to my feet to form the circle. The disease always returns. The longest I've been able to stay away from the statue is four weeks, and that pushes it to a level that is barely manageable. Your research might not need to include Sednamaroq, but I think you will find it useful if it does." Beverly's voice took on a tone of hopefulness as she talked.

"Yes, it might," Mateo said, his mind turning with the possibilities this new element might present, if true. "Since my nanobots are organic and based on algae, I'm curious what effect the statue's power might have on them."

"Yes, Mateo!" Beverly exclaimed. "That was my very first thought when I learned of your research. It has been a long time since I've had hope like this. Now, I want to show you the statue, then we will go to your apartment. I'll give you a few minutes to get settled, then we can look at the lab."

"Do you mind if we look at the lab first? My mind will want to start organizing my workspace, and that will help me relax once I get to where I'll be staying." Mateo requested.

"Of course, Mateo, of course," Beverly said as they entered the building.

The glass door that served as the main entrance to the building faced the dock. As they entered, Mateo turned to look back across the distance they had walked. He had a clear view of the dock, Beverly's transport boat, and an arriving cargo barge. The entrance foyer was small and had a single piece of furniture — a small side table against the left wall, topped with a small bud vase and a single flower made of Lego. Mateo made a mental note to ask Beverly about this at some point. Three solid doors led out of the foyer and into the building. Two doors framed either side of the small table on the left, and one door opposed the primary entrance door.

She quickly ushered him through the door opposite the one they had entered. The door led into a short hallway that contained another door at the end. As Beverly placed her hand on the handle to open the next door, she turned to Mateo and smiled. "The statue is in here. This next room is directly below the labs, so you will have direct access to it while working."

She started to push open the door, and Mateo suddenly realized the lack of security on the doors. There were no locks, no keypads, no access cards. He felt the need to address this before continuing. "Beverly. Wait a moment." Mateo said, placing his hand on the door handle and pulling it back to closed. "I don't see any security or locks. No access keypads, no access badges. What's that about?"

Beverly sighed, clearly frustrated at the question. "We don't need those things for several reasons. The island is private property; it is difficult to get here. We have cameras and sensors around the building and covering the island.

So, we know if there is anyone here that should not be. We also keep track of employees." Beverly pushed open the door and walked through. Mateo followed, briefly pondering her last statement. His momentary confusion was distracted by the space they had entered.

The room itself was large and circular and contained one item — the statue of Sednamaroq. The alabaster statue stood in the very center of the circle. Soft golden light emanated from a recessed channel that ran along the edge of the ceiling around the entire perimeter. To the right, a staircase was inset in the wall, evidently leading to the lab above. Mateo stared at the object. It scared him on a level that evoked memories of every horror movie he had seen as a child. At the same time, he felt a sense of peace underlying the fear. The combination of these two confused him. And caused him to want to know more.

"I don't know how to express what I'm feeling when I look at this thing. I want to turn away, but curiosity takes over." Mateo whispered.

"It has that effect on people," Beverly said in a normal voice. "I grew up with it and have a very different relationship with it than anyone else. And yes, there are times when it scares me. Nevertheless, I depend on it for my survival. You will get used to being around it, Mateo. I'm hoping you will tap into a part of it that we have not seen."

Mateo was silent, not knowing how to respond to Beverly's casual view of something that was so terrifyingly foreign. His doubts about the statue's powers faded as he moved closer to the outer wall to avoid being near it. Beverly motioned towards the staircase and started up towards the second floor. Mateo followed, curious what other surprises the building held. The access provided by the staircase emptied into a traditional-looking research lab. Well-equipped benches were arranged in clusters amongst various pieces of machinery used to analyze and create a variety of scientific things. Mateo recognized most of the equipment, and a few pieces seemed completely foreign to him. He was positive, however, that he would be able to discern their purpose with minimal observation.

"This is our main lab. There are currently six scientists working on a variety of approaches to find a cure. You will meet them tomorrow at our morning meeting, which occurs every morning at 10 a.m. at my house." Beverly was speaking quickly as she walked to the far end of the large room and pressed a button on the wall to summon the elevator.

"Your house?" Mateo questioned.

"I have a house that is near this building. Several years ago, I realized that I needed some separation from the facility itself. The house is my sanctuary, separate from the research and more importantly, separated from Sednamaroq." Beverly's voice had a tinge of nostalgia as she spoke. The elevator rose to the third floor, and the doors opened to a room similar in size to the one below. All the equipment that Mateo had requested was clustered in the center of the spacious room. Workbenches and desks dotted the remaining available space. Offices and small conference rooms surrounded the perimeter of the lab, all with floor-to-ceiling glass walls separating them from the lab.

"I wasn't sure how you might want things arranged, so I just had them put everything in the center. You have a staff of three assistants that will arrive in two days and will help you place things where you want them." Beverly stated, taking a sudden business-like approach to the conversation. "Anything else you need along the way, just let me know directly."

"Wow, I really didn't think you would be able to have these things here so quickly," Mateo said partially under his breath.

"Money makes things move." Beverly smiled at him. She walked over to a nearby office and opened the door. Etched on the glass to the right of the door were the words *Dr. Mateo Trujillo, Chief Scientific Officer.* "This is your office."

The office was neatly arranged with an L-shaped desk, a credenza against the side wall, an ergonomic desk chair, and two side chairs. A few pictures, a plant, and other knick-knacks had been arranged on the desk for him. Mateo saw the framed picture of him with his parents, and his eyes welled with tears. It was the last picture he had taken with them before his mother had passed. He walked over to the desk and picked up the frame, looking at it with love and longing. He clutched it to his chest, thinking how proud they would be of him. He was finally realizing his dreams. He was, at last, helping make the world a better place. He placed the frame back on the desk and turned to Beverly.

"Thank you for placing these things here. My parents would be so proud. As would yours, for what you are doing. I know there is a personal reason, but the simple act of hiring me and believing in my work — it just means so much to me. I won't let you down, Beverly." A single tear fell down his cheek as he spoke.

"I know," Beverly said as she stepped forward, wrapped her arms around him, and held him tightly. "We're going to do great things together, Mateo. You know that. I know you can feel it as much as I do." She pushed him back and held him at arm's length, her hands firmly on his shoulders. She looked him directly in the eyes. "What you're going to accomplish here will change the world."

Beverly released him and turned to walk out the door, pausing and rotating her head back to glance at him. "Let me show you where you'll be sleeping."

Mateo followed Beverly out of the office and back to the elevator, which they took to the first floor. The elevator opened into a hallway, which he assumed surrounded the circular chamber that held the statue. Beverly turned left and walked past several doors on the right until she reached one that was labeled with the number 23. She opened the door, which Mateo noticed did not have a lock. The space behind the door was a comfortable two-room apartment.

The first room was very comfortably furnished with an overstuffed and plush fabric sofa and a matching side chair in chocolate brown. Typical end tables and a coffee table of lighter ash wood complemented the setting. A TV hung on the wall and a kitchenette with a small fridge, microwave, a small sink, and a bistro-sized table with two chairs in wood that matched the other tables completed the living area. The next room housed a double bed with two nightstands, a combination dresser-wardrobe, and a leather chair with a reading lamp arching over the top from its floor stand. The bathroom was the most luxurious part of the small apartment. A custom tiled shower and separate soaking tub were separated from the toilet by a half wall, and the sink counter was fitted with quartz and rich wood cabinetry. The walls throughout the apartment were painted in warm hues of beige and brown. The walls were bare, leaving the only color to the throw pillows in the living room and the duvet on the bed.

"I made sure the bathrooms were perfect for relaxation. I like a long, slow bath. There are candles and bath salts available, if you like that. Sometimes when things are stressful, it helps to take a long soak in the tub. I've added some bath products for you." Beverly grinned as Mateo noticed the complete line of Los Poblanos lavender products on the counter.

"Thank you!" Mateo exclaimed. "I love this stuff." He walked over to the counter, wrapped his hand around the nearest bottle, opened it, and took a big sniff before extending it to Beverly to smell. "And I love taking baths."

Beverly laughed. "No thanks, I know what it smells like, and I like it too. I'm just glad this makes you happy. Your clothes and other things are all stowed in the wardrobe and dresser. I've also added some clothes with the institute logo. They're comfortable, and you'll need them as it gets colder. Just let me know if you need anything else. It usually takes about a week to get things. Take a few minutes to get settled. I'll be back in thirty minutes, and I'll show you where to eat and how to get to my house in the morning."

Beverly left the apartment, and Mateo looked through everything to see if there was anything that he might need imminently. He pulled back the curtains in each room and took a moment to appreciate the view of the wooded landscape. He wondered if bears or other wild animals ever wandered close to the building. In the distance, he could see a rather large bungalow sitting amongst the trees. He assumed it was Beverly's house. Everything had been taken care of in great detail. Something nagged at him, and he kept pushing it down. It all just seemed too good to be true. Beverly returned, as promised, and escorted him to the front end of the building, where a small dining room was located on the corner with beautiful views of the dock and shoreline. A large supply closet in the hallway contained a variety of supplies that he might need – various other toiletries, snacks, food, and beverages he could take to his apartment, and cleaning supplies. Beverly informed him that his apartment would be cleaned by the housekeeping staff once a week. If he needed to clean between those scheduled visits, he could use the supplies in the closet.

Beverly showed him the door that would lead him along a path directly to her house. With that final instruction, she told him good night and reminded him to be there at 10 a.m. Mateo returned to his apartment, still mildly disturbed by the lack of locks on the doors. He had also not seen another person since he had arrived. Wanting a snack, Mateo left his apartment and wandered down the corridor to the dining room, realizing that he had no idea what time breakfast was served. That question was answered by a neatly handwritten sign on the wall above the serving counter that listed the times of the daily meals.

He walked to the storage pantry next to the dining room and rummaged through the extensive selection of snacks and food. Reusable canvas bags hung on a hook near the door. Mateo took a bag and filled it with a few cans of tomato juice, two bottles of apple juice, four bottles of diet soda, and a variety of candy bars. He threw in a few bags of beef jerky and some snack crackers to complete his odd pseudo-shopping trip. He noticed a stack of lined notebooks and pens on a shelf and tossed a few of those in the bag at the last minute. As he reached for the door handle to exit the room, the door opened towards him, and he was face-to-face with a young Asian woman. She was considerably shorter than Mateo and did not seem shocked to see him. She walked in and allowed the door to close, looking around nervously as she repeatedly tucked her black shoulder-length hair behind each ear in turn with the fingers of her left hand.

"Find a reason to leave as soon as possible. The sooner the better." She said frantically and in a whisper. "This place is not what you think. Beverly will never let you leave if you wait too long."

"Who are you?" Mateo asked, not sure what to make of the strange instructions.

"Just leave when you can. It's not safe here. And she watches everything. This room is the only place she cannot see." The woman grabbed a random item from the nearest shelf and left the room, making sure the door closed before Mateo could follow her.

Mateo quickly opened the door, determined to follow her and ask more questions. What an odd start to his first day here, he thought. As he stepped into the hallway, his bag of snacks and drinks in hand, he looked in both directions, and there was no sign of the woman. He walked into the dining room and did not see her. Could she just be a disgruntled employee? Maybe someone whose research had reached a dead end? Still finding it odd, he walked back to his apartment and placed the drinks in the small fridge. He neatly arranged the snacks in the cupboard, reserving a bag of beef jerky for snacking, settled onto the sofa, and turned on the TV.

The streaming menu was clearly one that pulled from a local server and was not connected to anything off the island. This prompted Mateo to check his phone. No signal. He connected to the Wi-Fi, no password required, of course and opened his internet browser. He searched for a wide variety of subjects in turn and quickly learned that there was some sort of security program that limited which pages he could visit. Next, he opened his email app. Emails from Stephen and Beverly, but no others were coming through. No junk mail, which was very odd. He composed an email to a colleague, Marc, at the university to let him know he had arrived at the Baker Lake facility. The email seemed to go through. Now he would wait for a reply. Marc always replied to Mateo within a day or two, so he would have to wait.

Putting his concerns aside and choosing to focus on the lab, he chose a mindless sitcom and opened the beef jerky, letting his mind incubate on how to arrange the equipment in the lab. Within an hour, he had a clear plan. He turned off the television, walked to the bathroom, where he removed his clothes, tossing them in a canvas hamper that sat by the door, brushed his teeth, and peed. He smeared some of the lavender face cream all over his face and sighed at the delightful scent. Mateo climbed under the sheets, relishing in the high-thread-count fabric's luxurious touch on his skin. He had always slept in the buff, but never in bed linens this nice. He could get used to this. He fell asleep quickly, dreaming of getting the lab up and running and the possibilities of what might result from manipulating the algae DNA streaming through his head.

17

He had forgotten to close the curtain in the bedroom, and the golden light from the sun filtering through the forest woke him. Mateo sat up abruptly and panicked as he grabbed his phone. He had forgotten to set an alarm and fell back onto the pillows when he saw that it was only 8 a.m. He took a few minutes to gather his thoughts and finish waking up before getting out of bed and walking to the bathroom. He started the shower to let the water warm up and grabbed a towel from the cupboard and hung it on the hook attached to the shower door. He noticed that the shelf in the large shower already contained the coveted shampoo, conditioner, and shower gel.

When the water was sufficiently hot, he stepped into the shower, wet his hair, and applied the lavender shampoo, smiling while he massaged it in and simultaneously peeing down the shower drain. He rinsed out the shampoo and repeated the process with the conditioner, allowing it to sit in his hair while he washed his body with a loofah that he saturated with the scented gel. Feeling content and refreshed, he rinsed himself completely and turned off the shower. As he dried off with the towel, he thought how much of a difference high-quality fabrics made to the enjoyment of simple things. Not that he would have been able to afford such things in the past. But now, he was determined to always have these things. He ran a comb through his hair and walked back to the bedroom to get dressed.

His jeans, underwear, socks, and t-shirts were neatly folded in a drawer. He selected one of each and dressed quickly. He had noticed a dark green hoodie with the SISR logo, the four letters superimposed over concentric circles in wavy lines, hanging in the wardrobe and chose that to wear for the day. He pulled on a pair of hiking boots that sat on the floor nearby and paused to look at himself in the mirror. He liked the look. It fit with the location, he thought.

He left his apartment and walked down the hallway to the dining room. Six other people sat around a rectangular table, two women and four men. They all paused and looked up when he entered the room. He noticed the young Asian woman from the previous evening. Mateo held up a hand in greeting. "I'm Mateo Trujillo." He spoke.

The others raised a hand in greeting. One of the men who appeared to be the oldest in the group spoke for the rest of them.

"We will save introductions for the morning meeting. Beverly will want to introduce you to us properly and would not appreciate any introductions prior to that. In the meantime, please get some breakfast and join us." The man spoke softly and calmly.

Mateo stepped over to the service bar, which held a variety of fruits and cereals, as well as a hot tray with eggs and sausages. He took a plate from the stack nearby and loaded it with eggs, sausages, and a slice of melon. He noticed a basket sitting next to the hot tray and discovered rolls, biscuits, and warm tortillas. He took a tortilla and placed it gently on top of everything on his plate. He placed the plate on the table at a space the group had made for him and got himself a cup of coffee before sitting down.

Taking cues from the group, he ate in silence, his worry about the warning from the previous evening combined with the lack of locks on doors, concerning him more than it did yesterday. He held the tortilla in his hand and loaded it with eggs and sausage, finishing it with a healthy dose of hot sauce from a bottle on the table before rolling it up and taking a bite. He noticed the group staring at him.

"I'm from New Mexico." He said with a mouthful of food.

They nodded and continued eating their own food. Mateo found the food really good, as was the coffee. There was clearly no skimping on quality here. So, what was the problem? He wondered. Time would tell. For now, he was going to focus on the research.

"Do we get a say in what food is served?" Mateo asked.

"Yes and no." The older gentleman spoke up again. "If you want something, just tell Beverly, and she will communicate it to the chef. The food here is really good."

"Thanks," Mateo responded.

"If only good food were the answer to all the problems of the world." The young woman from the encounter in the pantry said, her tone sarcastic and low. The others stared at her with looks of sincere dislike but remained silent.

When everyone had finished eating, the young woman stood and walked to the doorway. Everyone else stood after her, and they walked single file down the long hallway, past Mateo's apartment, and out the door that led to the path to Beverly's house.

The walk took less than five minutes. It was five minutes of silence that allowed Mateo to appreciate the natural beauty of the island. A light mist swirled around the trees in the cool morning air. He could hear the scampering of small forest animals and wondered what it must have been like for Beverly's great-grandfather to discover this place. Beverly had glossed over the bear attack that had permitted the statue to revive him, and Mateo considered that it must have been terrifying, having the trauma of a painful death amongst such beauty.

The group of seven arrived at Beverly's house and walked up the long ramp to the porch. There were no stairs, and Mateo assumed this was to facilitate any difficulties that Beverly might have before her sessions with the thing. Following the lead of the group, he waited. He glanced at his phone and noticed that it was two minutes until the time of the meeting. They all waited in silence. At precisely 10 a.m., Beverly opened the door and motioned with her hand for them to enter. They followed her into an expansive great room lined with timber that perfectly framed the surreal view of the forest and the institute, with the lake in the background.

Seating consisted of eight leather chairs with inset cloth panels. The designs on the inset fabric looked to be of Inuit origin, representing fish, animals, and birds in the typical style of the native peoples. Rounded forms of solid and compact shapes formed interpretive visions of bears, seals, caribou, foxes, ravens, whales, owls, and sea birds. There were many other representations, but these were the only ones that Mateo recognized. The artwork reminded him of the images he frequently saw on native American pottery back at home.

Beverly took a seat in the chair that faced away from the large windows. She crossed her legs and looked around the room, smiling when her gaze met Mateo's. The other six people in the room stared at Beverly with fear, unaware of the stunning view behind her and seemingly not sure what to expect next. Beverly's demeanor, however, was chipper and elated.

"Let's get started," Beverly said firmly. "I'd like to introduce you to our new Chief Scientific Officer, Mateo Trujillo. Mateo's research involves growing organic nanobots using an algae base rather than the traditional frog cells. He calls them phyconanobots. I'm sure you will all have interesting conversations with him, and I expect you to collaborate with him when possible."

Beverly paused and waited for a reaction. The six other scientists nodded in agreement. Not waiting for a verbal response, Beverly continued by introducing the other six to Mateo, without their direct input.

"This is Susie Chen," Beverly said, motioning to the young Asian woman from the strange encounter the previous evening. "Dr. Chen has been with us for two years and has been focusing on a holistic approach to working with Sednamaroq, which seems to have reached a dead end. Correct?" She looked at Susie with a flat stare.

"There are still things to try. I have a new shipment of herbs and ideas for new tinctures to try. I think dead end is a strong statement to apply to my research." Susie floundered.

"We will see," Beverly replied. "Then we have Johanna Peck." Beverly motioned to the woman sitting next to Susie. Johanna looked to be in her mid-fifties, tall, thin, with salt and pepper hair pulled back into a tight bun. Mateo could not tell where she might be from, but could make a good guess of one of the Nordic countries.

"I found Johanna in Stockholm. She was working at the university there, attempting to get funding for mini particle accelerators that could be used in healthcare to alter cellular structures. Her work shows promise, and I'm looking forward to hearing about your week, Johanna." Beverly looked at Johanna and smiled.

Johanna smiled back and said very quietly, "Thank you, Beverly."

"Next up is Steven Basker." Beverly continued. "Steven is a physician from Montreal. He is trained in physical medicine and rehabilitation and is a specialist in PEMF, or pulsed electromagnetic field therapy, which shows great promise. Steven has been with us for just over six months now." Mateo recognized Steven as the one who had spoken for the group at breakfast. "Next to Steven is Yoshi Takahashi, from Tokyo. Yoshi is a micro-robotics expert. I think the two of you might share some common interests."

Yoshi nodded at Beverly and then turned his head to look at Mateo, giving him a thumbs-up with both hands. Beverly continued with the introductions, shifting her legs and turning her body to face the last two gentlemen. "Then we have Connor Smithson, from Alabama, in the U.S. Connor was working at the University of Alabama, Birmingham, studying the axolotl, or Mexican salamander. I specifically want him informed of your work, Mateo. His research has reached a plateau, and I think your phycobots might be the injection he needs."

Connor nodded at Beverly and addressed Mateo directly with a strong southern drawl, "I'm very excited to see what you're working on, Mateo."

Mateo smiled back at him as Beverly continued with the last of the six. "And lastly, we have Hugo Sosa. Hugo comes to us from Uruguay and specializes in xenotransplants. He's been working with interstitial shark cells, and his work shows promise. I think he will benefit from your work, as well. All our current team has been here for under a year, with the exception of Dr. Chen."

It did not escape Mateo that Beverly referred to all the scientists by first name, except Susie. It was clear that she was not happy with the direction that Susie's research had taken, and this explained why Susie had been so adamant about Mateo leaving. She needed more time to complete her work.

After the brief and uncomfortable introductions, Beverly listened as each scientist provided a recap of the efforts over the past week and detailed what they would be working on today. Mateo admittedly recognized the level of extreme micromanagement. But it was her institute — a privately held research facility at which they worked under her express invitation. If he were in her same position, wouldn't he manage it the same way? After all, it was her life they were trying to save.

Mateo was anxious to set up his lab. And was excited to have access to specialists in robotics and xenotransplantation. The axolotl guy was interesting. He could see how all these would fit into his research. Even Susie's research might be an interesting attempt at incorporating an extra element into his efforts. But it seemed Susie had already fallen out of favor with Beverly. When Hugo had finished telling Beverly about the growth stage of his shark cells, all attention turned to Mateo. He was not expecting to have to talk during this meeting. Beverly looked at him patiently, clearly waiting for him to speak.

"Uh, I'm going to start setting up my lab. I want to get the algae cultivation started since that takes the most time. If someone could come get me when it's time for dinner, I would appreciate it. I get lost in things sometimes, and I will need to eat. I also want to see what intersectionality might present itself amongst our areas of research." Mateo paused, waiting for someone to respond.

"I'll make sure you don't miss dinner. I can also help you set up the lab, if that's okay?" Connor spoke, looking at Beverly for approval. "My little guys still have a few days of limb re-growth before I can move to the next step."

"Of course, of course," Beverly said excitedly. "I really want you two to work together. Connor, if you can spare a day or two, please help Mateo out. His team will not be here for two days."

"Thank you, Beverly. I will gladly assist him." Connor said.

"Thanks, Connor," Mateo said, looking at Connor, whose eyes covertly darted towards Beverly, giving Mateo a cue to thank her as well. "And thank you, Beverly. For everything."

Beverly grinned. "I love this team!" She exclaimed as she stood. Everyone stood with her and walked to the door. "Now get to work. Same time tomorrow, yes? Oh, and Susie, can you hang back a minute?"

Everyone nodded as they walked past her and out the door, except for Susie, who walked back to the great room to wait for Beverly. The walk back to the Institute was quiet. Everyone went their separate ways as Connor followed Mateo to the elevator and eventually to the third floor. Mateo explained his vision to Connor, and they got started moving things around. As they worked, Mateo learned that Connor had been at SISR for ten months. He had maintained an interest in the axolotl since seeing one at a zoo as a child. In the course of earning a degree in biology from the University of Alabama and a subsequent PhD in integrative biology from the University of Texas at Austin, he returned to Tuscaloosa to be near his family and try to figure out where his career might be headed. A paper that he had published on a controversial topic had caught Beverly's attention, and she recruited him to work for the institute. The paper, a proposition that the axolotl DNA might be combined with human DNA to create a hybrid creature from which to harvest replacement organs for humans in need, drew too much negative attention from the religious right, and Connor was forced to maintain a low profile until he could figure things out.

Mateo shared his story, and the two men marveled at the similarities. They were close in age, and Mateo could see them developing a strong working relationship and possibly even a friendship. As they were moving a particularly cumbersome incubation chamber, Mateo decided to confide in Connor about the strange interaction with Susie on his first night. He told Connor the details, expecting a similar reaction.

"What do you think of her telling me that? She was so insistent. And so secretive." Mateo asked.

"Susie has done that with each of us. She told me that scientists never get to leave here. She believes that Beverly has them killed when they are of no use. Her assertion is that we are supposed to believe that they are sent home when they are actually disposed of like garbage. It's a stupid concept." Connor answered. "I mean, how would they make that work when we all know people that are NOT here and know we ARE here?"

Yes, I agree. It doesn't make sense. She was just intense!" Mateo said. "And when everyone was so quiet this morning, I started to think there might be something to her request that I leave as soon as possible."

"We were all quiet this morning because she goes on a rant if anyone says anything that might make the new guy feel like staying. She did the same thing with me when I started." Connor said. "I don't know if she really believes these things or if she thinks that limiting new research will allow her more time to prove hers."

"Well, she comes across as crazy." Mateo laughed.

Connor laughed with him, and they continued to arrange the workbenches and equipment. Mateo learned that Connor was his immediate neighbor, and they said good night as Mateo opened his door and watched Connor enter his own apartment. He had intended to ask Connot about the absence of locks, but it had slipped his mind. The next morning, Mateo met the group for breakfast, and conversation flowed to make up for the awkwardness of the previous day. Susie, however, was not at breakfast, and everyone assumed that her talk with Beverly had made her angry and she had decided to distance herself from the group.

Mateo and Connor walked together along the path to Beverly's house. Steven and Yoshi walked ahead of them and talked animatedly about the value of including a 1Hz pEMF device in a robotic prosthetic to force tissue change. Behind them, Johanna and Hugo discussed Hugo's latest breakthrough in incorporating the shark cells into human tissue. When they reached the house, the mood was significantly elevated from the previous morning. Beverly greeted them on the porch and ushered them inside. Her demeanor was also improved from the previous day and reminded Mateo of the Beverly that he had met in Albuquerque.

"First things first, as you might have guessed, Dr. Chen is no longer part of our team. She gave her research a good effort, but in the end, it had run its course. I think

I would have kept her on if her attitude towards the team effort had been in the right place, but it wasn't." Beverly sounded genuinely sad that it had not worked out. "Nevertheless, I am happy with the team that we have now, and it makes me happy to hear the conversations of collaboration. I want each of you to know what you mean to me. I have been very clear with you about our goal. My life is literally in your hands."

Beverly ended her soliloquy and asked each member of the team to talk about their work. The conversation was different from the day before. This time, it seemed more like an actual conversation. The scientists talked with one another as Beverly asked questions and posed new directions. When Mateo spoke, he described how Connor had helped him organize the lab and how each of their research fields might complement the other. Mateo left the meeting with a sense of belonging and purpose. The rest of the day was productive as he and Connor focused on calibrating the equipment and starting the algae cultures growing. Connor showed Mateo the room where his salamanders lived. Mateo was fascinated by the glass tanks full of the small white creatures swimming happily in the soft blue light of the room that made a poor attempt to recreate their natural habitat of the canals that led to the lake complex in Xochimilco, Mexico City. Connor was fascinated by Mateo's ideas and asked questions that made Mateo feel respected. He was finally part of a team that valued him and his ideas.

As the group sat down to dinner that night, none of them knew that Susie Chen's lifeless body floated westward in the cold waters of Baker Lake in a current forced by the rivers at each end.

18

The three research assistants arrived and wasted no time following Mateo's detailed instructions on getting the remaining equipment and supplies ready to start the real task at hand. Matt, Sara, and Jo were more competent than Mateo would have ever imagined. Beverly always got the best of what she wanted, and these three were no exception. Matt had been working in a biology lab at Yale, Sara had been working for a large pharmaceutical company in the Research Triangle Park area of North Carolina, and Jo had been poached from a military research facility that she refused to identify. They knew all the equipment and had read everything that Mateo had published or attempted to publish. And more importantly, they considered him the supreme authority on cutting-edge synthetic biology research.

In the next few weeks, at one of the morning meetings, Hugo requested more space for his work. He had taken over Susie's area but still needed more. Mateo suggested that Connor move to the third floor, since the two of them had found some common elements of their research that could be explored. Beverly agreed, and Connor made the move, with Mateo's help, over the course of the following week. Mateo felt a solid friendship developing between him and Connor. He was hoping that it might lead to more but did not want to risk the friendship by pushing it.

The algae cultivation went more smoothly than Mateo could have hoped for. With Matt, Sara, and Jo's help, he mixed his custom cocktail of algae substrate and placed it in the FP-PBR. Connor constantly questioned the acronyms that Mateo and his team used, so Mateo had adopted the habit of explaining them when he used them. In this case, he explained that FP-PBR meant flat panel photobioreactor, his preferred method for cultivating algae. Mateo further explained that some scientists used tubular PBR's but he preferred the flat panel for reasons that were too complicated to go into with basic conversation.

His custom creations promised to be the perfect base for the first batch of bots. The harvesting of the algae was a fun event. Sara had suggested that they make the harvest a party-like experience. So, they invited Beverly and the other researchers and acquired a few bottles of wine with Beverly's approval. Sara put some EMD party music on her portable Bluetooth speaker, and Mateo showed the other scientists how to harvest the algae, place it in the centrifuge, and ultimately, through the filtration process, isolate the cells. By the end of the day, everyone was laughing and having a good time. And Beverly seemed exuberant that the team was working together. The party ended with a usable batch of filtered cells and a happy research team.

With Connor's assistance, Mateo completed DNA amplification on three samples in three separate thermocyclers and sequenced them individually for analysis. A careful glance at the outputs told him that the samples were perfect for fragmenting. With Matt, Sara, Jo, and Connor patiently observing, Mateo separated the three samples into unique fragments and prepared three decks for TALEN. Mateo explained to Connor that TAELN stood for transcription activator–like effector nucleases and that it made more precise modifications to the DNA than the better-known CRISPR gene editor. Mateo decided to forego an explanation of CRISPR since it was inconsequential to their current process. They could talk about it later, if Connor showed interest.

This next step was the one that made Mateo nervous. The editing of the three samples had to be precise since they would need to work together, when combined, to build the bots. Mateo liked using the word 'build,' though 'grow' was a more appropriate term to describe the process. In theory, the three perfectly programmed samples would morph into an impossibly small organic machine. The goal of this first one was simply to survive.

The tension during the five-week wait was maddening. Connor kept Mateo calm and distracted by teaching him about the amazing axolotl and the advances towards understanding its unique ability to regrow limbs. He talked about removing a left leg from the salamander and transcribing the cells to an amputated right limb. The left limb would grow where the cells were placed. Harnessing the power of the axolotl's genetic code would have an impact on the medical community that would change the world. Connor had been successful in creating hybrid cells to grow a variety of organs, which did not survive. And he couldn't figure out why. He was considering giving up, then he met Mateo. Mateo's research gave him new hope.

During the TALEN procedure, Connor took a genuine interest in the details of the process. When the three days of target sequence selection and design were complete, Mateo explained the next phase of construction, which should take about ten days. After that, the expression validation should take five to seven days, depending on the outcome. Then, another short stage of transfection and genome editing. The final stage of selection and sequencing of the edited cells would be the longest, at two weeks. It was during this last period that Connor enlisted Mateo to actively assist him with the axolotls, mainly to keep him distracted.

Mateo cast the images of the first batch of bots onto a large screen mounted to a wall in the lab. The enhanced images showed a cluster of organic phyconanobots, various shades of fluctuating greens, moving casually in random patterns. There was a gasp from Jo, and an 'oh my God' from Matt. Connor smiled, his hand reaching up to Mateo's shoulder and giving it a gentle squeeze.

"You did it, Mateo," Connor whispered quietly.

 A single tear fell down Mateo's cheek.

Then they all watched as the bots attacked each other. Within seconds, the image turned to a grayish mass before hardening into a shiny black.

The silence permeated the space and drowned out the hum of equipment running in the background.

"What happened?" Sara asked?

"I don't know. And it doesn't matter. We just created the first batch of phyconanobots. And they lived, even though briefly, they lived. Now the real work begins." Mateo answered. "Let's take a break. We all need to process this incredible achievement. Meet back here in an hour."

Sara, Matt, and Jo ventured off together to take a walk outside. Mateo headed to the elevator, Connor following him.

"Do you want company or to be left alone?" Connor asked.

"Company. Please." Mateo answered, looking back at Connor.

They took the elevator down to the first floor and turned right towards apartment 23. Mateo walked into his apartment, followed by Connor. Mateo plopped down on the sofa; Connor sat down next to him and turned to face him.

"Look at me, Mateo," Connor commanded. Mateo complied. "It's just the first batch. There's still work to do."

Tears streamed down Mateo's face. "I know! I'm crying because I'm so happy. I never thought I'd actually see those bots. They lived, Connor! They were alive! We created organic nanobots out of algae! All those people that ridiculed me. They were ALL wrong. ALL of them! Fuck them all. I did it! I really did it!"

Connor leaned forward and hugged Mateo, holding him tightly.

"Okay, tonight, we celebrate!" Connor said, pushing back and using his right thumb to wipe at the residual of Mateo's tears.

"Yes! Let's go meet with the team and plan next steps." Mateo said, standing up and grabbing Connor's upper arm, pulling him along. As they exited the apartment and turned left towards the elevator, Mateo remembered something he wanted to ask Connor.

"Hey, why are there no locks on doors here? It's been bothering me since I got here." Mateo asked.

"I really don't know, but you get used to it." Connor answered. "I think there really is no need for them. We need to trust each other to work together. When that trust is no longer there, the work suffers. I think it forces us to trust each other, so maybe not a bad thing. Thoughts on that theory, Dr. Trujilo?"

"I think you're right, as usual." Mateo laughed.

The two of them took the elevator back up to the third floor to meet with Matt, Sara, and Jo. Between the five of them, and with Mateo's direction, they had a clear path forward to advance the research. Mateo texted Beverly the good news, and she showed up at the lab soon after with bottles of sparkling wine, glasses, and the other scientists. She was ecstatic about the speed at which Mateo had achieved this first step.

Over the next three months, Mateo saw steady improvements in the behavior of the bots. The tweaking of their programming was delicate, and he kept detailed and copious notes, as would any researcher. Beverly insisted that all the scientists keep their notes on a secure drive that was maintained on a server in the building, backed up to hard drives that were removed to a secure location elsewhere in Canada, and backed up to the cloud. Even handwritten notes, regardless of how petty they seemed, were scanned to digital files and cataloged. The dead bots, non-viable algae, and any other things that could be kept were stored in jars, trays, and containers in a storage closet directly off the lab.

When Mateo finally had a batch of bots that were as close to perfect as they could be without being programmed for a specific medical purpose, he stored them in a hermetically sealed tube that he had designed specifically for his phyconanobots. When he told Beverly about his idea for a storage container that would be better than the ones currently on the market, she quickly arranged a video call with an engineer whom she had met. Carl was a professor at Cal Poly and had a prototype ready within a week.

With the working bots securely in their sealed home, it was time to test what effect Sednamaroq might have on them. Beverly led the way down the stairs, followed by Mateo holding the bots, the three assistants, and Connor taking up the rear. Mateo and Connor had already set up an electron microscope on a cart in the statue chamber. Mateo turned on the microscope and carefully positioned the container under the lens. A small monitor nearby came to life, and the group observed the bots lazily moving around each other. Beverly had demanded that she be the one to roll the cart over to the statue. Mateo and Connor were fine with this, since the thing still gave them a weird, creepy feeling.

Beverly slowly rolled the cart towards Sednamaroq, almost as if she feared it might anger it. She stopped the cart close to, but not touching the statue. She stepped back and turned to the monitor. Within seconds, a light blue glow began to show between the cart and the statue. On the screen, the bots came to a complete stop. At first, Mateo thought the thing had killed them, then he noticed slight movement. The bots started forming a pattern. They grouped in squares of nine, three by three, repeated in a stacked, three-dimensional block within the substrate of the jar.

"Interesting," Mateo said, his fingers and thumb stroking his beard in thought.

"Why interesting?" Beverly asked. "Tell me what's on your mind, Mateo."

"Sorry, yes, it's almost like they're waiting to be told what to do like a holding pattern. The statue has organized them but doesn't know what it needs to do with them. Let's take them back upstairs and see if their pattern holds." Mateo said pensively.

Beverly walked over to the cart and rolled it back to the base of the staircase. Mateo grabbed the large vial gently and walked up the stairs first, heading towards the elevator at the end of the second-floor lab and then up to the third floor. When they arrived, he placed the container under another microscope. Their pattern remained intact.

"We're going to observe every fifteen minutes." Mateo addressed his staff. "Set up a schedule for the five of us, two-hour shifts." Matt, Sara, and Jo nodded and huddled to write out the watch schedule.

"What does it mean if they keep the structure?" Beverly asked the question that Connor was thinking.

"I'm not entirely certain, but I think it means that whatever the statue does to the bot, they will keep that behavior until they can be activated or used." Mateo surmised. "Now that we know the capability of the statue, we can work on more specific programming."

"This is very exciting, Mateo. I'm taking a short trip this next week, and when I return, we need to have a one-on-one to discuss the broader scope of what this means." Beverly turned and moved closer to Mateo, addressing him directly.

"Okay, Beverly. At this rate, I'll have more to share by then." Mateo said.

Beverly left to return to her house, while the research assistants went to their individual apartments after presenting the observation schedule, with Mateo taking the first shift. Connor decided to sit with Mateo for the first few observations, since his shift was later in the rotation. The pattern continued to hold throughout the entire rotation and into the next day. Mateo started developing ideas for the next step. He had been told by Beverly that, when she was a teenager, one of the scientists had insisted that she preserve various cell and tissue samples for use in later research. These samples were stored somewhere on-site. Once he had a fully programmed test sample, he wanted to test it on one of those tissue samples in the presence of the statue. That would give him a better idea of how to refine the DNA sequencing to counter the tissue's reaction to trauma.

Carefully extracting a small sample of the bots that had been organized by the statue, Mateo injected them into the reaction vessel that held a sample of Beverly's tissue. Connor had helped Mateo traumatize the tissue, and they could see the cells beginning to calcify and harden. When the bots encountered the tissue cells, they formed a single line along the expanse of the sample. Mateo, Connor, and the other three watched in silence as every other bot split from the line and moved in opposite directions to form what was now three single lines across the sample.

Then something unexpected happened. The bots replicated, something Mateo had not programmed them to do. Each line birthed a new line. This continued until the entire surface of the tissue sample was covered in a grid of the bots. A quick and subtle flash of green light completed the process, and the team watched as the bots absorbed into the tissue. What remained was a viable, living, healthy sample of tissue.

"Well, that was...unexpected," Mateo said softly.

"What did you think would happen?" Jo asked.

"Truthfully? I thought the bots would start repairing the sample and that it would take more time. I didn't expect them to replicate with this batch. Simply because they have not been told to do so. I also did not expect them to be absorbed by the tissue. I mean, it's ideal, and possible, but I did not program them to do those things." Mateo answered her.

"It must be the statue. That's the only explanation." Matt said

"Yes, I suppose so," Mateo said. "We need to see how long the effects last on the tissue sample. In the meantime, let's continue preparing more bots."

The repaired tissue sample maintained its healthy state for about three weeks, then it turned to stone. It was disappointing but not surprising since this was in line with how the statue had treated Beverly her entire life.

Later that evening, Connor suggested that he and Mateo have dinner and a movie in Connor's apartment. They took prepared plates of lasagna and salad from the dining room to his apartment and sat at the small table. They talked about the results of the research so far and ruminated over possible solutions. Connor cut a bite of lasagna with the side of his fork, pierced it with the tines, and raised it to his mouth. Just before taking the bite, he suddenly dropped the fork on the plate, placed both hands flat on the table, and looked at Mateo.

"Mateo! What if we activated the tissue sample in front of Sednamaroq?" Connor said.

"What?" It took a moment for him to recognize the change in direction of the conversation. "Um, wow. Yes, Connor, that is absolutely brilliant!"

Mateo put down his fork and stood from the table. "Let's go do it."

"What? Now!" Connor said.

"Yeah, why not?" Mateo smiled.

They left the uneaten food on the table and rushed to the third floor. Mateo texted Matt, Sara, and Jo:

<lab. now.>

By the time they had prepared the sample and moved the cart to the statue chamber, the assistants had sleepily arrived and were asking what was going on. Connor explained as Mateo focused on preparing the tissue sample. When everything was ready, the team moved to the chamber, and Mateo rolled the cart to the statue, avoiding looking at the thing as he moved. When the cart was in place, Mateo injected the bots and held his breath. They watch as the bots organize, replicate, and repair the tissue. Then the tissue sample itself started to quiver. In a surprising and disastrous turn, the tissue sample replicated itself. Two identical samples sat side-by-side in the reaction dish, pulsing with life. Mateo walked to the cart and rolled it back to the wall. The samples immediately hardened and died.

"What happened?" Sara asked."

"I think it overactivated the tissue repair. There's something I'm missing." Mateo said.

"I have an idea," Connor said. "I'll be right back. Mateo – prepare another sample."

Connor raced up the stairs, taking them two at a time. The team patiently waited for him to return, while Mateo walked calmly up the stairs and made his way to his lab. When they both came running back down the stairs, it was clear they had spoken.

"It could work. I mean, what do we have to lose?" Mateo said, talking mainly to himself.

Without telling the team what they were doing, Mateo placed the newly prepared reaction vessel under the microscope and rolled it to the statue, his trepidation about being near the thing overcome by this new direction. Connor walked over with him.

"Together?' Mateo said.

"Yes," Connor replied.

Simultaneously, Mateo injected the bots into the tissue sample while Connor injected a vial of clarified axolotl stem cells. They all watched as the bots absorbed the axolotl cells and turned a soft purple color. The glow from Sednamaroq was brighter than usual. The bots replicated so quickly that they covered the tissue sample with speed that resembled a thin liquid being poured rapidly over a solid surface. Within seconds, the tissue absorbed the purple goo of concentrated bots and pulsed with life.

Mateo and Connor stared at the monitor and turned to look at the statue. The blue glow intensified, flashed, and then disappeared. They both walked over to the cart and rolled it back to the wall. The tissue seemed to be continuing to thrive. Mateo took the sample and walked it back to his lab, his team following silently and in single file.

Mateo and Connor returned to the apartment and picked at the cold lasagna. The bond between them had reached a new level, and that night they took their friendship to the next level, as well. By the time Beverly returned a week later, the tissue sample was still alive and healthy.

19

The scientists gathered at Beverly's house on the morning after her return. She ignored the others as she focused on Mateo and his breakthrough. Mateo detailed the course of events over the past week, including Connor's idea to inject the axolotl cells into the mix.

"I could not have done it without Connor. "Mateo said. "We still need to observe the tissue sample to make sure it remains healthy, but as of now, it looks like this might be the solution we've been hoping for."

"This is unbelievable news, Mateo," Beverly said. "I'd like to meet with you and Connor privately. Everyone else, please leave and continue your efforts."

Beverly, Connor, and Mateo remained seated while the others left. Beverly wasted no time getting to the business at hand.

"Listen, guys, I'm over the moon with this discovery. I need to know two things. One, what testing is needed to make sure it's a viable treatment for me? And two, what are the other potential applications for this?" She waited while Mateo and Connor considered the questions.

"Well, first, I want to focus on what this means for you," Mateo stated. "We need to wait until we are sure the repaired tissue sample won't degrade. Considering the longest you've gone without the statue is four weeks, then I suggest we wait eight and re-evaluate. Then we need to test it on other random samples. We need to know how it reacts to a non-diseased cell. As for what that means for you, I'm honestly not sure. And we have no way of testing it unless you have another patient with FOP."

"I can arrange for another person with FOP for testing," Beverly said calmly.

"Really?" Mateo was shocked.

"Yes, Mateo. Really." Beverly said sarcastically. "I've been soliciting a database for years with potential patients ready to participate in a clinical trial. I can have three patients here within two weeks. Will you be ready by then?"

"No," Mateo replied quickly. "We really need eight weeks. And we'll need to inject the patient simultaneously with the axolotl cells and the phyconanobots, in the presence of the statue, of course."

"Okay then, I'll have them here in eight weeks. Be ready." Beverly stared at Mateo intensely. "What about my second question?"

Connor spoke up to answer. "The potential is unlimited. Whatever you need to cure, this process most likely will do it. There might also be potential to activate bots with the statue and then use them for other purposes. They will just need to be programmed to do that."

"Excellent. Just the answer I was hoping for." Beverly said.

"What are you thinking of doing with the bots?" Mateo asked.

"I'm going to sell them to medical research labs. Your names will be published in all the major journals, as well as many fringe publications, I'm sure." Beverly was direct with them.

"How do we maintain ethical boundaries?" Mateo asked.

"Ultimately, that is not our problem. Our liability ends when we sell them with a disclaimer." Beverly said.

Neither Mateo nor Connor believed this to be true, but did not argue. They left the house and walked back to the lab without speaking. Connor grabbed them coffees from the small break room off the lab, and they settled in one of the small conference rooms to talk. Neither of them mentioned the casualness of Beverly's outlook on medical research ethics. Instead, they focused on planning out the next eight weeks. Having a consenting test subject would be a game-changer. At this point, they willfully ignored the standards of ethical research and the need for an Institutional Review Board. As with everything else, they assumed that Beverly either had it handled or would find a way around it. They were too close to stop.

20

The next eight weeks passed quickly. Connor focused on making sure there were adequate axolotl cells for the foreseeable future, and Mateo, with the help of Matt, Sara, and Jo, performed as many tests as possible using the bots on anything and everything they could think of. The results were often surprising and frequently successful. It didn't seem to matter what damage had been done to any cell; the magic combination of Mateo's phyconanobots, Connor's axolotl stem cells, and Sednamaroq could fix it. At one point, Sara placed a half-eaten banana in a dish and injected it with the smallest number of bots and cells she could extract. The blue glow from the statue was dim and brief, almost as if it couldn't be bothered to fix it, but did it anyway to show her that it could. The whole unblemished piece of fruit that resulted was unsettling.

Mateo was the only one who made a comment. "Well, that's cool, but I'm not gonna be the one who eats it."

They all laughed, but no one ate it. The banana was preserved in a solution and placed in the storage closet with the other results of testing. Sara labeled the container as B1 and referenced it in her notes.

Mateo did not fully realize that eight weeks had passed until the morning meeting with Beverly when she announced that the three subjects for the clinical trial would arrive later that day. The morning's meeting concentrated on one thing – the process for testing these three subjects. The three people, one man and two women, would be staying in individual rooms on the opposite side of the building from the dining room and staff apartments. Mateo had never wandered to that area of the first floor and was interested to see the arrangement.

Beverly gave very specific directions on how the subjects would be treated. One person per day, with injections next to the statue and with the patients lightly sedated. There was to be no interaction with them otherwise. Beverly and a traveling staff hired specifically for the purpose of the trial were the only ones to have any contact with the subjects, except for the procedure itself. The subjects did not know the location of the institute and were not to know, under any circumstances. They would arrive by seaplane and were under the impression that they were traveling to a facility near a large city.

Once she was done laying out the rules, Beverly dismissed everyone except Mateo and Connor with instructions for them to stay in their apartments for the next four days. Food would be brought to them, and they could request any other items they might need. When everyone had left, Beverly walked with Mateo and Connor to view the rooms the subjects would be occupying.

The portion of the hallway on that side of the building had a door with a newly installed key card access pad on the wall to the right of the door. Beverly tapped a card on the pad and walked through, followed by Connor and Mateo. Connor gave Mateo a knowing look, suggesting that they would need to talk about the new security measures when they were alone. The hallway occupied the corner of the building closest to the front door and consisted of four service rooms and three hotel-like sleeping rooms, each with an ensuite bath. One of the service rooms was set up as a mini kitchen, one as a storage room, one as a medical exam room, and the final as a small conference room.

As they walked out the opposite end of the hallway, Mateo and Connor noticed that the door exited directly into the main entrance foyer. Beverly explained that the subjects would be rolled by gurney through this doorway and then through the perpendicular door into the statue chamber. Mateo noticed that these doors now had keycard access pads as well. When she was done talking, Beverly handed each of them a key card on a retractable lanyard.

"You will need these over the next few days." She spoke.

The two men took the cards and looked at each other, remembering their conversation about locked doors. They used the cards to access the door opposite the one for the patient hallways to access the side of the building where they lived. As they walked to Connor's apartment, they remained silent. Once they were through the door, Mateo flopped down on the couch and sighed. He had been staying at Connor's apartment more than his own and felt comfortable here. The relationship that had developed between them was comfortable and secure. Mateo wasn't ready to admit that he might be in love, but he was getting close.

"That was an unexpected turn of events. I mean, it makes sense that they don't want the subjects to have access to the rest of the building, but it seems like overkill." Mateo said.

"Yes, it does seem extreme since they are supervised anyway. But it might just be Beverly being cautious." Connor explained.

"I guess you're right, as usual." Mateo smiled. "We're prepared for the first subject tomorrow, so I'm just going to focus on that."

"Good idea." Connor agreed.

The morning started early. Mateo and the team prepared the injections and double and triple-checked every detail before moving the few items to the chamber. There was no contingency for medical emergencies. According to Beverly, nothing was needed. The experiment would either work or not. Mateo knew she was right, but it bothered him, nonetheless.

Beverly, Matt, Sara, and Jo stood in a line against the wall near the stairs as Mateo and Connor waited with a small rolling cart. On the cart were two syringes. The first was typical of one seen in interventional radiology suites and contained the axolotl cells. The second looked like something from an alien abduction movie. It was a miniature version of the bot containment vessel, fitted with a syringe on one end and a plunger on the other. The bots caused the glass of the syringe to glow a swirling green.

The door to the chamber opened, and an unknown woman with short platinum hair and black rectangular eyeglasses rolled in a gurney with the first subject, a female, covered in a sheet up to the top of her chest. She looked to be peacefully asleep. The woman rolled her into the room, set the brake on the bed, turned, and left the room, using a key card to open the door. Mateo and Connor walked the short distance to the subject. Connor disengaged the brake, and they both rolled the bed to be as close to the statue as possible. Mateo pulled back the sheet to reveal a woman who appeared to be in her mid-twenties. Her body was thin and frail, the evidence of her disease clearly manifested in her right arm, which had evidently experienced recent trauma and was rigid and locked, the tendons and muscles hardened like stone.

An IV had been inserted recently into her left hand, and Mateo suspected that the damage done by the needle was already provoking a response from her body. Without hesitation, Mateo connected a Y-split catheter to the IV and handed the axolotl syringe to Connor. Mateo himself picked up the syringe with the phyconanobots.

"Insert the needles into the hub." Mateo directed. "Push on my command."

They each inserted their respective needles into the sealed silicone hubs on each split of the tubing. Connor's thumb settled on the plunger, ready to deliver the crucial stem cells.

"On my mark, three... two... one... push," Mateo said clearly.

Each man pushed the contents of their syringe into the catheter and removed it when they were completely empty. Connor stepped back to join the others, while

Mateo remained, staring at the face of the young girl. He had either cured her or killed her. Either way, she would be delivered from a life of pain.

The phyconanobots immediately focused on the axolotl cells, incorporating them into their structure, absorbing their abilities. The bots found the heterotropic ossification within the woman's body and started repairing the damaged tissue, multiplying as they worked to accommodate the extent of the damage. Then the bots encountered a new set of instructions. The blue light that surrounded them altered their genetic composition in a way that enhanced their ability to interpret what they understood as repair. Their reproduction multiplied exponentially with this change. A few of the bots continued working on the damaged tissue; the remaining bots, which now numbered in the trillions, targeted the ACVR1 gene and removed the defect, correcting the woman's entire genetic composition to that of a normal, healthy female. When they were done, they dissolved casually into the surrounding healthy tissue. Their byproducts would be excreted through the normal process of her body's operations.

"Mateo," Connor called. "Join us."

"What?" Mateo replied groggily as he looked back at the others. Quickly gathering himself, he backed from the subject, turned, and walked briskly to join the others. By the time he reached them and turned back to the statue, a blue glow had intensified, becoming brighter than any of them had seen with the previous tests. As the light intensified, they all shielded their eyes, blinded by the bright light reflecting off the alabaster surface of the statue. Mateo could barely see the body through the blinding light, but he noticed the young woman stiffen and jerk violently as the light completely blinded him. Then the room went dark.

The lights along the perimeter of the circular room faded back into existence, and the body stirred on the gurney. Beverly was the first to rush forward. The young girl's eyes were wide with fear as she struggled to sit up.

"Be still," Beverly told her. "You're safe. Be still. Help me roll this thing back to her room." This last command was directed at Connor. Connor rushed over and released the brake. Beverly pulled the sheet back up to cover the young girl's naked body, but not before noticing that her right arm had returned to normal. Of course, that could just be the effect of the statue; only time would tell if she was cured completely. Connor helped Beverly roll the subject back to her room while the others waited in the chamber. When they returned to the group, Beverly suggested they meet in a conference room on the third floor.

"What's next?" Mateo asked Beverly once they had settled around the table.

"We wait," Beverly said. "The statue has the capacity to heal but not cure. We will observe for three weeks, then cause trauma to a part of her body. Maybe a light punch to the thigh. We will know soon after if her body will react."

"How long will all three subjects be with us?" Connor asked.

"Eight weeks," Beverly said quickly.

21

The other two subjects had similar responses to the treatment. The second, a boy in his teens, had no visible evidence of the disease. The third, a woman in her late thirties, had clearly endured great suffering. Her body was contorted with hardened sinew pulling her limbs in directions that were unnatural. After the treatment, however, her body was normal and pliable. Beverly seemed especially hopeful after the last subject finished the treatment. Over the next eight weeks, the team continued to prepare the bots and axolotl cells. Discussing progress at the morning meetings while Beverly told them about the progress of the subjects.

In week seven, the morning meeting began with just Connor, Mateo, and Beverly.

"I've sent the others home," Beverly said. "Their research was going nowhere, and I don't have any other research for them to do. They will be able to publish their work, failed or not, and become gainfully employed, if they choose. Although the pay they received will allow them to retire, which I suggested they do.”

“So, it’s just us?” Mateo asked.

“Yes, Mateo, it’s just us,” Beverly said. “We caused various types of traumas to the subjects. Nothing provoked a response. I think we can safely say your treatment worked. Of course, we will only know for sure over time, but knowing the disease and Sednamaroq as I do, I think I’m right in my assumption.”

Beverly clapped her hands together twice in rapid succession, and a young man appeared with a tray containing three glasses and a bottle of champagne. The bottle was dark green with a pink label, and Mateo recognized the Dom Pérignon name. The man placed the tray on a side table, expertly removed the cork cage, and used a white napkin to safely uncork the bottle. He poured a generous amount into each glass and picked up the tray, extending it first to Beverly, who took a glass. Mateo and Connor did the same.

“This is Dom Pérignon P3 Plénitude Brut Rosé. At just over five thousand dollars a bottle, it’s the perfect choice to celebrate this early stage in our victory. She raised her glass, extended it towards the two men, and smiled as the three glasses clinked together.

“Here’s to phyconanobots and axolotls!” She said, laughing cheerfully.

As they drank the expensive champagne, Johanna, Steven, Yoshi, and Hugo celebrated in a different way. A rope joined their feet, which connected them as a group to a large weight that sat on the lakebed in one of the deep coves of Baker Lake; their combined arms and heads floated outward and upward like a delicate flower undulating in the cold water.

22

The morning of the eighth week started slowly for Mateo. He and Connor woke and had breakfast in Connor's apartment. Connor looked out the window and marveled at the beauty of the contrast of evergreens against the snow. The cold season has started to set in, and the daily snowfalls seem to have frozen the island in time and place. The stillness of the scene calmed him. The tinge of fear that he had experienced during the same season the previous year had faded as he had become accustomed to life here on the island. And he had met Mateo, whom he saw as fate.

"We're going to need to bundle up for the walk," Connor said.

"Looks that cold, does it?" Mateo said, approaching the window where Connor stood.

"See for yourself." Connor stepped to the left to allow Mateo a clear view of the landscape.

"Yep, that looks cold," Mateo said, turning towards the wardrobe and suddenly realizing he wasn't in his own apartment. "I'll go get my gear from my apartment."

Mateo walked next door and retrieved his SISR-issued parka with its fur-lined hood, his insulated boots, and a pair of gloves. He met Connor in the hallway, who was dressed in identical gear. They walked slowly to Beverly's house, enjoying the stillness and beauty of the pristine snow. Mateo shielded his eyes as he walked, the sunlight on the snow nearly blinding him. It reminded him of the light from Sednamaroq when they were treating the trial subjects.

They arrived at Beverly's house, and she immediately let them inside, giving them time to remove their coats and enjoy a few sips of hot cider that had been offered by her butler. The three of them settled into large, overstuffed chairs by the roaring fire as they talked about the immediate future.

"When will you take the treatment?" Mateo asked bluntly.

"I'm going to wait until the subjects are three months out. They will be returned to their homes this week, and we will keep in touch with them over time to make sure the treatment is holding. Even if it will last just three months, it will be an improvement over what I go through now." Beverly seemed to be musing over possibilities and hope.

"That sounds good. So, what's next?" Connor asked.

"I've transferred your notes and the details of all the research to Chuck at BarsTech Industries. His team will begin to manufacture the bots in batches for specific purposes. They have an AI-driven manufacturing process that will be more efficient than what we do here. I want you two to see it when it's up and running. In the meantime, I've prepared new contract addenda for each of you. You will get royalties on each batch that is sold. By the end of the year, you both will be multi-millionaires." Beverly spoke with confidence and with a business-like cadence, reminding Mateo of her change in demeanor when she presented the initial contract to him in Albuquerque.

"That's very generous of you. Thank you." Connor said.

"Yes, thank you, Beverly," Mateo added. "Does that mean we will be leaving here after you take the treatment?"

"No," Beverly said. There is still more to do with developing the bots for other uses, and I want you around to guide that. I'm going to hire more people to assist you. If you'll stay, of course."

"Of course I'll stay. I want to see this through." Mateo said.

"Me too." Connor agreed.

Beverly walked them to the foyer and waited while they dressed for the cold walk back to the institute building. On the way back, Mateo remembered that he had wanted to ask Beverly about taking a period of leave to visit friends. He told Connor that he would join him shortly as he turned back towards Beverly's house. He walked up to the porch and raised his hand to knock. He heard Beverly talking to someone and stopped himself from knocking on the door. He could see her through the window, clearly talking on the phone. Mateo flattened himself against the wall of the house and listened to the conversation.

"Yes, of course they can be weaponized," Beverly said, remaining silent while the person on the other end of the line spoke.

"Well, if you're the highest bidder, then of course you will have exclusive use of them. And the technology." Beverly continued, waiting again for the response that Mateo could not hear.

"Don't worry about the researchers. I have all the notes and details of the research... No, don't worry. They will still need to work for me for a little longer, then I'll take care of it." Beverly disconnected the call and quickly made another.

"Hi Chuck. Yes, how soon can you have them to me?" She must be talking to Chuck at BarsTech, Mateo surmised.

"Four weeks is fine. But no longer. I have buyers ready to bid." Beverly paused for a longer time than usual.

"You'll get your cut, Chuck. Don't worry about that. Just make sure I get the bots. This is just the first of many." Beverly disconnected the call, and Mateo quietly made his way off the porch and down the snowy path to the building.

When he got to Connor's apartment, he told him what he had heard.

"This is serious, Mateo. What do we do?" Connor asked.

"I'm not sure. I think we need to keep going as if nothing is wrong while we figure it out." Mateo answered truthfully.

"We need a plan to get out of here," Connor said, his voice becoming frantic.

"We will figure this out. Let's let it sit for a day. We can talk tonight. Susie was paranoid that Beverly had cameras everywhere, and maybe she was right after all. She said the only safe place was the pantry near the dining room. We will talk there tomorrow." Mateo placed both hands on Connor's shoulder to reassure him.

The next day, Mateo and Connor went to the pantry to talk. Connor suggested that they present to Beverly that he was no longer needed here and ask her if he could leave. It was risky, but they had few other options. Connor told

Mateo his personal email and phone number and said that he would let him know when he was safe. Mateo repeated both until he had them in his memory.

In a meeting with Beverly later that week, Connor suggested that he return to his home after Beverly received her treatment. Beverly agreed and asked him if he needed to stay for the treatment or if one of Mateo's assistants could do it. Connor said that would not be a problem, and Beverly told him he could return home the following week if he wanted. She told him how valuable he was and that he always had a place here if he wanted to return.

Connor and Mateo spent the next week saying goodbye and preparing for his departure. On the day he left, Beverly joined Mateo on the dock to say farewell. The seaplane that would take off on the ice-covered lake waited at the end of the dock. Beverly hugged Connor tightly and told him how much she appreciated the work that he had done for her. She reiterated that he was welcome back at any time. Mateo hugged Connor, pulling him close and telling him how much he meant to him. Connor ducked into the low door of the plane and waved as it taxied to an appropriate place for take-off.

Beverly and Mateo walked back up the dock to the institute, Beverly's arm hooked affectionately in Mateo's. They were bundled in the SISR parkas, the dark green complementing the trees and snow, rather than providing contrast. When they were back inside, they went to the dining room to warm up. The three assistants were there, having hot cocoa and waiting for lunch. Beverly and Mateo joined them as Mateo prepared two mugs of steaming hot cocoa to help them warm up.

Beverly chatted casually with the now-smaller team about the plans for the next few weeks. She revealed to them the plans for a delivery from her manufacturing plant in California. These new bots would be programmed for new purposes, and it would expand their research into new and exciting areas. They talked briefly about Connor and how she hoped that he would one day decide to return to work with them on the new possibilities for research with the phyconanobots.

As they chatted casually over mugs of hot cocoa, the snow fell gently on Connor's limp and lifeless body draped over branches in the top of a tall tree in the forest several miles south of Bake Lake.

23

Two weeks had passed, and Mateo had not heard from Connor. He knew one possibility was the security of the SISR servers, but his instinct told him that Susie had been right, and Beverly had disposed of him now that she had no more use for him. He had to find a way to get away from the institute.

Beverly talked to him as if they were best friends, her speech manic and pressured. Mateo responded in ways that encouraged the strength of their friendship. As a result, she confided in him about her plans for his bots. She told him about the shipment from BarsTech and the details of the delivery itself. The bots would be delivered by truck to Thompson, Manitoba, where they would be transferred to a train and taken to Churchill on Hudson Bay, transferred to a seaplane, and ultimately delivered to the institute.

Mateo inquired about the rationale of using three modes of transport. Why not just put them on a plane and make it simple? Beverly laughed at the question, telling him the simplest plan was not always the best. Then she spent the next hour educating him on the intricacies of customs and transporting items that were, as she described them, delicate and misunderstood. In the end, she said the method she had chosen had been the one that provided the least risk, not only for prying government eyes, but also from potential bidders that might want to steal the merchandise rather than purchase it.

Regardless of Beverly's convoluted reasoning, Mateo now had the base for a plan. If he could talk Beverly into allowing him to assist with the delivery, he could use it as a chance to escape. He pleaded his case to Beverly, explaining that he was the only one who could verify the quality of the bots before they took delivery. Surprisingly, Beverly agreed and started planning for them to travel together to Thomson the following week. Mateo found it increasingly difficult to maintain his composure with Beverly, but it was his only chance to survive. His life depended on his ability to fake his relationship with the crazy heiress.

Mateo stood in his office on the third floor of the institute and considered what he wanted to take with him. Everything had meaning, but he could only take a few things with him. He removed the picture of him with his mom and dad and hid it in a zippered internal pocket of his backpack with the small amount of cash that he had in his pocket when he arrived at the institute. He had not needed cash while at the institute and had no ability to get any. He took the elevator down to his apartment and packed his backpack with a change of clothes and toiletries. He went next door to Connor's apartment to see if there was anything there that might be a memento of him. He suddenly realized that he had no photos of them. They had not even taken pictures on the phones the institute had given them. He remembered relinquishing his old phone when offered the newer model by Beverly several months ago. How could he have been so stupid?

He noticed a t-shirt of Connor's draped over a dining chair and remembered wearing it one night as Connor told him about it being his favorite. He stuffed it in the backpack, a single tear running down his cheek at the memories of a friend he would never see again. He grabbed his parka, gloves, and a scarf and made his way to the front entrance to wait for Beverly.

The vehicle that sat at the end of the dock looked like a custom-made contraption. And it was. Beverly called it her 'ice cube,' and Mateo admitted that it was exactly what it was. A miniature version of her water vessel, but perfectly square and bluish white. The 'ice cube' looked like a fake clock of ice on sleds. A custom dual-tread propulsion system worked to both move and steer the large cube. Beverly arrived, her mood elated and cheerful, and they walked carefully down the icy path to the dock and boarded the cube-shaped vehicle. Beverly removed her parka in the warmth of the cabin and settled into a comfy chair for the two-hour ride. Mateo removed his parka and gloves and joined her in a nearby matching chair. Sandra arrived soon after with a tray of light snacks and two warm whiskey cocktails.

"Here's to a bright future!" Beverly said, raising her glass towards Mateo. He reciprocated the toast and smiled at her as he took a sip.

"To possibilities." He said, making Beverly smile.

During the ride across the ice and the subsequent plane ride to the small airport north of Thompson, Manitoba, Mateo asked as many questions about the upcoming transaction as he felt safely possible. Beverly shared more than she should have. He learned that the truck driver would be arriving in an electric Volvo rig that had been fitted with a special charging generator designed by BarsTech. Beverly told him about the AI-driven manufacturing process at BarsTech and how impressed she was with it. Mateo showed genuine interest and told her he would like to see that someday. Beverly responded to all his comments and questions as if they would be best friends forever.

"We will stay two nights in Thompson, Mateo. The only hotels there are cheap chain hotels, so we will be staying in one of those." Beverly sounded discouraged, as if Mateo would feel she was letting him down with this news. They were thirty minutes into the ninety-minute flight, and Beverly seemed to feel the need to set expectations.

"It's okay, Beverly. We will do whatever is necessary." Mateo attempted to comfort her.

"I know, Mateo, but I've provided a certain quality of life for myself and for you. And it's difficult to reduce that at times. But we will suffer through it." Beverly mused.

"Can we walk through the plan? What happens when we arrive?" Mateo asked.

"Of course, of course," Beverly replied. "I have a driver arranged to take us to the hotel. There are some good local restaurants, so I thought we might have a nice dinner tonight and then go back to our individual rooms for an early bedtime. We will both need to get some rest since tomorrow will be a very busy day."

"That sounds good. Do you have a place in mind for dinner, or shall I find a place for us?" Mateo offered, hoping to manipulate the plan in his favor to give him more control over his options for escape.

"I have a place in mind," Beverly said. "There's a hole-in-the-wall steak house that I remember from the last time I was here. The atmosphere is rough, but the steaks are phenomenal."

"When were you here last?" Mateo asked.

"Last year. I bought a shipping business in Thompson that has a few warehouses. One of those is where we will take delivery tomorrow." Beverly said absentmindedly, obviously still reminiscing about the steakhouse.

"When are we meeting the truck tomorrow?" Mateo continued his questions, realizing that he might be asking too much.

"Noon. We might have to wait for the truck to arrive. Once you inspect the merchandise, we will move it to the train. The warehouse sits right on the Burntwood River, so it will be an easy transfer by small boat if transporting it by car proves to be risky." Beverly had regained focus and seemed annoyed by the question, and her tone turned quickly sarcastic. "And in case you didn't know, the Burntwood River empties into Split Lake, which joins up with the Nelson River, which then goes directly to Hudson Bay."

"That's fascinating. It's such an interesting area, with all the waterways joining together." Mateo softened his voice to ease the newly formed tension.

"My family has a history of exploration in Canada's North. So, it feels natural for me to talk about it. I forget that others find it so strange." Beverly had returned to normal, which relieved Mateo.

The plane landed at the small Thompson airfield, and the plane taxied to a private hangar where a black SUV waited to take them to the hotel. Beverly remained quiet on the short drive to the hotel. One of her many staff had already checked them into the hotel and had the keycards ready for them when they arrived. The hotel was clean and comfortable. Until Mateo had experienced the luxury of his stay at the small resort with the lavender bath products, he would have considered this hotel a nice one. Beverly took her keycard and gave Mateo instructions to get settled and meet her in the lobby in two hours. Mateo went to his room on the second floor, tossed his backpack on the king-size bed, and turned on the TV to have some background noise. In addition to the bed, the room was furnished with a dresser, a plush fabric chair, and a cabinet containing a mini refrigerator and a microwave. A single-serve coffee maker sat on top of the microwave with the promise of something that never really delivered.

He tore open the packet of coffee grounds and inserted the sachet into the tray in the coffee maker. He then removed the plastic wrapping from the paper cup and filled it with water from the tap in the bathroom, pouring it into the reservoir of the machine. He pressed the button to start it and stared at it while it did its thing. This was the first time in many months that he had not been on the island. He had not realized until now how restricting the institute had been. Connor had been there to keep him sane, but now what was there? Beverly? His only choice, if he had remained there, would be to descend into her craziness. When the coffee was done, he sipped the hot, bitter liquid that he could only describe a coffee-scented water and walked to the window. He pulled back the heavy drapes and looked out at the landscape of Thompson, Manitoba – a place he never imagined visiting.

The view was shockingly beautiful. Dark green evergreens pierced blankets of pristine snow. Rolling hills and small mountains layered the background, providing depth and character to a city that was unexpected. He knew there was a dirty side to the city, but he could not see it from here. Mateo walked back to the dresser and picked up a thin magazine that promised to tell him everything he needed to know about the small town. As the Hub of the North, Thompson had originally been created as a mining town and was one of the first fully planned cities in Canada. In addition to mining, the industries needed to support the community were the only other things that kept people employed. The city also boasted the largest marina in Manitoba. And there was a map. Mateo considered that this might be useful as he ripped out the page, folded it and placed it in his pocket.

He stretched out on the bed, thinking about how this might play out. He had no concrete plan and would need to improvise along the way to escape. Maybe he could find a place to hide here in Thompson until he could get a ride to another town? He wasn't sure, and the uncertainty was causing him to feel a combination of anxiety and fear that he had not experienced in a long time. He decided to take a shower and clear his head. He undressed and placed his clothes neatly on one side of the large bed. He walked to the small bathroom and started the shower, glancing briefly at himself in the mirror and realizing that he could do this. He must. Not trying was not an option.

The hot water felt good. It relaxed him and renewed his resolve. Now, he just had to keep up appearances with Beverly. That was the first key to his escape. If she suspected anything, she would send him back to Baker Lake... or worse. He thought about Susie's warning when he first arrived at the institute. When he was free, he would see if he could find any of the scientists who had left. If Susie had been right, they would all be dead, including her. This possibility did not surprise him. He had seen Beverly's insanity firsthand and knew it was only a matter of time before he fell out of her favor. He dried off with the sub-standard towel and walked back to the window, allowing his body to air dry while he pondered the contrast of his situation against the beauty of the river, trees, and snow.

Mateo dressed and walked down to the simple lobby. A sign advertised the included breakfast and pointed to an area that included tables and chairs, and a buffet area pre-set with chafing trays that sat empty at this time of day. Beverly was seated at one of the tables in the eating area, her legs crossed as she looked at her phone. She looked out of place in the environment and smiled when she saw him.

"Did you get some rest?" Beverly asked.

"Yes, and a shower," Mateo replied. "The landscape here, especially along the river, is more beautiful than I would have thought."

"It is. Thompson is a strange little town. It's a jumping-off point for much of the north. The waterways are confusing, but useful. They don't call it the hub of the north for nothing." Beverly laughed, throwing her head back and motioning with her hand as if she were presenting a five-star hotel. "Are you ready for dinner? I'm starving!"

"Me too!" Mateo grinned. "Let's get some steak."

The ride to the restaurant was short and pleasant. And the steak was as good as promised. As Beverly had said, it was a hole-in-the-wall, with mismatched tables and chairs and a clientele that was diverse. But the food and service were excellent. They both had ribeye, cooked medium, with loaded baked potatoes and corn on the cob. Choices of beverages included a single brand of beer – Labatt Blue – and water. They both had beer with their steaks, which seemed fitting for the atmosphere. Without asking, the waitress, a young local girl who looked to be in her late teens, brought house-made Nanaimo bars for dessert, telling them that her mother made them and they came with all meals. It was a nice treat.

The conversation during dinner consisted of Beverly talking and Mateo listening. She rambled on about a variety of things, including his research, the failure of the other scientists and how disappointed she had been, her favorite foods, the snow, and the advantages of being rich, among other topics. Her speech was constant and pressured at times, indicating to Mateo that she was experiencing some psychological elation resulting from whatever conditions layered her psyche. When dinner was over, she continued talking on the ride back to the hotel.

"Meet me here in the lobby at 11 a.m.," Beverly instructed. "They have a breakfast that is probably better than you would think."

Mateo agreed, and they went to their respective rooms for the evening. He fell asleep quickly, potential scenarios for escape playing through his mind.

The morning light woke Mateo before his alarm. He looked at his phone and saw that it was 7 a.m. He had attempted to look up the other SISR scientists on the phone's browser while connected to the hotel wi-fi, but the security measures installed on the phone limited what he could do. He got out of bed and dressed, looking out the window in the process. The sun had not yet risen, and the moonlight glistened on the white snow and slow-moving waters of the river. He left the room and made his way downstairs to have breakfast.

The crowd in the breakfast area was as diverse as the one at the restaurant the previous evening. A few families, miners, truck drivers, and business people occupied most of the tables, with a few having settled in on the two couches and four chairs near the reception desk, plates resting on their laps with beverages on the two coffee tables. Mateo pumped himself a cup of coffee into a heavy ceramic mug, trying to remember the last time he had seen this type of insulated coffee urn. A smaller table with a single chair was empty near a window, and he placed his coffee cup on the surface of the table, claiming it while he got some food. As Beverly had predicted, the breakfast selections were exceptional for being included with the room. Freshly cooked bacon, sausage, and scrambled eggs were complemented by warm biscuits, pancakes, and French toast. A variety of other breakfast breads, fruit, cereals, and yogurts are added to the choices. The only things missing for Mateo were tortillas and green chiles.

He loaded up a plate with sausage and eggs, a biscuit, and some fruit, grabbing a bottle of hot sauce on the way back to his table. While he ate, Mateo considered attempting escape by seeing if he could hitch a ride with one of the truckers having breakfast. It would be risky since Beverly could appear at any moment. He also had a strong desire to see the bots produced by BarsTech. It was foolish to ignore an opportunity to escape just to see the results of his life's work culminate into a mass-produced product, but he could not overcome it.

As he was taking his plate to the cart positioned against one wall for depositing dirty dishes, he saw Beverly step off the elevator. He realized that he would need to be careful with his plans. He refilled his coffee and greeted her.

"You were right about the breakfast." He spoke.

"Told you." She smiled. "I'm going to have some coffee and fruit. I think they might have oatmeal if I ask for it."

"Get your coffee and find a seat. I'll ask about the oatmeal and come join you." Mateo offered as Beverly smiled and walked to the coffee dispenser.

Mateo asked about the oatmeal and was told they would bring it out in a few minutes. He sat with Beverly while she ate, and they talked about the hotel and how it was not as bad as she had assumed it would be. When they were done, they went back to their rooms, with Beverly giving him a reminder about their meeting time.

Soon after 11 a.m. Mateo found himself in the back seat of the SUV with Beverly, on the way to the delivery. The driver pulled through the loading door of the large, empty warehouse and parked to one side, reversing the vehicle first so that it would be facing the door to facilitate an easy exit. Two other SUVs were parked on the other side of the warehouse. They waited silently for the next hour. Then, a vehicle unlike anything Mateo had seen pulled into the warehouse and parked in the very center of the vast space. The truck was dark gray and moved silently. None of the usual deep vibrations and industrial clatter of a typical truck of this size. The trailer that it pulled was short, appearing at odds with the large truck with its sleeper extension. Mateo could see the words "Cyber Wolf" printed in script on the side of the cab. Through the glass of the windshield, he could see two men who remained where they were after the truck had stopped. The door to the warehouse closed, and the doors of the other two SUVs opened, pouring out a total of six men and two women dressed in black tactical gear, carrying guns and full belts of other weapons.

It looks like the delivery has started, Mateo thought to himself.

24

Knox carefully reviewed the items before him. Everything was neatly arranged on the bed in his guest room. He did not typically stage things to this extent before a trip, but this one was unique. The winter weather in Barstow rarely dropped below freezing, and he knew the weather along the treacherous route to the north would be much colder. The setting sun reduced the light coming through the window, and he flipped the light switch for the overhead light so that he could continue packing. Ryder walked in with an armful of sweaters and tossed them on the bed.

"How many of these do you think I should take?" Ryder asked, smiling at Knox's clear annoyance.

"I think you should take all of them." Knox laughed. "We are close to the same size, so I can wear them too. I'll just take fewer of my own."

Knox had been elated since Ryder had agreed to go with him on this trip. He estimated the 2300-mile trip would take them around 45 hours if they were to drive straight through. So, considering stops for food, charging, and sleep, he had planned on eight days to get there. Ryder suggested they extend that to ten days to accommodate for any challenges along the way. If they got there early, they could rest or find other things to do until the scheduled delivery. The ten-day plan had them leaving in two days and trying to average six hours of active driving per day. If they could do more in a day, they would do that.

Knox's rig, Cyber Wolf, had been at BarsTech for four weeks getting fitted with the range-extending generator. When Knox picked it up three days ago, Chuck had instructed him on the simplicity of using the device. The generator had been hardwired to the truck's battery bank. When the charge was low and there was no access to a charging station, all Knox had to do was turn a dial. The dial had its own protective box that sat beside the toolbox-sized generator and had a locking cover that was accessible by entering a code on a mechanical keypad. There was an emergency key to open the cover, and Chuck suggested Knox hide that in the cab of the truck. Knox was no stranger to finding small hiding spaces for things in the rig, so he placed the key in a small pocket he had installed under the driver's seat.

Chuck warned that the generator was not designed to be used for constant charging. It needed time to rest between uses. Leaving it on for more than thirty minutes would cause it to overheat. It would, however, fully charge the truck's batteries in that thirty-minute time. If the generator overheated, it could lead to an explosion. He imparted this information matter-of-factly, ignoring Knox's shocked expression.

"I guess I just will have to remember to turn that dial back when it's done charging then," Knox commented.

"Yeah, that's really important," Chuck said.

"Anything else I need to know?" Knox asked.

"Nope. Just only use it if you need it. It's not tested for constant use. Like I said." Chuck responded. "Oh, and remember the security systems on the trailer itself. Same cameras, but the GPS tracking and motion sensors are enhanced to accommodate this haul. As long as your biometric readings are within range, and if the readings within the trailer itself remain within range, we will not intervene."

The drive to his house gave Knox time to work through the worry of having this device attached to his truck. The rules for operating it were simple, and he really had no reason to worry. He parked the truck in the driveway and told Ryder about the generator, providing the same instructions that Chuck had provided to him. Ryder's response was a simple 'easy enough.'

The day before their departure, Knox and Ryder spent several hours reviewing what they would need for the trip and carefully packing every available space in the truck. That evening, after a dinner of grilled steaks, mashed potatoes, and asparagus - courtesy of Ryder - they settled onto the couch to review the route. They would take I-15

North through Nevada and into Utah, catching I-70 East towards Colorado, where they would merge onto I-76 to Nebraska, and get on I-29 North up through the Dakotas and into Canada. Once in Canada, they would follow Manitoba Highway 75 North to Winnipeg before getting on the Provincial Truck Highway 6, also known as PTH-6, directly to Thompson.

Ryder had been reading that the roads were mostly kept clear for the trucks, but there was always a chance of storms that could cause driving to become difficult. He had also helped Knox map out charging stations, which would be available along the route up to Winnipeg, but not on the PTH-6. The 470 miles from Winnipeg to Thompson would be the most difficult and is where they would need the special generator. The City of Thompson had three charging stations, but they were not superchargers, and the truck would need to charge overnight, which might delay their return. Worst-case scenario, they would need to use the generator twice between Winnipeg and Thompson, once in Thompson if those chargers were not working, or if they were occupied, and two on the trip back to Winnipeg.

They had not decided where they would go after the delivery. Knox usually took a mini vacation after long deliveries. He had a full thirty days to return the trailer to BarsTech, so they had discussed heading to the west coast of Canada and spending a week or two there. The decision of where to go after the job had been left to Ryder. Knox told him nothing would make him happier than to let Ryder choose the destination, and Knox would make it happen. Ryder said he would have an answer to that before they arrived in Thompson.

The next morning, they did one final check of things and headed to BarsTech to pick up the trailer. They arrived at the guardhouse, and Knox was greeted by a guard that he did not know.

"Where's Janet?" Knox inquired.

"Day off. I'm Brad." The guard said, stepping up on the running board, his hand on the exterior handle. "I'm pretty new, so I don't think we've met."

"I'm Knox," Knox said, extending his arm out the window with his identification.

"Oh, I know who you are. You're a legend here at BarsTech." Brad laughed. "You and Cyber Wolf are well known."

Knox chuckled. "I'm glad my reputation is intact."

"I'm assuming your passenger is Ryder Garcia. May I see some ID, please?" Brad requested.

"Of course." Knox took the ID from Ryder and handed it to Brad, who looked at it briefly and handed it back.

"Okay, you two are good to go. Have a safe trip. I'll tell Janet I got to meet the legend." Brad smiled and opened the gate by pressing the screen on his tablet.

"Thanks, buddy. Hopefully, we will see you again soon." Knox smiled and winked at Brad, giving him a salute with two fingers and a touch to the brim of his ballcap.

Knox drove the truck through the gate and down the road to the BarsTech facility.

"I didn't know I was riding with the Legend," Ryder said, teasing Knox.

"You know it, babe," Knox said, trying to keep a serious face and failing.

As they approached the building, Knox provided instructions for Ryder. "When we park, we will wait until asked to exit the vehicle. Then will follow Chuck to a room where we will wait for them to connect the trailer. He will want to go over the route and delivery instructions. He may or may not want you to participate. Just go with whatever Chuck wants."

"No problem, Knox," Ryder said.

They entered the roll-up door to the loading area, and Knox pulled the truck up to a line on the floor at the far end, as he knew to do from the many previous deliveries he had made for BarsTech over the past two years. Within seconds of placing the truck in park and disengaging the electric motors, Chuck walked up to Knox's window and motioned for him to follow him inside. Ryder exited the truck on the driver's side and followed them into the building.

Good morning, Knox... Ryder." Chuck said. "Grab some coffee and let's all sit at the table to go over the route and delivery."

"Have a seat, Ryder. I'll make the coffee," Knox said, as he walked to the coffee machine. He turned to look at

Chuck, "We can start while I do this, Chuck. Ryder knows the route as well as I do."

"Sounds good. Tell me the route, and then we will go over the delivery." Chuck said.

Ryder detailed the route for Chuck, outlining where they would charge and when they would need the generator. He reiterated to Chuck his knowledge of the device, and that seemed to make Chuck happy. By the time Ryder had finished, Knox had taken a seat with them at the table with two mugs of coffee.

"Anything we need to know about the delivery?" Knox asked.

"Yes," Chuck replied. "This one will be different from the others. When you get to the destination, you will pull into the warehouse and exit the truck. You will need to be present while the merchandise is inspected. This is a request of the owner of the merchandise. Once the cargo is accepted and the trailer is re-locked, you may leave the warehouse."

Chuck paused, looking at Knox with uncertainty. "Knox, this poses a challenge for us that is different from your other deliveries. This delivery necessitates that I tell you what you are hauling." Chuck paused again, waiting for Knox to acknowledge the statement.

"I have no problem with that, Chuck. I'm assuming the numerous NDA's that I signed apply to this. So, I want you to know that I fully understand that I am not to disclose the information you give me." Knox said firmly.

"Knox's statement made Chuck grin. "You are right. And I would expect nothing less from you. In that case, here goes. The product you are delivering is phyconanobots. I will assume you do not know what those are and will explain. Phyconanobots are organic nanobots, or microscopic machines, that are made with a base of algae. They are very, very special and will be used in research that will change the world." Chuck continued to stare at Knox.

"Thanks for telling me, Chuck, but that means nothing to me. My goal is just a successful delivery." Knox was direct and honest. He made a mental note to have a conversation about these things with Ryder on the drive. He looked at Ryder, who seemed unfazed by the news of what they were hauling.

With the briefing over, Chuck pushed a stack of papers to Ryder. "Sign these, please."

Ryder signed them without looking at them and pushed them back to Chuck.

"We done? Can we get on the road now?" Ryder asked, appearing to be annoyed with Chuck.

"Yep, everything should be ready to go," Chuck said.

The three men walked back to the loading bay, and Chuck left them before Knox and Ryder got back in the truck. "Let's do this," Knox said as the door in front of the truck rolled up. Knox moved the truck through it, and they were on their way.

They were able to get in six hours on the first day. A brief break for food and to charge the batteries, put them in eastern Utah. The second and third days were more productive, with nine hours each day. Ahead of schedule at that point, they took a longer rest period in Grand Forks, North Dakota, and took an easy three-hour drive the following day to Winnipeg. They decided to get a hotel in Winnipeg to get adequate rest before the upcoming difficult drive to Thompson. During the time in Winnipeg, Ryder decided where they would go after the delivery.

"I've always wanted to see Calgary. So, I'm thinking we drive west, across the plains, and see what that part of Canada has to offer. What do you think?" Ryder asked.

"I think that's a great idea. I've never been to Calgary. Let's do it. I'll plan out a route for us." Knox seemed happy with Ryder's choice.

"Are you ready for the drive tomorrow?" Ryder said quietly.

"Yes. I'm ready. It looks like the weather will be bad, so we're just going to take our time. We're ahead of schedule, and that takes off some pressure." Knox said.

They started out the next morning on PTH-6 with weather that was cold and a sky that was overcast and gray. The first hour of the drive was uneventful, and they were making good time. Knox was careful on the switchbacks and was mindful of other drivers. Then the storm hit.

The sky darkened, and the snow flurries seemed light. Knox checked the charge level – sixty percent. The switchbacks and varying grades had used more battery than he had anticipated. They should be good to make it through the storm, as long as it doesn't last too long. He slowed their speed to accommodate the worsening weather. The flurries escalated to a full-on blizzard in a matter of minutes. With no other vehicles in sight, Knox pulled off onto the shoulder and placed the truck in park, leaving the climate control active to keep the cab heated.

"What do we do in a situation like this?" Ryder asked.

"I think the best we can do is wait it out," Knox said. "The batteries will keep the climate control intact."

They grossly underestimated the length and severity of winter storms in Northern Manitoba, which could last as long as three days. The snowfall enveloped the parked rig. Knox placed the insulating covers over the windshield and windows to keep in as much heat as possible and help reduce the strain on batteries that were already impacted by the severe cold. Over the next five hours, the two men became exhausted from the anxiety caused by the storm and fell asleep in the bed where they were huddled together. Knox was woken by a dinging alarm coming from the truck's warning systems. He sat up and looked at the information screen.

"Ryder, wake up." Knox placed his hand on Ryder's shoulder and shook him until he stirred and opened his eyes. "The batteries are at five percent. We have to use the generator."

"How, Knox? We're buried in snow!" Ryder started to panic.

"I'm going to go outside and figure it out. I have to. We won't survive otherwise." Knox said calmly, knowing what he said was the truth. "I'll be okay. Help me find the flashlight and gloves." Knox put on his boots and started putting on the heavy parka that was hanging on a hook. Knox zipped up the parka and pulled up the hood as Ryder handed him the gloves. Before putting on the gloves, he pulled the drawstring to close the opening in the hood and snapped the neck strap to protect as much of his face as possible from the deadly cold. When his gloves were on, he secured the flashlight's strap around his wrist and grabbed Ryder by the shoulders.

"It's going to be okay. It's only ten feet to the generator. I'm going to turn it on, then come back to the truck. Keep the door closed but not latched. I'm not sure I'll be able to open it otherwise." Knox tried to reassure Ryder and himself.

"Okay, Knox, just be quick and be careful," Ryder said.

Knox positioned himself in the driver's seat and opened the door. He pushed it against the packed snow and was only able to open it a few inches. He kept pushing until he could open it enough to squeeze out. Ryder pulled the door closed behind him, being careful to not let it latch. Knox hugged the body of the truck and pushed hard against the snow to move to his right. It took more effort than he had thought it would. The drifted snow seemed to push against him, needing him to fail, wanting him to die. Above his head, he could hear the whistle and moan of the strong winds. By the time he reached the generator, he was exhausted. He cleaned the snow from the area around the lock box, covering the dial, and looked at the mechanical lock. He tried entering the four number code with his fingers, but the gloves were too bulky. He pressed the button to clear the entry and tried again, this time using the knuckle of his pointer finger. Still didn't work. He was getting frustrated, and the cold was making it more difficult to move. There's only one thing that would work.

Knox used his teeth to grip the fingers of the glove on his right hand. He pulled it away from his hand, letting the empty glove dangle from his mouth. He quickly punched in the code, and the door popped open. He reached in with his bare hand and turned the dial all the way to the right. He heard a low hum followed by a deep pulsing tone as the generator engaged. The pulse was steady. Not wasting any more time, Knox slid painfully to his left towards the truck door. He reached up with his gloved left hand and firmly gripped the exterior support handle, pulling himself up and onto the running board. With his naked hand, he pulled open the door that was slightly ajar. One push with his feet to launch him into the cab of the truck took all the energy he had left. Knox crawled into the seat and over it to the open floor space. Ryder reached over him and closed the door completely.

Ryder noticed Knox's right hand was bare. It was bright red and looked painful.

"Why did you take off your glove?" Ryder asked.

"Couldn't punch in the code," Knox said, dropping the empty glove from his teeth and using them to remove the other one. Ryder loosened the hood of the parka and unzipped the body of the heavy jacket, helping remove it completely. He removed Knox's boots and pulled him onto the mattress, covering him with a blanket and examining the hand that had been exposed.

"I don't think it's as bad as frostbite, but you need to warm it up. Here, hold it between your thighs." Ryder placed Knox's hand in place and glanced back at the truck's information screen. "It's already at sixty percent. We need to go turn it off soon. If it overheats, our current situation will be mild compared to an explosion that kills us. I'm going out this time."

"No. I'll do it. I know how to get there. It doesn't make sense for you to do it. Without the lock to worry about, it will go quickly. I'll just turn the dial and leave the lock box open." Knox stated. Ryder knew it was the right choice.

Knox quickly bundled back up in his cold-weather gear and left the truck. The path he had made to the generator made the short trip easier. He used his gloved hand to turn the dial to the left. A red light at the top of the dial blinked frantically, warning that the generator was overheating. It seems he had turned it off just in time. He returned to the cab and removed the parka, gloves, and boots. He looked at the info screen and smiled at the one-hundred percent charge notification. He removed his jeans and shirt and climbed into the bed and covered himself with a blanket.

"We should be good for a least another twenty hours," Knox said. "Let's get some sleep and re-evaluate the situation when we're rested.

Ryder agreed and got in bed with Knox, and they slept soundly for six hours. Ryder was the first to wake and immediately noticed the silence. He pulled back the shade from the windshield and could see bright sunlight through the top third of the glass that wasn't covered in snow. The storm had stopped.

"Knox, wake up." Ryder shook Knox's foot that stuck out from the edge of the blanket. "The storm's over."

Knox woke, and they pulled down all the shades and stored them in a compartment behind the passenger's seat. They both got dressed in lighter jackets and pushed open the passenger door of the truck, since it seemed less snow had accumulated there. They trudged through deep snow to the front of the truck. The scene was not as bad as they had thought from inside the vehicle. The winds had pushed the snow up against the driver's side, the bank reaching almost to the top of the trailer and completely covering that side of the truck itself. It now made sense to both of them why getting to the generator had been so difficult.

Knox walked back to the other side of the truck and unstrapped the stack of orange Maxtrax skids from the rack on the back of the truck cab. He and Ryder placed one of the traction skids under each set of wheels. The ones on the side with all the snow proved to be difficult, and it took over an hour of hard labor to dig out enough snow to place them. They got back in the truck, exhausted from digging in the snow, but too motivated to get the truck moving to rest. Knox engaged the motors and tried to move the truck forward. At first, it did not seem that it was going to move at all, but the independent motors on each wheel did their jobs effectively, and the truck slowly inched forward. The right front wheel caught before the left, and there was a moment when Knox considered that the truck might skew and make their situation worse. He kept gently pressing on the accelerator, and the truck's smart-drive technology took over, changing the amount of energy being applied to each wheel to even things out.

After ten stressful minutes, the truck moved forward smoothly, and Knox pulled it a few hundred feet up the snow-covered road, stopped, and placed it in park. He and Ryder retrieved the skids and secured them with their storage straps. The road was still covered in snow but seemed drivable. As they prepared to get back on the road, another truck drove by slowly, giving a questioning thumbs-up to Knox, who returned the gesture to let the driver know they were okay.

The remaining three hundred miles went smoothly. Knox mindfully navigated the truck to Thompson, slowing carefully at switchbacks and sections of road that appeared uncertain. They arrived in Thompson two days before the delivery. Knox parked the truck at the Petro-Pass truck stop in the southern section of the small town, and they checked into a hotel a few blocks away to get some proper rest. They slept for ten hours before waking, showering, and getting a bite to eat at a pizza joint nearby. They checked on the truck before walking back to the hotel, even though Knox knew the trailer's security systems would alert BarsTech if anyone tried to tamper with it. They slept well that night and agreed to stay in the following day, watching movies and getting take-out. This would allow them to be fully rested for the drive west to Calgary in two days.

After two days of rest, they checked out of the hotel and walked back to the truck, making sure it was fully charged before heading to the delivery location. When they arrived at the warehouse list in Chuck's delivery instructions, they pulled through the large door and parked in the center of the cavernous expanse. The door closed noisily behind them. Ryder noticed two black SUVs on the left and one on the right. When Knox had disengaged the motors and put the truck in park, he and Ryder exited the truck and walked to the back of the trailer.

Two women and six men exited the SUVs to the left and approached the trailer. They were dressed in black tactical gear, and they all had weapons. From the SUV on the right, a woman and a man emerged and walked towards Knox and Ryder. The man looked to be in his mid-thirties, with dark close-cut hair and a well-trimmed dark beard. His skin was tan, revealing Latin descent in combination with his features. The woman was white with dark brown hair, neatly styled in a shoulder-length cut that looked easily managed. The man was dressed in jeans and a dark blue sweater with a southwestern motif in oranges, blues, and beiges across the chest. The woman was dressed in a classic dark brown pant suit with a cream-colored blouse. She looked wealthy.

"Ryder Garcia!" The woman in the pantsuit exclaimed. "It's been years. I was hoping you would be here for this."

"Beverly!" Ryder greeted her. "It's good to see you. You didn't think I would not show up for our most important venture in the history of our families, did you?"

"Ryder? What's going on?" Knox was confused.

"Ryder... you didn't tell your boyfriend about your connection to BarsTech? You have been very naughty!" Beverly laughed with that crazy laugh that scared Mateo.

"It didn't seem necessary, but I guess now is as good a time as any," Ryder said, turning to Knox. "Knox, I know you won't understand why I didn't tell you, but my family owns BarsTech Industries with the Seagram's."

"Who are the Seagram's?" Knox asked, his anger growing.

"Hi, Knox. I'm Beverly Seagram, and this is my Chief Scientific Officer, Mateo Trujillo." Beverly motioned towards Mateo and then stepped forward and extended a hand in greeting to Knox. "My family is Canadian, and we have an interest in many U.S. businesses, including BarsTech. You've become quite the legend amongst the BarsTech employees. I was hoping to see this magnificent truck of yours. And it does not disappoint!"

Knox pulled Ryder aside, his feelings of betrayal evident on his face. "Ryder, what's going on? What does this mean?"

"It doesn't mean anything, Knox. You know my family is involved in many things. This is just one of them." Ryder seemed smug in his answer. It was a side of him that Knox had not seen.

"And you didn't think it might be good for me to know this before this trip? Now it makes sense why Chuck didn't even blink when I told him you wanted to join me on this haul. This seems deceitful, Ryder. We have to talk about this after the delivery. I mean, really talk about it." Knox said angrily.

"We can talk, Knox, but it won't change anything. And me telling you ahead of the trip would not have changed anything. Let's just get this done, and we can sort this out later. Okay?" Ryder was firm with his request.

Knox and Ryder turned their attention back to the trailer and the group gathered there. One of the women in tactical gear walked up to the lock on the trailer and pulled a device from a cargo pocket. The device was the size of an old mobile phone, with a small stub antenna poking out the top. She punched in a series of commands and held the device up to the lock, which popped open with a mechanical click and whir of small gears moving inside. She removed the lock and placed both it and the device in separate pockets.

Two of the other men in tactical gear moved forward and opened the doors to the trailer. Inside were six tan Pelican cases, lined up two by two and three deep along the length of the space. Each case was strapped to a small platform, and each platform was independently supported by a series of shocks that were bolted to the floor of the container. Two other men climbed up in the trailer and started disconnecting the straps that securely held each case. When the straps had been removed, they carefully handed each case to the other six, who took the cases and placed them in line on the floor behind the trailer.

Beverly and Mateo stepped forward. Beverly motioned for one of her henchmen to open the cases. As each case was opened, they revealed the same thing. Each case held two containers of phyconanobots in the containment vessels that Mateo had help design. Mateo stepped forward, pulling a small portable electron microscope from the case that he had been carrying over his shoulder. The device was something that he had not known to exist until he had asked Beverly how they would inspect the bots. She had given him the microscope in response to his question. Like everything else Beverly used, it had been manufactured as an experimental device, and she had acquired it for her own use.

Mateo kneeled before the first case, activating the microscope and holding it close to the glass of the first vial. He observed the organic nanobots milling about, lazily co-existing with each other. They looked like his, but somehow different. The color was not the same. He had become familiar with the flux of shades of green of his bots. He knew the eccentricities of his bots like parents recognized the subtle details of their own children. These were like his, but not his. He looked up from the microscope lens, found Beverly's gaze, and gave her a thumbs-up. Mateo completed this process with all six cases, twelve vials in all. Each container of bots was slightly different. Mateo assumed that they had been programmed for things to which he was not privy.

Just as the last case was closed, chaos erupted. A black sedan, followed by a black pickup truck, raced into the warehouse, destroying the rickety closed door. A small army emptied from two vehicles, guns drawn. Four of Beverly's staff ran for cover, drawing their weapons as they crouched behind their own vehicles. The new guests wasted no time picking off the other four, killing them next to the cases they were there to protect. Beverly ran for her own SUV, entering it just in time to avoid the gunfire that riddled her bulletproof ride. Her driver raced past the commotion and out the damaged door.

Mateo saw his chance. In all the movement of cars and people, he dropped to the floor and crawled to the passenger side of Knox's truck. He opened the door and climbed into the cab, moving quickly to the back and covering himself with blankets. He took deep, slow breaths to calm himself. He waited. He saw Beverly's SUV leave with her in it, so if he waited here, the truck driver might be willing to give him a ride to Winnipeg, or further.

When Knox saw the door blown apart with the entry of the two vehicles, he knew it was time for him to leave. He had delivered the goods; now his job was done. He dropped to the ground and backed under the trailer, continuing to back up until he reached the cab. When he first hit the ground, his eyes looked up at Ryder, who had turned to look at him. Ryder's expression was one of sorrow and regret. 'I'm sorry,' Ryder mouthed as bullets tore through him. His arms windmilled as his body spun in a graceful circle before falling, back-first, onto the closest case of nanobots. Blood saturated the case, the deep red contrasting sharply with the tan of molded plastic. As Ryder's life left his body, his face fell to the side, facing Knox. His eyes were vacant as he looked at Knox for the last time.

Knox shimmied backwards and then sideways to get out from under the truck. He could still hear short bursts of gunfire. Pop-pop... pop... pop-pop-pop-pop. He stood next to the door to the truck and entered with urgency. There was no noise as he engaged the electric motors. Knox had learned many things about owning an electric truck, but the most important, at the moment, was the incredible and shocking speed that a heavy rig could achieve in a short time with an empty pup trailer. He pressed the pedal to the floor while simultaneously turning the wheel to the right. The rig accelerated so quickly that Knox almost lost control of it. The trailer tipped to the side with the sharp turn before over-correcting and returning to its upright position while in motion, the open doors in the rear banging against the sides. Knox steered the truck towards the busted door. His pulse raced with the adrenaline of escape.

Cyber Wolf burst through the damaged door of the warehouse, hitting the threshold with a force that caused the trailer to buck wildly as it exited. Knox maintained speed and didn't look back. He headed south on PTH-6 and kept to a speed slightly above the limit, unaware of the man hiding quietly behind him.

About an hour on the road, Knox looked in his side mirror and noticed flashing blue lights. The car pulled up behind him, and a voice on a loudspeaker instructed him to pull over. Knox complied, not sure what was going on since he had not been significantly speeding. He pulled over and put the truck in park, rolling down his window and waiting for instructions. He noticed the vehicle was a black SUV, which he found odd. The man who exited the vehicle was an RCMP officer; the distinct red coat was something that Knox did not expect to see. Why would a Royal Canadian Mounter Police officer pull him over here?

"Knox Creed?" The officer inquired.

"Yes, sir. May I ask why you pulled me over?" Knox attempted to be polite.

"No, sir, you may not. Please exit the vehicle with your hands visible." The officer instructed. Knox complied, opening the door and using the grab handle to back down the running board.

When he was firmly on the ground, he stepped back and looked between the truck and the trailer. He noticed another officer on the other side of the truck.

"Please remain here while we take a look at your vehicle." The RCMP officer said as he entered the rig.

Seconds later, the officer climbed down from the cab and motioned for someone to follow him. "You said you would come without resisting. Please exit the vehicle peacefully.

Knox was shocked when the scientist who tested the nanobots climbed down out of the vehicle, a look of extreme sadness on his face.

"I'm sorry." He looked at Knox. "You don't know what it's like working for her. I was trying to escape. Her reach is longer than I anticipated. I'm sorry I put you through this."

Knox nodded. He felt sorry for this guy. He didn't know what was going on and did not want to know. What he wanted was to get back in his truck and be on his way home. He had lost the person whom he thought was the love of his life. The one person whom he had trusted for a long time. The man who had lied to him. He knew this guy's sadness, but he needed to grieve on his own.

Knox watched as they kindly placed Mateo in the back of the SUV. He was given clearance to go, and he got back in his truck and started back on the road. He would go back to Barstow and figure things out. When he stopped for the night, he would call Chuck and find out if he would still get paid. And if BarsTech were still in business. He also needed to figure out what all this meant for him. And that would all come. For now, he just wanted to get home.

25

Pete Burns had been working for Seagram Industries for five years. His twelve years in the U.S. Navy, serving on SEAL Team Six, had prepared him for situations that other servicemen would find debilitating or would get them killed. The attempts on his life had been many, and he had survived them all. When he left active-duty service for an opportunity in private security, he had no idea the rewards it would bring. The few years with Beverly Seagram had been easy and enjoyable. He felt useful and needed as he discreetly followed her around and made sure her safety was his number one concern.

So, when Beverly had asked him to lead a special detail to protect the transfer of goods from a truck to a train, then to a plane, he agreed without hesitation. This was the type of operation that guys like him dreamed of. He put together a competent and capable team and made sure they were well-trained and well-armed.

He had anticipated an attack. Beverly had explained that there would be an auction for technology that was going to fetch a very high dollar amount. He was to expect an attempted theft before the auction itself. He just didn't think it would be so soon. He watched as the thieves picked off four of his team in a matter of seconds. Then they killed one of the truck drivers. He saw Beverly escape, so that was good. Pete and the remaining three of his team jumped into action quickly and had the intruders handled in minutes. Well, they killed all but one, which they currently had bound and gagged in the back of one of the vehicles. The remaining truck driver had left with the truck in a spectacular manner, right as Pete was hog-tying the surviving thief. He instructed his team to secure the goods, so they quickly loaded the cases into one SUV and huddled to debrief. One of them had seen the scientist get in the truck.

Pete called Beverly. "Are you safe? We have the situation under control. The goods are secure." Pete said.

"Excellent. Thank you, Pete. What else do you know?" Beverly asked.

"The truck has left. We think the scientist is in the truck with the driver. Unknown if the driver is aware. All but one of the intruders have been eliminated. What should we do with the one that we have in our possession?" Pete was brief and specific with his question.

"Kill him. And get the scientist. Meet me at the train with the goods and the scientist. We continue as planned." Beverly smiled to herself. Mateo thought he could get away. Maybe he was just trying to stay alive? She would find out on the train ride to Churchill.

"Will do, Ma'am. See you soon." Pete disconnected the call and barked at his team to take care of the remaining thief and to clean up the mess. They all got to work as Pete called a buddy of his with the RCMP. He smiled. Things were back on track. He had lost a few men, well, three men and one woman, but the mission was intact. And that felt good.

26

Beverly knew there was a risk that one of the bidders would try to steal the bots before the auction. But she did not anticipate that attempt to happen during the delivery from BarsTech. It was a stupid move on their part. They had lost. She supposed that Pete might be able to find out who was responsible, but it really didn't matter. The auction would go on. If the party that tried to steal the bots ended up being the winning bid, then their cost had increased with the amount they had just spent on a failed theft and loss of their team.

Beverly had her driver take her back to the hotel, where she gathered her things and made sure there was nothing in Mateo's room. He had his backpack with him, so his room was empty, as she suspected. From the hotel, she went to the train depot, deciding to wait for Pete in her private train car. Pete had other members of his team there, and she would be safe.

When she arrived at the train station, two members of Pete's team were there to greet her. They escorted her to the carriages, which were parked on a spur to the side of the main rail. Beverly's father had commissioned the three custom carriages before his death. She had never used them and had not considered them anything of value until this current venture. The custom coaches looked like every other ViaRail train car on the outside. Inside, however, they were fitted to be completely self-sustaining.

The leading car was used mainly for supplies and contained six crew berths, each with a small ensuite bath. The middle car held the galley, with an additional small crew bedroom and a large living and dining space for Beverly's use. The third car contained Beverly's private bedroom and bathroom, and a guest room. Additional storage rooms separated the two bedrooms. The furnishings were typical of the Seagram family lifestyle and would make the sixteen-hour trip to Hudson Bay comfortable.

Beverly settled into a chair in the living room and waited for an update from Pete. Sandra, Beverly's loyal attendant from the lake boat, was waiting for her and brought a tray containing a pot of tea, a porcelain cup, honey, fresh lemon, and a small plate of shortbread cookies – her favorite. She placed the tray gently on the low table in front of Beverly and asked if there was anything else needed at the moment. Beverly thanked her and told her she just needed to rest, pouring herself a cup of tea and adding honey and lemon.

Beverly had barely taken her first sip of the hot tea when her phone vibrated with an incoming call.

"We have the scientist," Pete said. "He was in the truck. The truck driver didn't know, and the scientist did not seem to know where he was. We should have him to your location, with the delivered goods within the hour."

"Thank you, Pete. I'm so relieved to hear this. Be safe. I'll see you soon." Beverly responded. She hung up and smiled at herself. Everything was going to be back to normal very soon. Mateo would be back with her, the auction would take place, and she would take the treatment so that she could be cured. She had been following the three subjects who had already received the treatment, and they had not relapsed. It was encouraging. Still, she was skeptical and wanted to give it a few more weeks to make sure.

By the time Beverly had finished her tea, Pete arrived with Mateo in tow. When Mateo entered the train car and saw Beverly, he rushed to her and hugged her.

"Beverly, I didn't know what to do. I hid in the truck to keep from getting shot, and the next thing I knew, we were moving. And moving fast! I begged the truck driver to stop, but he kept going. I'm so happy you found me." Mateo knew he had to get back to playing the game to survive. Beverly must always believe that he was on her side. Otherwise, he was positive she would have him killed.

"It's okay, Mateo." Beverly soothed him and rubbed his back, her voice soft and parent-like. "You're back now, and everything is going to be okay."

"Thank you, Beverly. Fill me in. What did I miss?" Mateo sat down on the sofa and leaned back, relaxing and crossing his legs. Sandra approached, and Mateo requested some hot tea. Beverly smiled at him like a parent would smile at a child who has exhibited proper manners. Sandra brought a fresh pot of tea and an extra cup, as well as an additional plate of shortbread cookies.

"That's a good question, Mateo. I was just going to ask Pete to fill us in. Pete, can you give us a recap of what happened and the eventual outcome, please?" Beverly looked from Mateo to Pete, who was standing in front of them.

"Yes, Ma'am, Ms. Seagram." Pete started, standing at parade rest while he spoke. "The most important thing to note is that the goods are safely onboard this train with us. We will connect to the next ViaRail train that leaves in two hours. The journey will take about sixteen hours. During the delivery, insurgents attacked the transaction and attempted to steal the merchandise. They killed four of my team and one of the truck drivers. The remainder of my team killed all the insurgents. At your request, we did not investigate the matter further. During the gunfight, the truck driver who survived left the scene. Unbeknownst to me at the time, Mr. Trujillo here was on the truck. I learned from one of my teammates that she had seen him enter the truck, presumably to avoid being shot." Pete paused and looked directly at Mateo before continuing. "I contacted a buddy of mine at the local RCMP office, and they were able to find the truck, which was on the way back to Winnipeg, and return Mr. Trujillo. They said that Mr. Trujillo was confused and scared but was nonetheless happy to see them and did not resist going with them."

"So, it all worked out. That's fantastic!" Beverly reacted to his recount of the situation as if she were a child being read a fairy tale. "What about the mess at the warehouse?"

"It's all taken care of. My team cleaned everything up and disposed of the insurgents' vehicles and their bodies. Another team is there now making sure the floor and other surfaces are sanitized. Further, I have been in contact with the other team members, and everyone is on alert for any negative actions that might disrupt the next two stages of our journey. If there's nothing further, Ma'am, I would like to get some rest before the train leaves." Pete finished.

"No, no, thank you for the recap, Pete. Please, go get some rest. Just check in with me when we are well into the train ride." Beverly waved him off, and Pete walked to the leading car to get some sleep, leaving Mateo and Beverly alone.

Mateo tried to gauge if Beverly believed him or if she was just stringing him along until they got back to the institute, and he could administer the treatment. The more she prattled on about the work they had done, how exciting the attempted robbery was, and what Sandra might be preparing for dinner, the more he became convinced that she did not think he had tried to escape. Eventually they moved to the dining table where Sandra served a delicious pasta with sauteed chicken and mushrooms, fresh salad, and an oaky Chardonnay. Tiramisu and decaffeinated coffee for dessert made them both full, so Beverly suggested they get some sleep to be rested for the next stage of the journey.

Mateo retired to the guest stateroom and fell asleep quickly, his exhaustion overtaking his worry that another interested group might try to steal the bots. When he woke, the morning light filtered through the transom windows. He looked at his phone and saw that it had been a full ten hours since he fell asleep. A quick calculation in his head told him that they had only four hours to Churchill. He curled up under the covers and considered whether there might be another opportunity to escape before they got to Baker Lake. His conclusion was that it would not be possible. There was too much scrutiny at this point, and he needed a different plan. Ideas rambled through his mind, and one kept coming back. He needed to sever the relationship with Beverly, whatever that might mean. He let this sit in his head and incubate. The solution would come to him. For now, he just needed to play along and be Beverly Seagram's best friend.

Mateo got out of bed, brushed his teeth, washed, and dressed. He walked the short distance to the next train carriage, where Beverly and breakfast were waiting for him.

"Good morning, sleepy head!" Beverly was unusually cheerful, manic even. "Did you have a good night?"

"Slept great. You?" Mateo tried to match her enthusiasm.

"Like a baby!" Beverly replied. "There are pastries and coffee. Sandra will cook eggs for you if you want them."

"No thanks. I'm good with the continental." Mateo smiled as he walked to the sideboard and placed a pain au chocolat on a small plate using the tongs provided and poured himself a cup of black coffee from the insulated carafe next to the pastries. He took a fork from the stack of silverware staged on another napkin-lined plate and took his place on the sofa, perpendicular to Beverly in her chair. He carefully placed the mug of coffee on a felt coaster on the coffee table after taking a sip and taking a bite of the pastry.

"How's this going to go today?" Mateo asked.

"Pretty simple. We arrive at the Churchill train depot in a few hours. We will need to switch engines to take us the rest of the way, since ViaRail only goes to the station. That will take about an hour. Then the cases will be moved to a seaplane." Beverly spouted off the steps casually. "Oh, and you'll need to ride with them on the seaplane. As you know, I don't do seaplanes. But I'll meet you at Rio House."

"Oh, okay. No problem at all." Mateo said, his mind turning to see if there might be an opportunity in that plan for escape. He could not see one.

Pete walked in while Mateo was getting more coffee.

"I have an update, Ma'am," Pete said.

"Good morning, Pete. I trust you had a restful night?" Beverly greeted him.

"Uh, yes, Ma'am, my night was fine. We will be arriving in Churchill in two hours. As you know, we need to switch to a different locomotive to go to the end of the line. It won't take long. I've confirmed that the seaplane is waiting. The transfer of the cases and Mr. Trujillo to the seaplane should take less than 15 minutes. Once the cases are on the seaplane and it has taken off, my team will transport you to the airfield in Fort Churchill for your flight to the Baker Lake airfield. My question, Ms. Seagram, is whether you would like for me personally to travel with the cases, or with you?" Pete stopped talking and waited for Beverly's reply.

"That's a great question. I would rather you travel with the cases and keep Dr. Trujillo company." Beverly answered.

"Will do. And my apologies, Dr. Trujillo. I have been addressing you incorrectly." Pete looked at Mateo.

"It's fine, Pete. And since we're going to be on the plane together, please call me Mateo." Mateo offered.

Pete looked at Beverly for approval. "It's okay, Pete. You may call him Mateo." Beverly sighed, smiling at Mateo as if she had given in to the requests of a petulant child.

"Okay, then. Mateo, please have your things ready to go by the time we arrive. There will not be time to wait once the train stops at the final depot." Pete looked at Mateo sternly.

"I just have my backpack. I'll be ready." Mateo said.

"Roger that. Please wait in this space until I come to get you." Pete said, then turned and walked back to the other car.

The train pulled slowly into the station at Churchill and stopped. Beverly had returned to her cabin, and Mateo had not seen her since breakfast. Mateo had brushed his teeth and washed up, packed his backpack, and returned to the living room area to wait. He felt the carriages move as they were uncoupled from the ViaRail train and then a hard bump as they reconnected minutes later to an independent locomotive. The uncoupling and re-coupling had taken less than fifteen minutes. The locomotive and the three private cars jerked forward and picked up speed quickly. The journey was short, and they arrived at the end of the rails in ten minutes.

Mateo looked out the left windows and saw a series of warehouses sitting by a seemingly abandoned industrial marina and the blue water of Churchill harbor beyond. The train moved slowly past a road sign letting him know that they were crossing Axworthy Way. He was surprised at the depth of color in the dark blue water and how it contrasted with the tans of the buildings and the white of the snow. The water looked serene and very cold.

The train slowed to a complete stop, and Mateo waited. He watched out the windows as the security team loaded the six cases into yet another black SUV. Pete walked into the living space with purpose.

"Good morning, Pete," Mateo said.

"Mornin', Mateo. Let's go." Pete wasted no time now that the cases were on the move.

Mateo followed Pete out the door of the carriage and down the two metal steps to the waiting SUV. He got in the back with one of Pete's security team. He recognized the person as a woman who had survived the gunfight at the warehouse. Pete got in the front with the driver, and the car moved alongside the warehouse until they encountered an alleyway that connected the train platform to the harborside dock. When the car got to the harborside, the driver accelerated towards the end of the industrial pier and the seaplane that Mateo could see waiting at the end.

The vehicle came to a stop, and Pete opened the door, simultaneously making a 'let's go' gesture by pointing his index finger in the air and making rapid circles.

"Mateo, wait here until we get these loaded. I'll come get you when we're ready for you. Don't leave the vehicle. Understood?" Pete was quick and firm with his demand.

"Yes," Mateo said.

Pete and the female loaded the cases into the plane. Mateo watched as they managed two cases at a time, moving them rapidly from the SUV to the cargo door of the Cessna 208B Grand Caravan EX. Pete trotted back to the vehicle and motioned for Mateo to join them. Mateo shouldered his backpack and jogged behind Pete to the plane. He climbed in the open cargo door and walked past the cases to the four seats. He removed his backpack and plopped down in the seat on the right that was closest to the back. Pete entered after him and motioned for him to move towards the front. Mateo complied, moving to the seat in front of where he had sat. Pete took a seat opposite and behind him, and the female, whom Pete called 'Smith', sat behind Mateo.

The pilot closed the cargo door and buckled into the left pilot seat. He started the props and taxied to the open water of the harbor. The plane accelerated and rose into the air. Mateo looked out the window over the empty seat opposite him and noticed an old fort on the left. It sat on the peninsula opposite the marina where the train had stopped. Mateo wondered out loud about the fort, and Pete absentmindedly said that it was Prince of Wales Fort and was very old. Mateo nodded and turned his head to the right to look out his own window. He looked back to see the train and noticed Beverly stepping off the train and into the SUV that had parked just a few feet from the door.

The 450 nautical miles to Baker Lake were uneventful. There were moments of rough air during the two-and-a-half-hour trip, but the pilot expertly navigated the turbulence and landed smoothly on the icy waters at the eastern end of Baker Lake. As they taxied to the dock, Mateo saw four additional security team members waiting.

Pete must have had them here at Rio House the entire time, waiting for the delivery. As soon as the seaplane was tied to the moorings, the pilot shut down the engines and opened the cargo door from the inside.

Pete slid the cases to the edge of the door, and the two men on the dock moved them to a motorized cart waiting nearby. Snow covered the area around Rio House, but the path to the building had been cleared, including the path that diverted to the right and wound around the building to the back and towards Beverly's house. When the cases were all loaded onto the cart, Pete, Smith, and the two other guards moved with the cart up the path.

"Lead the way, Mateo," Pete said. "We're going to take these in the back door and up to the third floor. You know the way."

"Okay," Mateo said simply as he started to walk along the path.

They walked along the path in the cold. Mateo's light jacket was not sufficient for the temperature, and fortunately, the walk only took a few minutes. Pete and the other guards seemed unfazed by the cold breeze that blew off the water. When they reached the back entrance, Pete tapped his access card to the pad beside the door. This level of restricted access was still relatively new to Mateo, and he wondered if he still had access to all the doors. He would need to test that soon.

Pete and his team carried the cases, one by one, through the door and to the elevator. When all the cases were safely in the elevator, Mateo joined Pete and Smith as the other two resumed their sentry at the front of the building. The elevator door opened into Mateo's lab, and he appreciated the comforting moment of familiarity at seeing his equipment. Pete and Smith moved the cases to an unused room at the front and the opposite end of the building.

"Is Beverly here?" Mateo asked as Pete walked by.

"No. She will be here in about two hours. I just got a notification that she's on her water vessel and en route." Pete answered.

"Thanks. I'm going to do some work. Will you be around?" Mateo inquired.

"Okay, Mateo. I will be near the merchandise until Beverly tells me otherwise." Pete answered, taking a seat on a stool nearby. "I won't interrupt your work."

Mateo turned and walked to his office, pretending to check on things. He returned to one of the workbenches and started preparing three syringes for Beverly's eventual treatment. He walked over to the storage room and retrieved a vial of bots that he had used as a control in one of the early experiments. He brought it back to the bench and carefully transferred them to a syringe that he had previously marked with a permanent marker. He had drawn a single line around the top of the dark metal band of the containment syringe. When sitting beside an unmarked syringe, the difference was only noticeable if you knew exactly what to look for. Otherwise, it appeared as a slight shadow.

He placed the syringe in a drawer and prepared another with the treatment bots and placed it beside the one in the drawer. He could barely tell the difference between the two and had to look closely to see the mark that he had made. Finally, he prepared a syringe with the axolotl cells and placed it beside the others. With an unexpected urge, Mateo filled a fourth syringe with a bot neutralizer that one of the research assistants had prepared during one of the tests to stop bots that had gotten out of hand. The neutralizer would allow the bots to live but would remove any programming, making them unusable. He placed the fourth syringe in the drawer with the others and then retrieved it and placed it in his pocket. He was ready when the time came.

27

"Beverly will be disembarking at the dock in ten minutes," Pete said, looking at his phone. "Let's go greet her."

"Of course," Mateo said, grabbing his jacket from the hook that was fixed to a nearby column.

Pete, Smith, and Mateo took the elevator to the first floor and walked the circuitous route along the hallways to the front entrance. They left the building and walked down the path to the dock. The air was turning colder, and snow flurried around them. Beverly's boat pulled up soon after they reached the dock. Beverly stepped onto the dock before the boat could even be moored to the pilings.

"All secure?" Beverly asked, looking first at Pete, then at Mateo.

"Yes, Ma'am," Pete said. "All secure."

"Great. Let's go inside and talk about tomorrow. We will all need to be on the same page to make this go smoothly." Beverly talked as she walked to the building.

Beverly scanned her keycard to access the building and walked directly into the chamber with Sednamaroq. She walked briskly to the stairs and up to the second floor. Judging by the look on Pete's and Smith's faces, they had never been in the chamber and were unsure what it meant. Beverly led them to a conference room off the empty second-floor labs. She typed on her phone as they walked, and within minutes of everyone sitting around the conference table, one of her attendants arrived with a rolling cart containing hot cocoa, coffee, hot tea, hot apple cider, and a variety of cookies. Beverly took a mug of cider and a shortbread cookie, encouraging the others to do the same. Pete and Smith reluctantly took mugs of hot cocoa. Mateo settled for coffee and a cinnamon sugar cookie.

When they were all settled, Beverly talked to them about the upcoming auction.

"Tomorrow at 10 a.m., I will open the bids online by presenting a live video of the phyconanobots." Beverly started. "Mateo, I will need you with me for the video to verify the validity of the bots. There will be an hour after the video for questions, which I will answer personally and privately with each anonymous bidder through the bidding portal. Mateo will be by my side to answer any technical questions. When the bidding opens, it will commence for a period of two hours, and the bidders will operate within the portal without my involvement. At the end of the countdown, the highest bidder will be sent a validation code and instructions for wiring the money." Beverly paused. "Any questions so far?"

Everyone shook their head no.

Beverly continued, "Once I have verified the funds have been sent to my account, I will send the pickup location to the winning bidder. The bidding portal will falsely promote the location of the auction as a place far from here. And the bidders think the products are located separate from the auction. This is the information that has been promoted all along for the auction. Now, considering the attempted theft that we all experienced, it is possible that one or more of the bidders know the actual location. So, Pete, have your team on alert."

"Yes, Ma'am." Pete nodded.

"When I send the location to the winner, they will most likely arrive to collect them within a few hours. Pete, I will need you and your team to take the cases to the dock for delivery. I will provide a code for you that must match the code they give you. Verify the code before turning them over. Mateo, you will need to be out of sight when they arrive. I don't want to risk them taking you as part of the deal. You will need to stay in your apartment after the auction until everything is finished. Do you understand?"

"Yes, Beverly. It's not a problem. I appreciate your concern about my safety." Mateo responded. "When will I know it is safe to come out?"

"Just stay in there until the morning. Meet me at my house at 11 a.m. tomorrow, and we can talk about what's next for us." Beverly seemed completely unconcerned that she would not have eyes on Mateo for such a long period.

Mateo nodded in understanding. Thinking this might give him a chance to escape. Beverly dismissed them, and they went their separate ways. Mateo assumed that Pete and his team would guard the bots, and Beverly would go to her house. He went to the pantry and stocked up with food and drinks for his apartment, made himself a simple dinner of microwave rice, a can of black beans, and salsa. He ate it with flour tortillas, which were always in the pantry since he had started at the Rio house. After dinner, he lit a candle and took a long bath with the lavender bath salts, enjoying a cold beer in the hot tub. He tried to calm his mind so that he could get good sleep. He would need to be rested for the next day.

The next morning, after a very restful night, Mateo had breakfast in his apartment – coffee, oatmeal, and a banana - before joining Beverly in the conference room with the cases on the third floor. The room had been converted to a digital studio; several monitors sat in the corner like a command center. Three cameras on tripods were focused on different angles of the six cases, which had been moved to raised tables and opened to reveal the vials. Pete stood watch outside the door to the room and simply nodded at Mateo as he entered the room.

Beverly greeted Mateo and handed him a portable microscope with a cable attached.

"When I start the video, I'll need you to explain what you are seeing and why the bots are viable. The image will be cast to the video feed in a frame with you and the microscope. As I'm sure you know, the bots in each vial are programmed differently. You don't need to explain this. The programming details are in the info that has already been sent to the bidders. Understand, Mateo?"

"Yes, Beverly. Of course. I'll present well, I promise." Mateo made himself sound as professional as possible.

"Of course you will, my dear. Of course you will." Beverly said vacantly, as she adjusted her hair and makeup in the mirror of a handheld compact. She snapped the compact closed and dropped it casually in her pocket.

"Show time!" Beverly said. She pulled Mateo into view of the cameras and clicked a remote in her pocket to activate the recording.

"Hello, everyone." Beverly began. "The twelve containers behind me contain the items as detailed in the information that you have all received. My Chief Scientific Officer will now visually validate the items."

Mateo turned on the microscope and placed the lens over the first vial. "As you can see, the phyconanobots are alive and active. They are casually moving around each other, which is how they act when in stasis." Mateo moved to the next vial. 'You can see the same activity with these; you will notice a slight variation in coloration between this batch and the previous batch." Mateo panned back to the first vial and then back to the second. "The variations in color indicate differences in programming. This one has greens that are darker and fluctuate at a different rate. You will notice differences as we move from batch to batch." Mateo continued with each of the twelve vials, describing the variations in color. When he was done, Beverly escorted him off camera and spoke to the bidders herself. "As agreed, bidding will commence at the hour.

Best of luck to you all." Beverly clicked the remote and ended the recording.

"Now we wait," Beverly said to Mateo.

When the auction started, Beverly sat in front of the three monitors, waiting calmly to see what would happen. She motioned for Mateo to pull up a chair, which he did, sitting beside and slightly behind her. The screen indicated nine bidders, each only identified by a single one-digit number. Beverly explained that all bidders had been vetted by an independent banker whom she trusted implicitly. The first bid came in five minutes after the auction started.

Two billion dollars.

"How dare they start with such a low-ball offer!" Beverly exclaimed. "I should eliminate them from the auction."

"Is there a figure you have in mind for an opening bid?" Mateo asked hesitantly.

"Well, I was expecting a minimum of six billion to open, so two is low," Beverly responded.

A second bid came in — four billion.

"Now they're testing the waters." Beverly leaned back and crossed her arms, smiling. "They will all enter bids within the next few minutes, then it will sit until someone has the courage to move the needle."

She was right, the other seven made bids within seconds of each other. The maximum bid now stands at 8.7 billion U.S. dollars.

"Why U.S. dollars? Mateo asked.

"The exchange rate is better, and the bank I'm using for this is in Switzerland," Beverly said, as if it were a common sense answer to a stupid question.

"Now we sit for at least an hour. Do you want some lunch? I feel like a sandwich. Do you want a sandwich?" Beverly texted on her phone, seemingly not interested in Mateo's answer to the questions. Ten minutes later, a cart of sandwiches appeared, with a variety of beverages. "Pete!" Beverly called. "Come get yourself a sandwich."

Pete entered, grabbed a sandwich and a soda, and went back to his post. Muttering a thanks as he took the food. The look he gave Mateo was classic. It said, 'Yeah, I know she's crazy, but she pays me a lot to put up with it.'

There was no movement in the auction until ten minutes before the end. The countdown clock on the screen read 9:57, 9:56, 9:55... Then a new bid came in. 9.9 billion from bidder number one. Bidders two, three, eight, and nine withdrew, their profiles on Beverly's screen indicating their withdrawal by a single red line through the number. Three more bids arrived, 10 even from bidder four, then 10.2 from bidder five, then 10.3 from bidder three. Bidder number six remained silent. The countdown clock continued: 1:58, 1:57, 1:56...The silence continued until the clock reached 0:28. Then the bid came in from bidder number six – 100 billion dollars. Red lines immediately appeared on all other bidders.

"Looks like we have a winner," Beverly said, masking her shock at the final bid. With a few clicks, the account information and confirmation of the winning bid were sent to the buyer.

"It will take a few minutes for the funds to come through. I'm going to take a bathroom break. Mateo, close the cases, please." Beverly asked and walked out of the room.

Mateo walked over to the cases, looked at the cameras to make sure they were off and glanced over his shoulder to watch Beverly enter the restroom at the far end of the room. Pete continued his guard with his back to Mateo. Mateo pulled the syringe of neutralizer from his pocket and injected a small amount into each vial as he closed each case.

When Beverly returned, Mateo was sitting at the desk, looking at the screen. "I can't believe someone paid a hundred billion dollars for the bots I made. All thanks to you, Beverly."

She smiled at him. "I told you we would do great things."

Beverly moved Mateo aside and logged into her bank account. The money had arrived, and she sent the location for pickup to the buyer. The response she got back was that they would arrive in three hours.

"That's my cue to make myself scarce," Mateo said. "See you at 11 tomorrow?"

"Yes, have a good night, dear," Beverly said, smiling at him with that crazy smile that made him feel dirty and sad.

Mateo took the elevator down to the first floor and entered his apartment. He prepared his backpack as he had for the last trip, knowing that whatever he took with him was what he would have. He waited two hours, then quietly made his way to the dining room, thinking that if Beverly saw him there, he would tell her that he needed to eat and pretend to not understand her instructions to stay in his apartment. He could see the dock from the window in the dining room. He closed the door and took a seat where he could see out the window, but where it would be difficult for anyone outside to see him.

The seaplane that pulled up to the dock was unlike any that Mateo had ever seen. It was the size of a small commercial aircraft and had two jet engines mounted to the top of the wings, rather than under, like most jets. It was painted in a muted gray that made it blend in with the water and softly swirling snow. The door opened on the plane, and two men dressed in black tactical gear exited. This must be a standard uniform for the henchmen of the rich and famous, he thought. The two men stood on each side of the door, and a man exited who looked like he was the epitome of the Russian oligarchy. His shaved head, muscular build, and sunglasses – despite the waning light – were overshadowed by his mere presence. The man exuded power and confidence. He walked forward and waited. Pete and Smith walked toward them. When they met, the buyer pulled out a phone and showed it to Pete, who most likely acknowledged the code, and then there seemed to be a heated exchange. Pete furiously texted on his phone, probably to Beverly. Then they all walked to the building.

Now was his chance. Mateo listened to make sure they were not in the foyer before he exited the building. He ran along the path, praying that no one would see him. When he got to the plane, he climbed through the door without thinking about what might be on the other side.

The interior was cavernous. He looked to the left and saw the pilot facing away from him at the far end of the large space. To his right was a door. Without thinking, Mateo quietly opened the door and went through. The door led to a toilet and sink, and another door. He opened the other door, which led to a cargo space.

The cargo space was filled with things that looked like they had not been used, nor checked, in a very long time. Bundles of musty rope, bags of safety gear, and life preservers that were covered in mold. The letters on the equipment looked like Cyrillic, which supported his assumption about the origin of the buyer. Although he did not speak Russian, it was the closest he could come to an answer. At this point, it didn't matter. Mateo closed the door behind him and climbed over piles of things he could not identify to hide himself as far back in the tail section as possible. As he waited, he considered that he did not know where the plane was headed. If the buyer was Russian, again, a wild assumption by Mateo based on the look of the guy, that means the plane was headed for Russia. Surely it would need to stop and refuel at some point. He would need to get out of the plane at the next stop, regardless of where that was. He started to rethink his plan, then he heard commotion up front. They were loading the cases. It was too late for him to abandon this action.

There was more movement, and Mateo heard the door to the plane close, the distinct series of heavy clunks sealing his fate. The noise from the jet engines of the Be-200 Altair was deafening as it took off from the cold waters of Baker Lake. Mateo curled up amongst the life preservers and moldy bags to stay warm. He soon fell asleep from the stress and exhaustion of the escape. He woke when the large plane touched down in the Tanana River near Fairbanks, Alaska. The plane taxied to an industrial dock near the small town of North Pole, just southeast of Fairbanks.

Mateo was not sure where they had landed and assumed they had stopped to refuel. He looked at his phone and saw that four hours had passed. He had another twelve hours before Beverly would fully realize that he was missing. He also considered that Beverly would be able to track him with this phone, and he panicked, picking up a large metal carabiner from a nearby looped rope and smashing the phone. He shoved the pieces under a pile of canvas bags and listened for movement in the plane. He heard the door open and then calm talking from three people. They all seemed to exit the plane, leaving the pilot. He opened the door and slowly crawled into the bathroom, pressing his ear against the door to the main cargo hold. He could still hear the voices, but they seemed to be diminishing. He secured his backpack to his back, hooking the chest strap to make sure it would stay in place.

He opened the door slowly and peered into the cargo hold. He could see the six cases strapped to the floor in the middle of the cavernous space. The pilot was at the far end, facing away from him and apparently engrossed in a task sorting and repairing wires that required immense focus. Mateo looked to his left and out the wide cargo door. He could see the three men in the distance, past the front of the plane. One of them was on the phone, yelling. Mateo created a scenario in his mind where they had stopped for fuel and the refueler crew was not waiting for them, as promised. He had no way of knowing that his assumption was correct.

Without hesitation and in a moment of sheer panic, he slipped out the door and dropped his feet off the gangway and into the icy cold water between the plane and the dock. His pulse raced, and he felt his heart was going to stop as the just-above-freezing water saturated his clothes. He took slow, deep breaths as he grabbed the edge of the seawall, the edge of which was just above his shoulders, praying that neither the three men nor the pilot would see him. Adrenaline fueled his body as he inched his way along the bulwark, making his way in the direction of the tail end of the plane. When he was past the rear of the plane and the end of the concrete dock, he tried pulling himself up into the grass and snow above the seawall. The cold water had all but disabled the use of his legs. He briefly thought that this might be the place and time of his death. Not willing to accept that he had come all this way to die in the cold waters and not even knowing where he was, he mustered every ounce of strength and hoisted himself to the top of the wall. His belly rested on the top board of the seawall as his legs dangled off the edge.

His fingers dug into the frozen ground to find purchase so he could pull himself all the way onto land. He collapsed into the tall, snowy grass, his face frozen to the ground. Maybe he could stay here until the plane left? How long would that be? It did not matter since he had no strength left to move. He hoped that he would not freeze to death before he could figure out what to do. So, he rested and drifted off to sleep.

When he woke, he tried to move his legs. They seemed attached to the ground. Where was he? As awareness slowly regained purchase in his mind, he pulled hard at his arms and legs and separated them from the frozen earth. He sat up and looked around, his legs, hips, and spine screaming in pain. The huge plane was nowhere in sight. Now, he had to figure out where he was. He saw a small building in the distance. Figuring he had nothing to lose at this point, he raised himself to his knees and carefully stood. It took him almost an hour to make it the hundred yards to the building, and there were moments when he thought it would be easier to allow himself to fall and die.

When he eventually fell against the door to the building, the thud caused the person inside to open the door. Mateo looked up and saw a stocky female looking down at him. She was wearing dirty tan coveralls, muddy boots, and a stocking cap with stringy hair poking out the edges.

"What the hell do we have here!" She exclaimed.

"I need help. Please." Mateo said weakly as he collapsed into the open door.

She grabbed him by the top strap of his backpack and pulled him into the building. She closed the door and sat Mateo up against the wall, grabbing a wool blanket and wrapping it around him.

"What's your name?" She asked. "I'm Jenny. Tell me your name."

"Pete," Mateo said weakly, saying the first name that came to mind. "I'm Pete. Where am I?" Mateo looked around at the rather large office, which contained a desk that was messy with papers and a well-used sofa. An old TV sat on a filing cabinet in the corner next to a pile of boxes. A cast-iron wood stove maintained a roaring fire and provided a nice heat.

"Well, Pete, we will talk more when you are warmed up. But you're in the North Pole, Alaska. Near Fairbanks." Jenny said. She left him for a few minutes and returned with a mug filled with hot tea, sweetened with honey and a lot of cream. "Sip this."

Mateo took the mug and slowly sipped, coughing as the hot liquid hit his lips.

"Easy," Jenny said.

"Thanks," Mateo said. "I guess I need to explain how I got here."

"Yep, let's start there. Then we'll figure out what to do with you. I manage this dock, and I pretty much know everything that happens here, so you're a mystery, for sure."

"I got involved with some bad people, and they put me on a big seaplane. I was knocked out, and the next thing I knew, they were tossing me into the water. I don't know how I got there, but I woke up in the grass and snow. Sat up and saw this place. And here I am." Mateo hoped she believed him.

"I knew those guys were trouble. They stopped here to refuel and wouldn't tell me anything. They paid cash, a lot of cash. And I've never seen one of them planes like that. I didn't know there were seaplanes that big." Jenny said. "I think they were Russian. The plane had writing on it that looked Russian. Like I know what Russian looks like!" Jenny laughed.

"I made very bad choices," Mateo said.

"Yeah, it happens to the best of us," Jenny said, appearing to remember her own choices. "Here, we need to get you out of those wet clothes. Come with me, I've got some coveralls you can wear while they dry."

Mateo followed her through a door that clearly led to the place where she lived. They walked through a small kitchen and into a small living room. Jenny told him to wait while she got the clothes from the other room, which he assumed was a bedroom. The living room had a recliner, a sofa, a cabinet with a more modern television, and another wood stove.

She returned with a pair of coveralls that were clearly too big for him and motioned towards a bathroom off the living room. "You can change in there. There's a shower if you want to wash up. You hungry?"

"Uh, yes. Thank you." Mateo hung his head in humiliation. This woman was being so kind to him, and she didn't even know him.

"Just wash up and change. Throw your old clothes out the door, and I'll hang them by the fire to dry. I'll make us something to eat. Take your time, Pete. I don't have any other work today." Jenny said kindly.

Mateo took the clothes she had given him into the bathroom and placed them on top of a small stool. He took off his wet clothes and opened the door just enough to place them on the floor in the living room. He unpacked what was in his backpack – everything was soaked. He locked the bathroom door and sorted out everything from the backpack on the floor. His wallet, which he emptied to allow things to dry — driver's license, a bank card, one credit card, and two hundred dollars in cash. Two pairs of underwear, two t-shirts, an extra pair of jeans, two pairs of socks, and an intact vial of his phyconanobots.

He showered, feeling like he was going to pass out when the hot water first hit his skin, then he allowed the water to wash over him with sensations of relief and comfort. He did not linger in the shower, unsure how long might be considered by Jenny as taking advantage of her kindness. He toweled himself dry and put on the coveralls and a pair of his extra socks that were mostly dry. He carefully repacked his backpack except for the jeans and shirts. When he came out of the bathroom, Jenny was waiting in the recliner. She had moved chairs from the kitchen to stand in front of the wood stove, and his clothes were hanging there.

"Do you mind if I hang these here too?" Mateo held up the jeans and shirts. "It's my extra clothes from my backpack."

"Of course not," Jenny said. Come into the kitchen when you're done. I have some soup for us." She stood and left the room while Mateo hung the jeans and t-shirts by the fire.

Jenny had warmed up cans of beef stew, which bubbled on the gas range. She ladled generous portions into two bowls and placed them on the table with a sleeve of saltine crackers. "It's not much, but it'll do."

"I appreciate this. You don't know me, and I haven't done anything for you to be so kind to me." Mateo said as he picked up a spoon and started eating.

"It doesn't take much to be kind, Pete. Just don't murder me and take all my riches." Jenny held up her hand and motioned around the kitchen as they both laughed."

"How long have you lived here?" Mateo asked.

"Thirty years," Jenny said. "My dad owned this land and serviced seaplanes and river barges here. He died a few years back, and business is not what it used to be. The new docks in Fairbanks offer more modern services. But I have what I need. What about you, Pete? What's your story? Consider it payment for the kindness." Jenny smiled, showing he didn't have to tell her if he did not want to.

"It's not too complicated. I grew up in Texas, studied engineering, and got hired by this company in Winnipeg. I moved up there, and it turned out they did a lot of illegal stuff. I tried to get away, and they didn't like it. They told me they were going to take me to a different location to work. Next thing I know, I'm on that weird plane and then here. There's a lot I don't remember." Mateo worked hard to sound convincing. "You said we are near Fairbanks?"

"Yes, near Fairbanks. That's a sad story, Pete." Jenny answered him.

"Can you help me get into Fairbanks, Jenny? If I can get there, I think I can make my way back to Texas."

"Yes, I can drive you there. I have things I need to do there that I've been putting off. It's about a thirty-minute drive. But my truck is old, and it takes me about an hour. I'm not up for it tonight, though, and it's getting dark. You can sleep on the couch tonight, and we will go first thing in the morning." Jenny seemed firm in this decision.

"Okay. Thank you." Mateo said as he finished his soup and crackers.

When they were done eating, Jenny washed the bowls and gathered a pillow and blanket for the sofa. She spent some time in the bathroom and eventually went into her bedroom. Mateo heard the sound of the door being locked after she closed the door. He fell asleep quickly and woke early the next morning with light, noise, and the smell of bacon coming from the kitchen. Jenny's bedroom door was open.

He stood up and walked to the bathroom to pee. When he returned, he folded the blanket and placed it neatly on top of the pillow at one end of the sofa. When he entered the kitchen, Jenny was cooking bacon and eggs and had a pot of fresh coffee ready.

"Good morning!" She said cheerfully. "Coffee?"

"Good morning. Yes, please." Mateo took the mug she extended to him and filled it with hot coffee. "The bacon smells good. I don't remember the last time I had bacon."

"It's not much, but it'll get us going. We'll leave after we eat. Any idea where in Fairbanks you want to go?" Jenny asked.

Mateo thought for a minute. "I think maybe the train station is a good start."

They ate, and Mateo grabbed his backpack. They got in Jenny's old Ford truck and started towards Fairbanks. The weather was good, and the road was clear, helping them arrive in forty-five minutes, rather than the hour Jenny had anticipated. She pulled up in front of the train station and put the truck in park.

"Good luck, Pete. If you ever make it back to the North Pole, stop by and say hi." Jenny said.

Jenny, I don't know how to thank you. I don't have anything to give you." Mateo said.

"It's okay. I didn't help you so I could get something out of it. Just take care of yourself." Jenny smiled at him. "Now, get your ass out of my truck and back to Texas." She laughed.

28

ateo entered the train station and found a paper brochure with train schedules. He found a place to sit and decide what he should do next. The reasonable thing seemed to take the train to Anchorage, and then he could take a plane from there. He also knew that traveling under his real name was dangerous. He started developing a plan in his mind. He walked to a sales kiosk and asked if he could borrow an ink pen. The clerk begrudgingly gave him a pen, which he took back to his seat and made a list in the margins of the paper schedule.

- Get cash

- Find a place to stay for a few days

- Get a fake ID

- Open a new bank account

- Transfer money from the old account

- Travel under a new identity

- Where?

He needed to reduce the risk that Beverly could track him. Getting cash would identify his location, so he would have to withdraw a substantial amount, but first, he needed to find out how to get a fake ID. He observed the people moving around him in the train station and noticed those who clearly hung out in here to either be begging for money or because they had nowhere else to go. He removed a twenty from his wallet and approached a man who looked like he could use the cash.

"Hey, buddy. Do you know where I might get an ID?" Mateo asked, holding out the bill.

The guy took the money, folded it, and put it in his pocket. "Yeah, I know a guy. Follow me."

The man walked towards the exit, and Mateo followed, thinking that this could end badly. But his choices were limited. They walked around the station to the side where groups of people were waiting for buses. The man approached another man and motioned for Mateo to hang back. The two men talked for a few minutes. Mateo took another sixty out of his wallet, being careful not to draw attention to himself. He placed two twenties in his left pocket and one in his right. The man that he had approached inside the station walked back to Mateo, the second man following close behind him.

"I know someone." The second man said. "The info will cost you."

"How much?" Mateo asked.

"Fifty." The guy said.

"I have forty. It's all I have right now." Mateo offered.

"Okay. Hand it over." The guy held out his hand, and Mateo noticed the first guy had left. Mateo reached into his right pocket and handed the guy the two bills.

"Follow me. It's a couple of blocks." The guy said.

Mateo followed, again realizing the potential danger and knowing he had no choice. They walked in silence, and a few minutes later, the man stopped in front of an old burgundy Chevy Suburban with blacked-out windows, rusted and looking like it might not be able to move from where it was parked. The window rolled down, and the man spoke to the person inside for a few minutes.

"Ruben here will help you out." The man said to Mateo.

Mateo approached the window to see a young kid, maybe in his late teens. Blond, with piercing blue eyes that betrayed an intelligence at odds with the situation.

"What do you need?" The blond kid said.

"Driver's license, social security card, passport, if you can do it," Mateo said.

"I can do it. It's gonna cost. You picky about the name?" The kid asked.

"No. How much?" Mateo responded.

"If you're not too picky about the name, then $15k for all three. It'll take two days. I'll get the age close. You in?" He asked.

"Yep, I can have the money for you when it's ready. What do you need now? I can give you $100. It's all I have on me? Mateo admitted.

"I usually ask for half, but that will do. You look trustworthy. Hop in the back and I'll get some pics." The kid said.

Mateo opened the back door and got in, still not sure he wasn't going to be abducted. The setup inside the large SUV was elaborate, and not something that a kid on the street could have put together. It was thoughtful, professional, and efficient. A neutral backdrop hung from the interior of the roof between the two seats of the second row. In the front, a top-of-the-line camera had been permanently mounted. A dimmable light bar was mounted above the camera, with additional lights on each side of the front seats. The interior of the vehicle was clean and well-kept, in sharp contrast to the outside.

"Sit in the center and look forward. I'm going to take several pictures. There are two button-up shirts in the seat beside you. I'll take three sets, one with what you have on now, and two more with each of the shirts. Let me know when you're ready." The blond kid said, his tone professional, as if he were hiring Mateo for an executive position with a reputable company.

Mateo ran his hands through his hair and smoothed his beard. "Ready."

The lights came on, and the kid dimmed them from a control in the center console. A small monitor let him see the camera so he could focus and adjust the image. Mateo looked forward and did not smile. The digital camera made three sounds that mimicked the shutter of a traditional camera. The kid looked through the images and seemed to be satisfied.

"Put on the first shirt, please."

Mateo complied. More pics, more checking.

"Second shirt."

Mateo changed, and the kid took the final series of pics. Mateo removed the shirt and folded them, placing them neatly back in place. The kid looked at him in the rearview mirror and smiled. "Thanks. You're one of the rare professional customers that I've had in here. Usually, it's just high school students wanting fake IDs to buy booze."

"Should I meet you back in this same location?" Mateo asked.

"No." The kid said. "I'll meet you at 5 p.m. in the pickup zone at the train station. Two days from now. I'll pull up, you'll get in, I'll drive to a quiet place and go over everything. Have the cash."

"Okay. What makes you so sure I'll show up?" Mateo could not help but ask.

"I know a person in real need when I see it. I'm guessing these are a matter of life and death for you." The kid looked directly at Mateo, his expression caring and concerned.

"You have no idea," Mateo replied. "See you in two days."

Mateo got out of the vehicle and walked back to the train station. There, he asked a ticket clerk for help in locating a bank. Mateo had used a national chain bank for many years, and that decision made long ago has now paid off. There was a branch only a few blocks from the train station. He walked there and met with an account manager. He explained that he had been out of the country for over a year and needed to withdraw $20k in cash so that he could get housing. After a series of questions and verification of identity, the account manager left and returned thirty minutes later with the cash in four envelopes of $5k each. Mateo asked the account manager if he knew of anyone who could rent him a room for a few nights while he looked for an apartment. The manager was kind and made a call to a friend who lived downtown. The guy had several short-term rentals that he managed and agreed to let Mateo stay in one for a week if he could pay cash up front.

Mateo jotted down the address and agreed to meet at the apartment in an hour. He placed the envelopes with the cash in an interior pocket of his backpack and left the bank to walk to the apartment, which was four blocks away. The apartment was in an old house that had been converted to four studio apartments. The unit was clean and simply furnished, and the transaction was simple – $500 for five nights. Cash up front. The man handed him the keys and told him to leave them on the kitchen counter at the end of the five days, and make sure the door was locked.

There was a convenience store on the corner near the apartment, and Mateo walked there to buy a few toiletries and food. His plan was to stay inside as much as possible. When he returned to the apartment, he showered and brushed his teeth, luxuries that he realized he had taken for granted. By now, Beverly must have realized that he was gone. He knew that she would stop at nothing to try to find him. He must be very careful over the next few days.

For two days, he stayed in the apartment. He watched TV, slept, and tried not to think about what would happen if Beverly's henchmen found him. Would they kill him? Or simply return him to her? His guess is that Beverly would force him to give her the treatment. With his most recent deception, he knew that she would need him to oversee the injections. The risk of something going wrong was too great otherwise.

He walked to the train station on the evening of the second day was maddening for Mateo. He looked over his shoulder every few seconds and hid in the shadows while waiting for the blond kid to pull up in the beat–up SUV. When he finally drove up to the passenger pickup area, Mateo wasted no time getting in the back seat. The kid drove off without speaking. He drove for about five minutes to a cheap hotel near the river. He parked and turned off the truck. "You have the cash?"

Mateo handed him three envelopes. The kid counted the cash and handed Mateo a large white envelope. Mateo opened the envelope and pulled out a Texas driver's license, a passport, and a Social Security card incorporated into the letter the Social Security Administration used to mail them.

Mateo's new name was Tanner Michael Kingman.

He was surprised at the quality of the fake IDs. The security features on both the driver's license and passport were intact.

"Wow, how do you do this? This is amazing." Mateo asked.

"It's all about skill and having the right resources. I'm a hacker at heart, but this pays the bills. You'd be surprised at what kind of supplies and equipment you can buy on the black market." The kid said.

"Well, you may not know it, but you've saved my life," Mateo said. "Do you mind if I ask how old you are?"

"Thanks. And 17." The kid said. "I'm glad I could help. I can drop you off somewhere if you want?"

"That would be great." Mateo gave him the address of the apartment.

Mateo kept looking at the name. Tanner Michael Kingman. Not bad. He could live with that. Should he introduce himself as Mike? Or Tanner? Tanner. He liked that. He slept better that night than the previous two. The next morning, he walked to a bank different from his own and opened an account, depositing the minimum amount to open the account. He told the accounts manager that he would be transferring money from another bank in town. She gave him the wire information and said to have the manager call her directly before the transfer. They printed a debit card for him before he left. Mateo left and went to his old bank. He met with the branch manager and told him that he wanted to close his account and move all the money to the other bank, to an account in a different name. It took over an hour to convince the manager that he knew what he was doing.

Mateo had to make up a story about the new account being his brother's, along with crazy reasons that made no sense, even to him. This seemed to confuse the bank manager, who talked about tax implications and how complicated this would get when his brother filed his taxes. In the end, and a lot of paperwork later, the money was wired. The total amount was just over three million dollars.

On the way back to his rented room, he stopped at a drugstore and purchased a beard trimmer, razors, shave cream, a pair of sunglasses, and a ballcap with the logo of the Ice Dogs, a local junior hockey team. When he got back to the apartment, he used the trimmer to shave off his beard and the hair on his head. He used the razor and shave cream to finish the job, looking at himself in the mirror. He laughed at his appearance. Mateo had not had a clean-shaven face in a very long time, and he had never shaved his head. The look made him completely unrecognizable.

His plan was simple and short-term. He would take it day by day until he felt reasonably safe from Beverly. He knew he would never feel truly safe, but he thought he could elude her until he could figure out a way to live under his new name. He packed up his backpack, cleaned the apartment, and put on his new ballcap. He left the keys on the kitchen counter and walked to the train station. On the way, he ducked into a retail store and made an impulse buy of a pay-as-you-go mobile phone. He chose the more expensive version that would allow him to access the internet. When he arrived at the train station, he purchased a ticket to Anchorage and figured he would plan his next steps on the 12-hour train ride. He wanted to maintain a low profile on the train, so he purchased a bottle of water, two bottles of diet soda, a few snacks, and two pre-packaged sandwiches for the trip.

He boarded the Denali Star towards the tail end of the 14-car train. He quickly learned that the train was full of cruise ship passengers returning to Anchorage from their add-on trip to Fairbanks. It should be easy for him to blend in. He settled into a seat and looked around to see if there might be a way to enhance his disguise. Most of the tourists had tote bags branded with their respective cruise lines. And all of them wore either a lanyard or a small sticker on their clothes that identified them as part of a tour group. Mateo had no idea how to acquire one or more of these items. He had no street skills that would relate to petty theft or pickpocketing, but fortune smiled on him when he made a trip to the restroom to pee. One of the tourists had left a tote bag in the small washroom. He looked through it, and it contained a lanyard with the name of the ship and a group number, a few brochures about the tour, an ink pen, and a handful of small chocolates. Nothing that anyone would miss. He shoved the bag in his backpack and went back to his seat.

Finding the bag gave him an idea. He pulled out the burner phone, opened the packaging, and removed the phone, SIM card, and instructions. He spent the next hour activating the phone and purchasing the most data allowed using his new Tanner Kingman debit card. Once the phone was activated, Tanner opened the internet browser on the phone and searched for the cruise line listed on the bag that he had found in the washroom. The ship that was currently in port in Anchorage departed the next day for Whittier, then would make three more stops before returning to Seattle in five days. This was the perfect opportunity for him to disappear for a few weeks and plan. He booked a last-minute cabin on the ship leaving the next day. This prompted him to look at other cruise lines. There was another cruise by a different company that left Seattle the same day he arrived, and traveled to Baja California, Mexico, making stops along the California coast before returning to Seattle. He could disappear for at least three weeks and take time to decide where he wanted to go. He booked both cruises, feeling confident that he would be able to avoid Beverly's reach for a short period.

As the train pulled into the station in Anchorage, Tanner pulled the cruise line tote from his backpack and added a few items from his backpack to it to make it appear as if he had done some shopping. He put the lanyard around his neck and put on his new sunglasses. The map on his phone indicated that it was an easy 30-minute walk from the train station to the cruise terminal. The weather was cold, but the sky was clear, which made the walk simple and gave Tanner time to prepare for the next stage in his journey.

Tanner checked in for the cruise and boarded the ship. He avoided the greetings from the crew and made his way to his cabin, which was on one of the lower decks. The cabin itself was nice, with a large window looking out at the dock. Tanner watched as guests boarded the ship, his guard up as he searched for anyone who might have caught on to his plan. He did not see how any of Beverly's henchmen would have found him this soon, but it was still at the front of his mind. He considered that it always would be. What kind of life would he have? Always looking over his shoulder. Always wondering if he would be found and returned to her. He just knew that he had to keep going. He had to try.

The next three weeks helped reduce Tanner's worry and anxiety. He fully immersed himself in the lie of his new identity and in the activities on board the cruise ship. He connected with people under his new identity, avoiding going ashore at any of the port calls, and took time to read books from the ship's library and map out a plan for his future. He purchased new clothes on board, as well as a small suitcase and the toiletries he needed to maintain his new, clean-shaven appearance.

The idea for his next move came to him when they pulled into port in Los Angeles. The cruise still had three days left on the journey back to Seattle, but he would depart the ship here. He informed the guest relations desk that he would not be back on the ship when it departed that evening and rolled his small piece of luggage off the ship with his backpack securely on his shoulders. He got a taxi to LAX and purchased the next non-stop flight to

Albuquerque. It was a crazy idea, but it might be the last place Beverly would look. She would not expect him to return to his home. He was sure of that. Well, mostly sure.

29

The blizzard approaching Rio House was mild compared to Beverly's wrath. After a peaceful night in the glow of a successful multi-billion-dollar deal and a pleasant morning watching the snow flurries build to a full-blown storm, all from the warmth of her living room, Mateo had not arrived for their scheduled meeting. She texted Pete to stop by Mateo's apartment and see if he had overslept. It was unlike Mateo to miss a meeting with her, and her initial reaction was one of concern.

Pete showed up at Beverly's house thirty minutes later and reported that Mateo was nowhere to be found. He had briefly reviewed the video feeds and needed more time to determine where he might be. Beverly's concern turned to sincere worry. She told Pete to review the security camera files as quickly as possible and to report back to her. She continued to text and call Mateo, with no answer. It did not occur to her that Mateo would try to leave. Where would he go? And how?

Pete returned ninety minutes later and told Beverly what he had learned. The security footage showed Mateo in the dining room when he was supposed to be in his apartment. Then he walked out the front door. The outside cameras showed him heading to the dock, but the weather prevented knowing where he went after that. Pete suspected that Mateo had fallen in the water and was dead. Beverly wasn't so sure.

"Could he have gotten on the plane with the Russians?" Beverly asked.

"I doubt it. And if he did, they would have found him by now. And that means he's already dead." Pete said with conviction. "They wouldn't bother finding out who he was. Being in the same space with the merchandise they paid that much money for would not afford him any consideration."

"Why would he leave? He had everything he could ask for here." Beverly mused, more to herself than asking a question. "We should still consider that he ran away. I've never been convinced that he ended up in that truck by mistake."

"It's possible. It just doesn't make sense that he would try to escape from here. And especially right after the auction. That would take some balls that I don't think he has." Pete laughed.

"Well, maybe. Something about it doesn't feel right to me." Beverly said. "Can you investigate this and see what you can find? Maybe see if the Russians stopped anywhere before they flew home? Of course, if he did get on the plane and didn't get off before they hit Russian airspace, then he's as good as dead anyway."

"That's true, Ms. Seagram. But I'll investigate it anyway. I'll also have someone perform a sonar scan of the waters around the island. If he accidentally fell into the water around the island, his body would still be nearby. The waters are close to freezing right now. And as you know, the current from the river is only on the north side of the island. Since the building and dock are on the east-southeast side, anything that falls in the water there just stays there." Pete rambled, more to himself than in explanation to Beverly.

"Sounds good, Pete. Just keep me informed. Unless you have new information, come see me tomorrow morning." Beverly said. "Now, can you escort me to the institute? The weather is getting bad, but I need to go there, then come back here."

"Of course, Ms. Seagram," Pete said, waiting while Beverly put on a heavy parka, boots, and gloves.

Pete walked with Beverly to the building, noticing that she seemed to have more trouble walking than usual. When they got to the building, she walked them to the dining room and asked him to wait there while she went to the statue chamber. Pete was happy to comply; he hated going into the chamber. That thing made him feel all kinds of strange and uncomfortable.

Beverly started to leave, then turned to make one more request of Pete. "Can you find the three research assistants for me while I'm in the chamber, please? I need for Jo to stay and help with things until we find out what happened to Mateo. Tell her I will meet with her after the storm clears. The other two are free to go home."

"Will do, Ms. Seagram. You know they will not be able to leave in the storm?" Pete queried, hesitantly, knowing what Beverly was saying and hoping that she might correct it as a misunderstanding.

"I know that, Pete. I just don't want them here. Their job is done. So, send them home, please."   Beverly gave Pete a look that was clear — Matt and Sara were to meet the same demise as every other researcher who no longer worked for her.

"I'll take care of it, Ms. Seagram," Pete assured her.

"I know you will, Pete. You always take care of things for me. That's why I pay you so much." Beverly laughed lightly and smiled in that crazy way that let Pete know she had other people who could take care of him, as well.

Beverly left the dining room and walked to the chamber. She stood just inside the door as it closed behind her. The statue glared at her, knowing she needed it. She could not wait to rid herself of this need. But she did need it until she could get the treatment. Then she would need it one last time. She walked to the statue and knelt in front of it as if in prayer. She painfully lowered herself to the ground and turned on her right side, placing her belly firmly against the base of the statue. His hand instinctively reached around the stone and rested lightly on her bent knees. This was a posture that was so familiar to her that she did not even know she was doing it. Her mind was preoccupied with thoughts of Mateo. What if he actually was dead? Would Jo know enough to properly administer the treatment? She would explore that with her tomorrow. She didn't think Mateo was dead. She could feel it within herself. The lifetime of contact with Sednamaroq had given her a heightened instinct about these things. Whether real or not, the feeling was real to her.

The soft blue light that surrounded Beverly was comforting to her. She felt the power of the statue course through her, healing her. She wondered if the treatment would be like this. Or maybe more intense? The three subjects from the trial reported that it felt like electricity running through their bodies. A pleasurable pain was the way one of them had put it. Regardless, it would be worth it. She communed with Sednamaroq for another thirty minutes, falling asleep as she usually did, and waking up refreshed. When she was done, she nimbly got to her feet and walked back to the dining room, where Pete was waiting for her.

"I sent Matt and Sara home," Pete said blandly. "Then I told Jo that they had been sent home earlier and that she was to meet with you tomorrow. She acknowledged the request."

"Thank you, Pete. Any indication that there might be a problem with Jo?" Beverly asked.

"No, Ms. Seagram. I'm positive she understands her duties and loyalties." Pete replied succinctly.

"That's good. It's nice when everyone knows their place. Now walk me home. I want to curl up in front of the fire with a good book. It's perfect weather for that, don't you think?" Beverly said her delusions came through strongly in her statement.

"Yes, Ma'am. Perfect weather for that." Pete said as he helped her into her parka and gloves.

They walked back to Beverly's house in a storm that was getting increasingly worse. Pete made sure Beverly was settled before he left her house to walk back to the institute. After Pete had left, Beverly settled down by the fire with a glass of whiskey and a book. She could not focus on reading. The more she thought about Mateo, the more she became convinced that he had escaped her care. She needed him, and he needed her – whether he realized that or not. She ruminated on it until she thought that she would go mad with the uncertainty. The storm prevented any immediate actions, but she would meet with Pete tomorrow and have him ramp up his search.

The storm lasted four days, preventing any movement between the house and the institute. The snow and wind eventually settled and presented the pristine landscape that always made Beverly thankful to have the solitude of Rio Island. She summoned Pete and Jo to meet her at her house that afternoon. She would speak with Jo first, with Pete present, then she would meet with Pete privately to talk about Mateo. When they arrived, Beverly acted like the consummate hostess, offering hot cocoa and shortbread cookies. Pete, as usual, declined. Jo accepted and casually sipped the hot drink as they talked.

"We've misplaced Dr. Trujillo." Beverly started the conversation.

"Excuse me?" Jo reacted.

"We don't know where he is. He was here before the storm, and now he's not. I fear that something has happened to him. I am very worried. Do you know anything about where he is or what might have happened?" Beverly was curious if Jo might actually know something.

"No, Beverly, I spoke with him just a few days ago when the two of you returned from your trip. He seemed normal and even talked about new directions for research. He was very excited about all the things we could do." Jo seemed genuine in her response.

"It's such a mystery. We were supposed to meet the next morning, and he didn't show up. Everything is in place in his apartment and his office. Nothing seems to be missing. Just him." Beverly again seemed to be talking to herself and not necessarily to Jo or Pete.

"I really hope he's okay/" Jo said.

"Me too." Beverly continued, looking directly at Jo. "What I need from you is to know if you can perform the treatment for me if we can't find him?"

Jo paused before answering. "I think so, I would need to review his notes. It's risky to attempt it without fully understanding any intricacies that might pose a problem during the procedure."

"I think that's a smart approach. How long do you need?" Beverly asked.

"Honestly, Beverly, at least a few months. I just don't think it's worth the risk. We might only get one shot at it." Jo said.

"Yes, I agree," Beverly said, looking out the large windows at the snow-covered lake. "Start today, if you can. I know it will be a lot of work with Matt and Sara not here, but do your best. Pete will make sure you have access to what you need. You and I can meet weekly to talk about your progress. Agreed?"

"Agreed," Jo said. "I'll get started right away."

"Thank you, Jo, I don't know what I would do without you," Beverly said. "You can go now. I need to speak with Pete, and then he will meet you in the lab."

Jo left, taking a cookie for the wait. As soon as she closed the door, Pete turned to Beverly. "The sonar of the waters around the island did not show anything of significance. So, I'm assuming he did not go into the water."

"Did you check on the plane?" Beverly asked.

"Yes. It landed outside Fairbanks, Alaska, to refuel. The refueling took place at a seaplane dock that is not frequently used. There is only a slim chance that he would have been on the plane unnoticed. And an even slimmer chance that he would have been able to get off the plane in Fairbanks unnoticed. Even if he did, it would be challenging to survive there without resources." Pete paused while Beverly processed the information.

"My gut tells me he's still alive, Pete. Six months. I want you to make this your priority for six months. Follow every lead and use whatever resources you need. You have a blank check for this investigation. Do you understand?" Beverly was speaking with a force that Pete had not seen.

"Yes, Ma'am. I will start in Fairbanks and see what I can find. How often would you like reports?" Pete asked.

"Don't contact me until you have information, or the six months expires," Beverly said directly. Pete had a feeling his expiration was also tied to that deadline if he did not uncover something.

Pete had secretly been hoping that Mateo had escaped. He also had been hoping that Beverly would think that he had died and would move on with other things. He now knew that it was his life or Mateo's. And he wasn't ready to die for a scientist who had escaped from Beverly's grasp.

30

Tanner boarded the plane at LAX. As he settled into his seat for the flight to Albuquerque, he looked in front of him to see if anyone might be looking at him. He had chosen a seat in the very last row so that he could observe the other passengers. The two weeks on the second cruise ship had given him a sense of safety that he knew was premature. He remained alert until all the passengers had boarded the mostly full flight.

The days in the sun on the cruise ship had darkened his skin. He had allowed his hair to grow to a short stubble but had continued to shave his face. He would need to be cautious about his arrival in Albuquerque. He had turned the situation over in his mind more than necessary and had a plan that he thought would allow him to determine if he was in danger. It would not be a pleasant life at first, but he would endure. The decision to live as a homeless person would help him avoid notice in social circles until he could get a better sense of his safety.

When he landed, he walked to a cheap hotel near the airport and paid cash for a room for two nights. He would need to plan his approach to living homeless. He settled in the room and left only to get take-out from a nearby restaurant. His first action was to get his bike and a sleeping bag from his storage unit. He spent the first evening paring down his belongings to what he could fit in his backpack and shoved everything else in the small rolling suitcase. He took a taxi to the storage unit, having the driver drop him off close enough to the storage complex for him to observe the entrance without being seen.

The storage unit building was a small three-floor warehouse. It was one of the kind where all the units were accessed by interior hallways, and all were climate-controlled, with the loading/unloading area being covered and secure behind the gate on the first level. Stephen had suggested that it would be the most secure, and the climate-controlled units would make sure his belongings remained in the best condition possible for his long absence. That had been almost two years ago. He had remembered the code to the entrance and had kept the key in a hidden pocket of his backpack the entire time he had been gone. That key was now securely in his front pocket.

There was no movement at the entrance to the building. He waited. A family pulled into the underground parking with a small moving truck, and he took a chance to try to blend in with them, just in case someone was watching. He punched in the code to the pedestrian gate, just as the family pulled through the main gate. He walked to join them, smiling and waving as he walked past them to the elevator. Another code in the freight elevator, and he was on his way to the third floor. He exited the elevator and turned right, walked down a short hallway and made a left. His unit was the first on the left. He unlocked the padlock, unhooked it from the door, and slid the locking bar to the left. He rolled up the door just enough to duck under it, shoving the small suitcase in before him and quickly lowering the door once he was inside the large unit.

Tanner rolled the suitcase neatly to the side and looked over the bicycle that hung from a hook attached to the wire frame separating the storage units from the warehouse ceiling. He gently pulled down the bike and examined it. The tires needed air. He looked around for a few minutes and found the air pump, which was conveniently next to a bag of bike stuff that he used to take with him on bike rides. He opened the bag and removed a small bottle of chain lube and a tool kit. It took him thirty minutes to service the bike. It took much longer to find the sleeping bag.

The sleeping bag fit perfectly under the straps of the bike backpack, with the bike pump nestled securely between the two. Tanner put the backpack on his back, hooked his arm through the straps of the bike helmet he had removed from the bag, and rolled up the door, looking carefully down the hallway and around the corner before moving the bike out. He rolled the door down and re-locked the padlock, placing the key back in his front right pocket. He walked the bike to the elevator and took it down to the ground level. When he rolled the bike out, the family was still unloading their truck. They seemed to be having an argument about things that should have been taken to the trash, and paid no attention to Tanner as he went through the pedestrian gate, mounted the bike, and rolled off.

He took a circuitous route back to the hotel. Taking his time and enjoying the freedom of being on the bike. He was happy to remember the trails and shortcuts to get around the city. In the past, he had frequently argued with non-bike riders about how easy it was to get around Albuquerque on a bike without getting on major roads or highways. After two hours of easy riding, he arrived back at the hotel and took a shower to wash off the dust from the ride. After the shower, he dressed and walked to a chain restaurant down the street, where he got enough food to last for the next day. Warmed-over burritos weren't ideal, but the minifridge and microwave had been nice to have.

The TV provided background noise while he looked at the map on his phone. It was the same phone that he had gotten in Alaska, and he considered whether he should replace it. He had not given the phone number to any person, so he decided it would be safe to keep, for now. His purpose in looking at the map was to find an area of the city where he could live outside but still have access to amenities. He decided the area to the north would be best. The village of Los Ranchos de Albuquerque was one that had few homeless people, and Tanner suspected that he would be unnoticed if he kept himself clean and did not beg for money. It was also the area of the lavender farm with his favorite bath products. He suspected that Beverly would not direct her search in a place where their contract had been signed. He was willing to admit that his logic might be flawed, but his gut told him that he was right.

The next day, he checked out of the hotel and rode his bike north. He found a fitness center that was part of a national chain and purchased a membership, paying for the year in advance for their highest tier. His rationale was that he could go there daily, do some sort of workout or other physical activity, and have a place to shower. He would find a place to sleep and spend his days in coffee shops or other public spaces where he might remain anonymous.

His first week was rougher than he imagined. Sleeping on a park bench was uncomfortable, and the nights were colder than he remembered. He was able to keep himself busy during the day and visited a barber shop to get a trim on his hair and beard that had been left to grow. He tried several places to sleep and finally settled on a cluster of metal benches that were on a path that joined Rio Grande Blvd to the trail that ran along the river. He had been sleeping there every night for a week and had noticed many of the same people running and biking on the trail. People occasionally gave him money, but usually did not make conversation. Then there was Jake.

It had now been three months since Jake had approached him. He found himself needing to quickly make up a backstory about why he was homeless and what he did for work. He also had to leave the house each weekday and pretend to go to work. The worst of it all was that he had become very attached to Jake and didn't know what the future might hold for their relationship. He would eventually need to decide whether to tell Jake the truth or continue living the lie. It had been five months since he had escaped, and he was becoming more and more confident that Beverly had either given up on finding him or considered him dead. If she had talked one of the research assistants into performing the treatment, she might have been healed and would have moved on with things.

Then he thought about the sabotaged bots. She would not be able to come back from that. The Russians would not only want their money back, but they would also want blood. If fate were to smile on him, they would kill her, and he would not have to worry about her finding him. Part of his daily routine was to search online for Beverly, always hoping the search results would return news of her death.

His life was going in a good direction. He had a new identity, a new love, and a new life. He was confident that he would figure out how to move forward, both with him and with Jake. It might mean another lie, but it would be for the best possible outcome.

31

Pete thought that he had reached a dead end in Fairbanks. Then he came across a panhandler who seemed to remember someone fitting Mateo's description. Several years later, Pete found himself being introduced to Ruben Stafford, a blond teen who had made a very lucrative business out of creating new identities. Ruben had not been swayed by cash. But he had been broken, nonetheless.

It took Pete and one of his buddies just over a day to get the information from Ruben. By the end of that time, Ruben was barely conscious, so he did not notice when Pete ended his life. The local police had been investigating Ruben, and they were not surprised when the blackened body in the torched Chevy Suburban was positively identified as the kid. The fire destroyed any evidence that Ruban had maintained in his vehicle, and he had kept everything about his business there.

Now that Pete had the name of Tanner Kingman, things would get easier. It also confirmed Beverly's suspicions. Pete had called Beverly that evening with the news. It was the first time he had talked to her since she had directed him to investigate Mateo's disappearance, and her only words before she hung up were clear - "Find him and bring him back to me."

And that's what Pete intended to do. He used all his resources, including a lot of cash, to get information. He traced Tanner Kingman to the train and then to Anchorage. Finding the connection to the cruise ship was more difficult. But Pete learned that if you talk with enough people, the truth usually comes out.

Once he learned that Tanner Kingman had taken the first cruise, learning of the second cruise was easy. Finding out that Tanner had departed the ship in L.A. was more difficult, and a few people got roughed up, but Pete got his way. The money that it took to hire a hacker to find out which flight Tanner had taken from LAX was an amount that Pete found absurdly expensive, but it wasn't his money. And Beverly had been very clear about the unlimited nature of his budget.

And that was the journey that left Pete in his current situation. He watched patiently, as Mateo — A K A Tanner Kingman — enjoyed his dinner on the outdoor patio of a brewery in Albuquerque, New Mexico. The guy sitting with Mateo was clearly more than just a friend. Pete would scope out this situation until the time was right. It might be a two-for-one. He didn't see a safe path for bringing back Mateo and not his friend with him. The thought briefly crossed his mind that he could just eliminate the second guy and bring Mateo back. Pete knew the advantage of maintaining leverage, and that's just what the second guy would be. Beverly might not agree at first, but if Pete was right, she could use the other guy to maintain Mateo's compliance.

He observed the two men for three days before making his move. He had already been in their house while they were away and knew it would be the best place to act. He waited until they left home one evening and then let himself into the house, waiting patiently in the second bedroom for them to get home. This bedroom was directly off the door to the garage, where the two men usually entered the house. Pete lightly touched the four prepared syringes of midazolam with his fingers. They were arranged in a neat row in a small pocket on the right leg of his black tactical cargo pants. In his right hand, he maintained a firm grip on the bright yellow TASER 7 CQ. He had a backup gun attached to the belt on his left side, but he only needed the one. The 7 CQ was the most expensive electroshock weapon on the market and had the perfect feature for disabling two people — two cartridges. It was designed to provide a backup in case the shooter missed the target the first time. But Pete wouldn't miss. He would, however, need to be very efficient in his movements.

He heard the garage door open and then the double clunk of two car doors closing. The garage door started closing just as the door into the house opened. Pete stepped out of the bedroom and fired the TASER at Jake, who convulsed and dropped to the ground. Pete fired the second shot into the man he knew as Mateo before Jake's body hit the ground. Pete quickly let the TASER fall to the ground. He had five seconds to administer the midazolam. He fell to his knees while simultaneously pulling two syringes from his pocket with his right hand. It took less than 2 seconds for him to remove the caps with his teeth, switch one syringe to his left hand, and shove the sharp needles into the torsos of both men. Then he stepped back and waited.

Jake tried to stand but fell on top of Tanner. Tanner pushed Jake to the side and tried to stand to no avail. The strong dose of the drug took about a minute to work. Within five minutes, Jake and Tanner were completely unconscious. Pete pulled out his phone and typed a quick text. Within minutes, Pete's team of four had loaded the bodies into a waiting dark blue minivan. Pete sat in the passenger seat as they drove away. The two members of his team sitting in the back of the van wrapped duct tape around their wrists and ankles of the two unconscious men, strengthening them with zip ties. With their wrists secured behind their backs, extra zip ties were used to connect their hands to their feet. The drug would wear off in less than two hours, maybe sooner, but Pete had two other doses if he needed them.

The drive to the small airport south of the city in the small town of Belen took about 45 minutes. The driver pulled the minivan into a private hangar, and the final two members of Pete's team closed the hangar doors. The plane that sat in the hangar was a Gulfstream G550 and was the largest one that Pete could charter last-minute in L.A. He had paid in advance for the use of the jet, including a pilot, for a month. It was more luxurious than anyone on his team needed, but the space it provided was necessary to transport the two men to the SISR facility.

A padded wrestling mat had been placed on the ground next to the plane. Beside the mat, in a compact and neat pile, were two industrial rolls of plastic wrap, a clear tube of black zip ties, and four rolls of duct tape. Pete's men moved Jake and Tanner to the mat. The two men were starting to stir, and Pete rushed forward, pulling the last two syringes out of his pocket. He took his time with the injections, the escapee first, and his friend second. Once the men were fully unconscious again, Pete's team worked quickly to cut the zip ties and remove the duct tape. They re-taped each man's ankles and wrapped tape around their waists, securing their arms to their sides. Then they wrapped them in plastic wrap, completely immobilizing them and using duct tape to create handles, making them easier to move from place to place. The final touch was a long single strip of duct tape across each man's mouth, wrapping completely around each head so that it would stay securely in place. Pete would prepare more syringes once they were in the air. He anticipated the journey on the boat from Baker Lake airfield to the institute to be easier for everyone if the men stayed drugged.

The four-hour flight was uneventful. The men woke briefly towards the end of the flight, and Pete injected them again, hoping it would not be enough to kill them. He would never know the thin line he approached towards almost ending their lives prematurely. The two men were completely unconscious when they were transferred from the plane to the waiting boat. The reinforced hull of the XO 260 Cabin Cruiser cut through icy waters with ease, and Pete had the men unloaded at Rio House before they regained consciousness. Beverly was waiting at the dock when they arrived.

"Take Mateo to my house and lock his friend in one of the rooms on the third floor. And remove their restraints, the plastic wrap is a bit much, but I understand why you did it." Beverly's voice was calm and firm as she spoke.

"Yes, Ma'am," Pete said. "You sure you want to remove all restraints?"

"Yes, where would they go, Pete?" Beverly said sarcastically.

"Yes, Ma'am. I'll take care of it." Pete knew better than to argue when Beverly's tone turned to sarcasm. He instructed two of his men to take Jake to the third floor and unwrap him. He gave explicit instructions to lock the door to the room and stand guard. Pete himself loaded Mateo onto a rolling cart and took him to Beverly's house, waiting until he had him inside before he removed the plastic and tape. He positioned the still unconscious Mateo in one of the chairs in the living room. Beverly arrived soon after and sat quietly while waiting for Mateo to regain consciousness. She asked Pete to stay close by in case Mateo got angry.

Mateo slowly regained consciousness; the repeated doses of the strong drug left him confused and groggy. He remembered pulling the car into the garage but did not remember getting out of the car. Where was Jake? They had been in the car together. His vision was gradually returning to focus, and he looked up to see Beverly smiling at him. How did he get here? This was what he had feared most. He had no idea how Beverly was going to react to his escape.

"Welcome back, sleepy," Beverly said scoldingly. "You've been a very bad boy, Mateo."

"Beverly, how did I get here? Where's Jake?" Mateo said, his speech slurred.

"Pete found you and brought you back home. And Jake is fine. He's in a room near your office." Beverly continued as if Mateo had only been gone a day, not months. "We still have a lot of work to do. I need you to administer my treatment, and we need to talk about what we want to do next with your bots. Jo is still here to help you, but the others were sent home." Beverly rambled.

"Okay, Beverly, I'll do whatever you want. I just need to know that Jake is safe." Mateo said, knowing that trying to do anything other than what she wanted was pointless.

"He's doing fine," Beverly said, picking up her tablet from the side table and navigating to the extensive network of video cameras. She pulled up a camera of the room where Jake was being held and showed the video to Mateo. Jake was seated in a conference room chair, his arms on the armrests and his head tilted forward and resting on his chest. He clearly had not regained consciousness. Mateo started to cry, soft tears falling quietly down his cheeks.

"I never meant to hurt him," Mateo said.

"I know, Mateo. But you made bad decisions, and other people get hurt when you do that. Now he's involved, and that's on you. He will be okay, as long as you do your job. Do you understand?" Beverly talked to Mateo like he was a child.

"Yes, Beverly, I understand." Mateo's response was demure and submissive.

"Excellent! Now, let's get you something to eat and drink, and we'll get to work." Beverly said cheerfully as she rose from her chair and motioned for Mateo to follow her to the kitchen.

Mateo tried to stand and immediately fell on the floor. Pete stepped in from where he was waiting in the next room and helped Mateo to the kitchen, seating him in a chair at a small bistro table near a window looking out on the forest.

"Do as you're told and everything will be okay. You know I take my orders from her. Just remember that." Pete whispered in Mateo's ear as he helped him sit in the chair."

Mateo nodded in agreement. Pete stepped back to the other room as Beverly joined Mateo at the small table, placing a prepared tray with small sandwiches and two cloth napkins in front of them. She walked back to the kitchen counter and returned to the table with two mugs of hot apple cider. As she sat in the chair opposite Mateo, she picked up her mug and sipped the warm liquid. Mateo did the same, his arms shaking as he gripped the mug tightly with both hands. The warm cider felt good going down his throat. He picked up a sandwich, suddenly ravenous, and shoved it in his mouth. The seasoned chicken, mozzarella, and pesto tasted wonderful, and I swallowed it without chewing it sufficiently. The wave of nausea that washed over him caused him to momentarily lose consciousness. Beverly's hand steadied him.

"Easy, Mateo. Eat slowly while you recover." Beverly comforted him.

"Okay, thanks. Can you make sure Jake has food, as well?" Mateo said.

"Oh, of course." Beverly spoke, aware that she should have done this already. "Pete, can you make sure Mateo's friend has food and something to drink?"

"Of course, Ma'am." Pete texts on his phone.

"Thank you," Mateo said.

"Let's talk about next steps." Beverly's tone converted to that business-like voice that she used when she needed to focus on encouraging people to comply with her instructions. "When can we complete my treatment?"

"I need at least two days to recover to make sure the mix is right. And I will need to coordinate things with Jo so that she understands everything as well. So, the day after tomorrow?" Mateo said, his speech slurred as he tried to sound like he was back to being a part of the team, knowing it was his only chance to keep both himself and Jake alive.

"That will work. Pete will take you to your apartment. Jake may join you there after we've had a talk with him. You will be escorted between your apartment and your lab and will always be under Pete's watchful eye. I'm sure you understand." Beverly said.

"Yes, Beverly. I understand." Mateo said quietly. "I need to rest and recover, then I'll be as good as new." He smiled at Beverly.

"Pete – please escort Dr. Trujillo to his apartment. Make sure someone is always outside his door. He may go to his lab when he wants, as long as he is escorted. Understand?" Beverly stood and addressed Pete directly.

Pete helped Mateo to his feet and supported him as they walked back through the snow to the institute building. When he was in his apartment, Mateo sat on the couch to think. He would play along until he could make his next move. But first, he must make sure that Jake remained safe. As possible strategies played through his mind, he drifted off to sleep.

32

Pete rushed into Beverly's house, not bothering to knock.

"Beverly!" He yelled. "The Russians are here. I need to get you to safety."

"What do you mean, the Russians are here?" Beverly screamed, running out from her bedroom in her flannel pajamas.

"They landed in a small seaplane and stormed the dock. They've already killed two of my men, and they keep calling your name. The one guy keeps shouting that you sold him defective merchandise. I don't know what they mean by that, but they are ransacking the building. My men are trying to take care of it, and I'm confident they will. Until then, I need to get you to safety." Pete said frantically.

Beverly grabbed a heavy coat from the coat rack in the foyer and rushed back to meet Pete in the kitchen. She opened the pantry door and pulled on a set of shelves, revealing a set of steps going down into a dark void. She flipped a switch on the wall, and a soft amber light illuminated the stairway. Pete followed Beverly down the stairs, and she punched a code into the keypad to the side of a heavy steel door. The door popped open a few inches with a hiss of the escaping positive air pressure. The code lived only in Beverly's head. She feared that anyone else outside the bunker might be convinced to reveal her hiding place. Pete had developed a hand gesture that would warn her if it was safe to open the door. Once locked inside, she would be able to see the stairway through a closed-circuit camera. If the coast was clear, Pete would touch his pointer finger lightly to his forehead in a natural gesture. If he were under duress, he would hold his arm loosely in front of his torso.

Beverly reached her fingers inside the door and pulled with some force to swing the door open enough to enter. As soon as she was in, Pete pushed the door closed as it locked automatically. The bunker had been built beneath the house during its construction. It had never been used but was always kept stocked. The bunker itself was a single room, well furnished with a bed and sofa along one wall and a long counter across the opposite wall. The shelves above the counter contained shelf-stable food for two people for three months. Beverly figured if anything happened that caused her to need the bunker longer than that, she would succumb to her disease, and her life would be over anyway. A small box contained a set of small vials of liquid specifically for this purpose. She was determined that she would not suffer if it came to that.

Books, several energy-efficient tablets, and memory sticks loaded with entertainment options would ease the pain of being underground for any extended length of time. A monitor to the left of the door contained squares of images that showed fifty of the hundreds of cameras around the island, institute, and her house. The images that she had chosen included the labs, the areas surrounding the two buildings, and the dock. It was the monitor that consumed Beverly's attention.

She watched a small cadre of men enter the front door of the institute. Four others waited by the dock with the two small seaplanes bobbing in the dark water. Suddenly, the four men at the dock dropped, three of them falling into the icy black water. Another figure ran towards the dock, crouching low as he moved. Pete's team was hunting the insurgents. The figure rolled the fourth man into the water and ran back to the building, entering the front door with caution.

Motion caught Beverly's eye on another section of the monitor. It was the third-floor lab. Men were running through the space as lights flickered, and machinery was destroyed. It was difficult to determine which of the men were on Pete's team as they fired at each other. She noticed a different person crouching in a doorway. It must be Mateo's friend. The man ran across the lab and into the storage closet, closing the door behind him. More flashes of light as the other men continued to fire at others from an area that Beverly could not see. Then stillness. She waited. Pete walked through the lab, his gun lowered, and two of his men following him. They must have subdued the Russians, she thought, as she watched Pete walk to the storage room door and try to open it. He kicked it with his booted foot – once, twice, and a third time hard enough to dislodge the door from its frame.

The man who had entered the room earlier kneeled on the floor; his hands held up in self-defense. A quick jab against his head with the butt of Pete's rifle made him fall to the side. Beverly watched as Pete turned and walked a few steps away to make room for one of his men to retrieve the unconscious man. Pete's teammate grabbed the back of the man's shirt and dragged him to the conference room that Beverly had used for the auction. Pete yelled something into his walkie-talkie and turned on his heels, making his way across the disheveled lab to the stairs by the elevator.

Moments later, there was a loud pounding on the door to the bunker. Beverly looked at the small monitor above the door and noticed Pete standing there with his finger casually resting on his forehead. She punched in the code to open the door. Pete pulled the door open, stepping into the room.

"The Russians are all dead. You are safe now." Pete said. "My team is taking care of the aircraft now. They will sink them at the western end of the lake. I have Mateo's friend in the large conference room on the third floor. One of my team members is retrieving Mateo to join him. I want to have a talk with them. Would you like to join us?"

"Yes, I want to know what the hell is going on," Beverly said as she rushed past Pete and up the stairs.

By the time Beverly and Pete reached the conference room. Jake and Tanner were sitting in chairs, facing each other. They were not tied to the chairs since four of Pete's men stood in four corners around them, their guns raised.

"Why would the Russians attack us?" Beverly asked Mateo, standing between the two seated men and facing him.

"I don't know Beverly. Why would I know?" Mateo said.

"They were saying the bots were defective. What does that mean?" Beverly continued.

"I have no idea. Maybe they don't know what they are doing with them and disabled them?" Mateo knew better than to admit that he was the one who sabotaged the bots.

Beverly turned to face Jake. "How long have you known Mateo?"

"Who's Mateo?" Jake asked, clearly confused.

"Jake. I'm Mateo." Mateo said, leaning his head around Beverly so that Jake could see him.

"What? I don't understand. You're Tanner. Who's Mateo?" Jake shook his head in confusion.

"Well, this is interesting," Beverly said, stepping to the side so the two men could see each other. "See, Jake, the man you know as Tanner Kingman – that's the name, right?" Beverly looked at Pete, who nodded in agreement. "The man you know as Tanner is actually Mateo Trujillo, my Chief Scientific Officer here at the Seagram Institute for Scientific Research." Beverly paused, waiting for a response from Jake.

"Is this true, Tanner?" Jake asked, looking at Mateo, the expression of hurt on his face causing Mateo to break down and sob.

"Yes, Jake, it's true," Mateo said through his tears. "My real name is Mateo Trujillo. I am a scientist. I created a new version of organic nanobots using algae, and Beverly funded my research. I left here without her permission and tried to create a new identity. I never intended to get you involved in all this. I'm sorry, Jake. I'm so sorry."

Jake sat silently, staring at Mateo, unsure what to say. His anger and confusion consumed him. He turned his face to Beverly. "I clearly don't know what's going on here and evidently do not know the man sitting in front of me. What do you want with me?"

"It's a valid question, Jake. I don't want or need anything from you." Beverly answered.

"If you send him away, I'll never do the treatment on you, Beverly. You'll have to start over with a new scientist and hope they know what they are doing. Let Jake stay. Let him live, and I'll do whatever you want. I promise." Mateo looked at Beverly with sincerity.

"Oh, Mateo, if he's that important to you, then of course you can keep him. Besides, you will need a distraction over the coming days, and it might be good for you to have a pet since Connor left you. Beverly's tone was condescending and parental.

Mateo looked at Jake with a look that said, 'I hope you see the crazy we're dealing with.' Jake's expression told Mateo that he understood.

"Jake, will you be good and stay in my apartment if I ask you to? You can still call me Tanner. It'll be like a game we have." Mateo laughed lightly.

"Of course, Tanner. I just want to be with you. I can be good. I promise." Jake responded, understanding what Mateo was trying to do.

"See, Beverly. He'll be a good boy. I promise." Mateo smiled brightly at Beverly, mustering all the skills he had learned to deal with Beverly.

"Well, okay. But this is the last stray you bring home. Understand?" Beverly was spiraling into a level of delusion that neither Mateo nor Pete had seen before.

"Thank you, Beverly. I'm happy to be back home, and I'm ready to start working." Mateo said. "It looks like the lab needs straightening up. Can you call Jo to help me? And I can show Jake how to help as well, unless you think it better that I put him away until after I finish work."

"Yes, we need to get the lab in order. I'll help. And Jo can help. And yes, Mateo, your little friend can help as long as he behaves." Beverly conceded.

"Then let's get started. May we have some food and music while we work? Like we used to?" Mateo asked.

"Excellent idea!" Beverly exclaimed as she texted furiously on her phone.

They all moved to the lab, Jake staying cautiously close to Mateo and remaining quiet. Jo arrived and greeted Mateo with trepidation and started checking the equipment. Mateo found a Bluetooth speaker and connected it to Beverly's phone as she started a playlist that they used to listen to when working together. Mateo gave Jake basic cleaning tasks, whispering to him that they would have a chance to talk later. A worker that Mateo did not recognize delivered trays of sandwiches, pretzels, fruit, and beverages. As he moved about, directing the efforts to get the lab up and running, he opened the drawer where he had placed the prepared syringes. They were intact. He could still distinguish the subtle mark that he had made on one of them.

Several hours later, the lab was in working order, and Mateo motioned for everyone to huddle near his personal workbench. "Good job, everyone. I think we are ready to move forward. Beverly — if it's okay with you, I think we should take a break until morning. Jo and I can start preparing for the treatment. We should be able to get it ready in two days now that everything is working."

"Of course, Mateo," Beverly responded. "Good job, everyone. I'll stop by tomorrow to check on things."

Mateo turned towards Jake. "You'll need to stay in the apartment while I work tomorrow. I'll make sure you have food, and there are plenty of entertainment options."

Jake nodded, and Beverly smiled.

Beverly walked off, presumably back to her house. Pete and his team dispersed, with only one of them remaining to look over Mateo and Jake. Jo told Mateo she would be in the lab at o-nine-hundred in the morning before going back to her apartment. Mateo and Jake walked to the elevator and took it down to the first floor, joined by the remaining female member of Pete's team. Jake and Mateo entered the apartment as the security guard took up her place outside the door.

The door closed, and Jake stepped towards Tanner, hugging him tightly.

"I'm so scared, Tanner," Jake whispered in his ear.

"I know, Jake. I'm so sorry." Tanner whispered back, barely loud enough for Jake to hear. "We can't talk openly here, but there is a place. Just follow my lead on things. I'll explain everything."

Jake hugged him tightly. They moved to the kitchen area, and Mateo took inventory of the few items that were there.

"We'll need to go shopping so that you'll have food for tomorrow. And for dinner tonight." Tanner said, walking to the door and motioning for Jake to follow him.

"Where do you think you're going?" The security guard asked roughly.

"We need to get food from the pantry. You can follow us." Tanner said, pushing past her and continuing down the hall, Jake following close behind him.

They reached the dining room, and Tanner noticed that several plates of food sat on the serving counter, insulated covers keeping the food warm.

"Looks like they prepared dinner for us. Let's eat here, then we will go shopping." Tanner said, turning to look at the guard. "There's food for you, too, if you want. We're going to sit by the window. You can eat by the door. I promise we're not going anywhere. I mean, what's the point?"

Tanner and Jake took plates of food, gathered napkins and silverware, and took a seat by the window. The meal was meatloaf, mashed potatoes, and green beans. Simple and very tasty. The guard hesitated but eventually took a plate and sat at a table by the door, eating slowly and keeping a careful eye on the two men. When they were done eating, they moved the dirty dishes to the serving bar, and Mateo told the guard they were going to the pantry to get food for the apartment. The guard walked into the hallway and took a look in the small room to verify there was nowhere else for them to go once in there and then allowed them to enter. She remained outside in the hallway while they shopped.

Tanner entered the room, grabbing two canvas totes from the hook on the wall as they entered, allowing the door to close behind them. As soon as the door closed, Tanner moved close to Jake and spoke softly. "This is one of the few places where there are no cameras. We can talk here; we just need to keep our voices low and put stuff in the bags as we do. Understand?"

"Yes, I understand. Now tell me what's going on." Jake demanded, grabbing a pack of crackers from the shelf and throwing them in his bag.

"It's a much longer story, but the short version is that I was not getting my research funded at the university. Beverly came along and offered unlimited funding if I came to work for her. I took it because I trusted her. And I had no other options. She has an incurable disease, and I found a cure using the phyconanobots that I created. We tested the treatment on others but waited to do it on her to make sure it lasted." Tanner continued to pick things off the shelf: cans of soup, shelf-stable microwave meals, and candy bars.

"That's very complicated," Jake said.

"It gets worse." Tanner continued. "There's a statue in a chamber on the first floor. That's a much longer story, but it's ancient and has powers. The treatment must be done near the statute to be effective. There's so much more to this Jake, there just isn't time right now to tell you. You must decide whether to trust me or not. You need to know that my feelings for you are genuine. The only thing I faked was my identity."

"It's bizarre, but I believe you. I'm not sure why, but I do. "Jake said. "And I love you so that might be clouding my thinking. Nevertheless, how do we move forward?"

The double entendre was not lost on Tanner as he continued. "I have a plan. Just be ready to stay near me when I come to get you. It might take a few days. Just always be ready. Understand?"

"Yes. Now let's get out of here before Atilla out there gets suspicious." Jake laughed nervously.

They quickly filled up the bags and opened the door. Tanner teased Jake about how many candy bars he took. The guard motioned for them to continue down the hallway to the apartment. Another guard had arrived and took up the sentry duty. Jake and Tanner entered the apartment and prepared a snack of cheese and crackers while they settled on the couch to watch a movie. The night was spent without talking, Jake's mind trying to avoid thinking about their situation, and Tanner's going over his plan.

They both slept well that night, the exhaustion from the previous few days overtaking them. Tanner woke at 7 a.m. and showered, brushing his teeth and moisturizing his face before getting dressed. Jake snored softly in bed. Tanner woke him to let him know that he was leaving. Telling him to take a bath and relax for the day, assuring him that nothing would happen today. Then he kissed him goodbye, left the apartment and walked to the lab. Two security guards were outside the door to the apartment. One stayed, and the other escorted Mateo to the lab.

33

When Mateo arrived at the Lab, Jo was focused on validating a batch of new phyconanobots, the monitor in front of her showing the recognizable creatures moving lazily around one another. Mateo walked to his bench and opened the drawer with the three syringes, pretending to search for something before closing the drawer and opening another. He took a pair of headphones from the second drawer, looked at them, realized he had nothing to connect them to, and tossed them on the bench.

Jo wandered over to Mateo's bench after finishing her work. "Where do we go from here?" She asked.

"We prepare to give Beverly the treatment," Mateo said blandly.

"I think you know what I mean, Mateo," Jo said firmly.

"I think our focus right now should be to prepare the syringes. We can talk about the rest later. Right now, can you verify this and double-check these calculations, please?" Mateo opened a paper notebook and started writing, positioning his body next to Jo's to shield any camera from seeing what he was writing.

I have a plan; it will happen quickly tomorrow. can I trust you? Mateo scribbled rapidly on the paper.

"Yes. That is correct. I'll be ready to help administer the treatment tomorrow." Jo said as she turned away and walked back to the area where she was working.

Mateo released the breath he did not realize he had been holding. He continued to write in the notebook, making fake notes over his scribbled message to Jo in an attempt to cover it if anyone else decided to look.

Beverly showed up a few minutes after Mateo's interaction with Jo. She was chipper and laughing as she flitted about the lab, looking at things, she clearly didn't understand and talking with Jo about her understanding of the procedure. Beverly eventually made her way to Mateo and prattled on about how well she slept and how nice it was for Mateo to have Jake here to keep him company. She finally exhausted herself with her manic behavior, and her tone turned serious.

"Tell me how this will go tomorrow." She said, talking about the treatment.

"We will have everything prepared by the end of day today. We should get started tomorrow mid-morning, let's say 10 a.m." Mateo suggested. "Rather than preparing you in a separate room as we did with the others, you can just come prepared, and we will do everything in the chamber. We will have the gurney and injections ready, and Jo will place the IV port when you get here."

"That sounds good. Do I need to be naked? I really would rather not. I have a white tunic I can wear that will give you access to the IV port." Beverly asked.

"That will be fine, Beverly," Mateo reassured her.

Happy with the answers, Beverly left to return to her house. Mateo and Jo decided to take a break for lunch. Mateo stopped by the apartment to get Jake, and the two of them met Jo in the dining room, accompanied by the guard stationed outside the apartment door, as well as the guard who had been in the lab. The three of them ate salads with grilled chicken in silence. When they were done and Jake had cleared all the plates, Mateo looked at Jo.

"Do you have any questions about the procedure tomorrow? It will be straightforward; we just need to be prepared for any anomalies. Beverly's situation is different from the others. She has decades of relationship with the statue. The others had just met it. That's the one unknown in this." Mateo spoke.

"No questions. I'll be prepared for whatever happens." Jo looked at him, showing understanding of their cryptic conversation. "I need to get some things from the pantry. Jake, do you need anything since you're holed up in the apartment?" Jo looked at Jake.

"I do, actually. I'll join you there." Jake said. "Tanner, you should join us, too, since we can't be left alone or separated without supervision." Jake made eye contact with one of the guards, who simply stared back without emotion.

The three of them entered the pantry, Jo and Jake taking a bag as they entered. Once the door had closed, Jo took a few random things from the shelves, as did Jake.

Mateo pulled them into a tight huddle and spoke quickly. "I can't tell you my plan, but there will be chaos during the procedure tomorrow. Jake, you need to be ready to go tomorrow. Be dressed and ready. Understand?"

Jake nodded.

Mateo continued. "Jo, get a bag ready tonight and have it ready to go. Don't bring it to the lab, just have it ready in your apartment. The one variable I have to deal with is Pete. But after tomorrow, I'm positive he will be on our side. Just be ready to go."

Jo and Jake nodded again. They exited the room laughing, as Tanner and Jake had done the night before. Jo teased Jake and Mateo about eating too much junk food. The guards escorted them to their apartments and then, after a short rest, escorted Jo and Mateo back to the lab. The two scientists busied themselves for the remainder of the afternoon preparing for the next day. They arranged the rolling bed in the statue chamber, alongside a rolling cart to hold the syringes. On the cart, Jo placed the sterile pre-wrapped supplies to insert the IV port into Beverly's vein.

The next morning, Beverly arrived at the lab at 9:30 a.m. with Pete accompanying her. She was dressed in a black cloak that brushed the floor. Mateo and Jo had already been there for an hour. Mateo had taken the marked syringe, and the axolotl cells syringe from the drawer and placed them on a tray on his bench. While Beverly waited in the lab with Jo, Pete escorted Mateo to the chamber with the syringes. Mateo placed the syringes on the rolling cart next to the gurney, both of which sat against the wall and well away from the statue.

"That thing still gives me the creeps," Pete said.

"Me too." Mateo agreed.

Mateo decided to take a chance and attempt a conversation with Pete.

"Hey Pete, I know you were just doing your job, but you understand why I ran, right?" Mateo asked.

"Yes, Mateo, you know I understand. But you are right that I was just doing my job." Pete answered kindly. "I think you also know that there are times when I would leave, if I could."

"We are in the same boat, for sure," Mateo said, laughing at the similarities in their predicaments. "Anyway, on to the task at hand. Things could be worse, right?"

"Yes, I suppose so," Pete said, offering a rare smile.

They walked back up to the lab, where Beverly was anxious to get started. With everything ready to go in the chamber, Beverly led the way down the elevator Jo the first floor and walked the long, circuitous route to the front entrance to the chamber, rather than taking the stairs from the second-floor lab. Mateo and Jo followed her, with Pete bringing up the rear. When everyone was in the chamber, Beverly unclasped the black cloak and let it fall to the floor. She was dressed only in a pure white silk caftan that shimmered in the amber glow of the lights in the circular room. The material moved like liquid around her as she sat on the edge of the gurney. Jo moved the back of the bed up so that Beverly could extend her legs and be in an upright position while she installed the IV port.

Resting Beverly's arms on her thigh, Jo cleaned Beverly's right hand with an alcohol pad and opened the sterile kits containing the items needed to install the port. She wrapped a temporary tourniquet around Beverly's upper arm and, with a quick and expert motion, Jo pushed the butterfly contraption into a vein on Beverly's hand, securing it with tape. She then attached the Y-split to the port and gently placed Beverly's hand by her side on the bed.

"I'm going to lower the head of the gurney and roll you to the statue. The procedure will happen quickly. In just a few minutes, you will be free from your pain and suffering." Jo informed Beverly, attempting to be kind.

She rolled the bed to the statue and engaged the lock. Mateo followed with the rolling cart containing the two syringes. As he approached the gurney, he hit the wheel lock with his toe, disengaging it.

"Are you ready, Beverly? It will happen quickly." Mateo asked.

"Yes. Let's do it, please." Beverly said nervously.

Mateo handed Jo the syringe with the axolotl cells and then picked up the other syringe.

"Insert your needle into the hub, please," Mateo instructed.

Jo inserted the needle into the split of the port, and Mateo did the same with his in the other side of the split.

"Push on my mark," Mateo instructed. "One... Two... Three... Push."

They emptied both syringes into the port. Mateo let the syringe fall from his hand as he grabbed the edge of the gurney and pulled it back towards him. Then, with as much force as he could gather, he pushed the gurney away from him. The wheeled bed rolled silently to the other side of the room, far away from Sednamaroq. Everyone watched in silence as the bed rolled, not sure what was happening. Beverly looked confused.

"Mateo! What's happening? Mateo!" Beverly screamed. She tried to sit up, but her body stiffened, the force throwing her back onto the bed. The alternate solution that Mateo had prepared had very specific instructions – ossify all available tissue. The bots eliminated the axolotl cells first, turning them to gravel flowing through Beverly's circulatory system. Then the bots started to reproduce, working on any available tissue as they multiplied.

Pete, Jo, and Mateo watched as Beverly's right hand turned the color of the statue, matching the silk cloth draped over her body. It took less than two minutes for her entire body to turn to stone. Her screams softened as her lungs collapsed. What living tissue remained convulsed until the conversion reached it. Her brain was the last to ossify. Her head was turned in the direction of the others, but her focus was on the statue. There was no blue light coming from it. It did not know that she needed help. Like all others in her life, it had ultimately abandoned her.

"Mateo, what did you do?" Pete mumbled.

"What no one else would. We need to act quickly. Pete – Do you have the means to destroy this building? I don't mean just a little, I mean level it?"

"Uh, yes. It will take some time, but yes." Pete said.

"Do you have a way to leave, with or without your team?" Mateo continued.

"Yes. What about you? Pete asked.

"I need to go to Beverly's house and get her phone. I'm going to pretend to be her and schedule a flight for us. I should have thought this through. I'm hoping her face will still unlock the biometrics of the phone." Mateo said, his anxiety showing.

"I'll go get the phone," Pete said. "You two get ready to leave. I'll tell you how to get across the lake when I get back. Once you get off the island, I'll take care of everything here."

"What about her body?" Jo said. "I don't want it anywhere near the statue."

"I'll take care of that as well," Pete said, rushing off to get Beverly's phone.

"I'll stay here. Go get your bag." Mateo said to Jo.

Jo ran out of the room and returned moments later, just before Pete arrived with Beverly's phone. Pete activated the phone and held it towards Beverly's body. The phone unlocked.

"Okay, I really didn't think that would work," Mateo said.

"Well, it did. Now what?" Pete said.

Mateo took the phone from Pete and opened the list of text messages, scrolling through to find the one for her pilot. He typed out a message letting the pilot know that she would be sending three people, two men and one woman, who needed to fly to Winnipeg. When he was done, he was to fly back and wait for her. The three would be arriving later this afternoon.

"Fingers crossed that actually works," Mateo said. "Okay, Pete, how do we get to the airfield?"

"There's an emergency ice sled. It will work on the ice or in near-freezing water. It's located in a building along the shore about a hundred yards from the dock. It's designed to auto-navigate to the western end of the lake. Beverly had it installed before the auction as a backup to get off the island. Get your things, and I will meet you there." Pete's tone had softened.

"Thanks, Pete," Mateo responded. "Jo, come with me to get Jake. And from now on, please call me Tanner."

"You got it, Tanner." Jo smiled at him as they walked briskly to get Jake.

Pete walked over to the gurney and wheeled Beverly's dead, ossified body out the door and into the front of the building. He had frantic and terse words with his remaining team, telling them briefly what had happened and instructing them in what to do with the body. He left the team to take care of Beverly's body and went back inside, walking down the corridor to the storage room that Beverly had assigned to him on his first week working for her. He grabbed two large duffel bags and emptied them of the survival gear inside.

He gathered every incendiary device he had collected over the past year and tossed everything into the two bags. He had accumulated a substantial supply of grenades, blocks of C4, and small, remote operated devices to access locked doorways. He had forgotten, however, about the two nukes. It had been an impulse purchase. He came across them on the black market and used his unlimited budget to have them delivered. They were small, each contained in a case the size of a carry-on suitcase. The instructions that had accompanied them were in Arabic, and he had spent several evenings with an online translation tool to help him understand how to work them. Ultimately, the operation of the devices was very simple. Once the case was open, there was an on/off switch that activated the arming system. Next, a timer had to be set. The maximum time was sixty minutes. The arming button, which was covered with a metal cap that had to be flipped up to work, was the last step. Once that was pressed, there was no turning back.

After the devices had arrived, Pete could not think of a use for them, but, like everything else, he never knew what she would need. And now he knew the purchase to be one of fate. This was their intended use. He placed them in the duffel bags and struggled to carry the heavy bags to the second floor, where the canisters of gases were stored. The cylinders of Argon, Helium, and Nitrogen were under pressure, and that would help. But the bigger bang would be noticed from the oxygen, hydrogen, ammonia, and methane. Of course, the nuclear devices would do enough damage on their own, but Pete wanted the island decimated, not just destroyed.

He scattered the variety of devices around the room, pushing some behind the cylinders and leaving room for the two nuclear devices in the center. With everything in place, he would make sure that Tanner, Jake, and Jo were on their way, then he would arrange his own exit before activating the weapons.

34

Tanner, Jake, and Jo waited at the ice sled. The conveyance looked like a flat-bottomed boat with a small shipping container sitting on it. As Pete had said, it was inside a small shed at the edge of the lake, not too far from the dock. The rectangular watercraft had windowed doors at each end and a very simple interior of padded benches along each side. A small console in one corner contained a touch screen and a start button. There seemed to be no way to steer it or otherwise operate it.

The door to the shed had been unlocked, so the three survivors sat quietly on the benches inside the ice sled until Pete arrived. Pete's entry to the shed startled them. He entered the cabin with them and pressed the start button. The screen came alive, and a low hum indicated that something was working beneath them. Pete touched the screen and selected the destination from a short list.

A green square appeared on the screen with the word 'GO' in it.

"When you press this, it will automatically go to the airfield at the western end of the lake. The journey will take about three hours, but the cabin is heated. There are two propulsion systems – treads for ice and a small propeller for water. I can only delay the explosion for an hour once I start the sequence. I need to prepare for myself as well, so you should be about ninety minutes along when it happens. You will feel it. And see it. I'm telling you this so that you are not surprised." Pete's instructions were quick and direct. "Any questions?"

"Be safe, Pete. And good luck. I'm hoping that if we see each other in the future, we can have a chat." Tanner said.

"You bet, Tanner." Pete winked at him. "Now, off you go. Press the button as soon as I leave."

The door to the shed closed, and Jo reached over and pressed the green button on the screen. The wall of the shed closest to the water lowered, and the vehicle slid forward into the icy water. The propulsion system engaged, and the sled moved smoothly along. A map on the screen showed their location, the estimated time and distance to the destination, and the status of the power supply.

Pete walked calmly to Beverly's house. He knew there were other boats near her house at her private dock, and he would take one of those. He vaguely remembered her telling him the keys to all the boats were in her kitchen, hanging on the inside of the cupboard door. He entered the house, found the keys on the back of the fifth door he opened, and decided to look around to see if there might be anything of value that he might take. The house was full of valuable things, but nothing that would translate to spendable cash when he was off the island. Surely Beverly kept cash somewhere? He looked in her bedroom and then in her closet. Then he saw it – a light glint of shiny black through the hanging clothes. He spread the clothes and revealed a sizable safe. It had a typical old-fashioned wheel and dial. Pete knew that most wealthy people who kept things in safes like this rarely locked them. It seemed it was just too much trouble to open each time they wanted a little spending cash or the diamond necklace to wear to a party. And Beverly was no different. Pete turned the handle, and the door pulled open with only a small amount of effort.

When the door opened, strips of LED lights illuminated the interior. The top shelf of the safe contained a small bag of loose diamonds, a Glock P17 pistol, and a stack of documents. The remaining selves were stacked with cash, from many countries, predominately Canadian and American dollars. Pete looked around the closet and found a large black hard-sided suitcase and a matching carry-on. He neatly placed as much of the cash in the suitcase as would fit and tossed the diamonds, documents, and gun in the smaller bag with whatever remaining cash he could fit.

He rolled the designer luggage to Beverly's private dock and looked at his options. All the keys from the back of the cupboard door were in the left cargo pocket of his pants. His choices were limited to several flat-bottomed skiffs and a sleek cabin cruiser. He fished the keys from his pocket and selected the one that looked like it might belong to the most expensive boat. It was a more substantial key attached to a teak keychain engraved with the letter 'S'. He loaded the luggage onto the speedboat and inserted the key. It was the correct choice, and the engines started with a rumble and a low thrum.

Pete released the mooring ropes and walked back to the helm. He moved the lever forward and piloted the boat the short distance to the main dock. After he shut off the dual engines, he loosely moored the boat with a single line and walked back into the building. His team had all left, as he had instructed, and the environment was eerily quiet. Avoiding the chamber with the statue, he raced up the front stairs to the second floor and to the room where he had staged the explosives.

Pete knelt in front of the two cases. He opened both of them and pressed the activation button on them at the same time. He set the timer for sixty minutes on the first and then on the second. He raised the metal caps covering the arming buttons and pressed them both simultaneously. The countdown started.

As he raced to the dock, he used the voice command to set a timer for fifty minutes on his smart watch. He jumped on board the boat, released the mooring line, started the engines and pushed the lever all the way forward. The boat jerked forward, gaining speed as Pete navigated the waters in the dimming light of evening. The V-shaped hull of the speed boat pushed through the slush of the icy water with ease. Twenty minutes into his journey, he did not notice when the boat traveled over the stone-like body of Beverly Lynn Seagram, lying prone in the soft mud beneath him.

Jake looked at the screen and noticed that they had been en route for almost two hours. Shouldn't they have heard the explosion by now? The screen said they had fifty minutes to their destination. He turned to look at Tanner, who had fallen asleep. He reached to wake him when a low rumble sounded. The noise woke Tanner and Jo, who had also fallen asleep.

"What was that?" Jo asked.

"Assuming it was the explosion we were expecting," Jake replied.

"Seemed underwhelming," Jo said curiously.

Tanner started to speak when the shockwave hit. The ice sled rocked and jerked, moving forward at a terrifying speed before resuming its previous trajectory. The screen flashed red, then yellow, with a notification that there was a course correction in progress.

"I was going to say that there might be a shockwave if the explosion was strong enough." Tanner chuckled.

The three of them stood and looked out the rear of the craft. The darkening sky was illuminated by a fierce orange glow accented by a small and strangely shaped mushroom cloud immediately recognizable as resulting from the detonation of a nuclear device.

"I didn't realize Pete had nukes," Jo said, her comment casual and portraying a lack of surprise.

"Does it really surprise you?" Tanner joked, as they all laughed.

There was a feeling of comfort in the explosion. If they could make it to Winnipeg, they might all be free, at last.

The mood lightened for the rest of the ride. They discussed how they would get from Winnipeg to Albuquerque. Jo said she wanted to join them until she figured things out. Both men agreed that it was acceptable. Commercial air travel seemed the simplest, and that's what they decided they would do. Then the conversation turned to the more immediate concern. What if the explosion triggered some warning to the pilot, and he refused to take them? How would they get away from Baker Lake?

The small dock was quiet when they arrived at the western edge of Baker Lake. Jo slung her backpack over her right shoulder and exited the ice sled's small cabin. She pushed her left arm through the other strap and secured the front strap across her chest as she stepped onto the dock. A single light mounted to a tall post barely illuminated the immediate area around the dock and shoreline. In the near distance, she could see other lights, presumably from the airfield itself. Tanner put on the backpack that held both his and Jake's things and followed Jo onto the dock. Jake hesitated, looking around carefully before joining them.

"How do we get to the plane?" Jake asked.

"We might have to walk," Tanner said, looking around to assess their situation.

"Wait, what's that?" Jo pointed past the end of the dock to a dark object at the edge of the light provided by the streetlamp.

"It looks like a truck," Jake said, as the three of them started walking towards it.

The snow and ice along the edge of the dock and on the dock itself indicated that it had not been used since the last storm. The hundred yards to the object were treacherous and cold. Deep drifts of snow-covered layers of ice made each step uncertain. They arrived at the object, and it was, indeed, a truck. A newer Ford F-150 that had been fitted with special tires to accommodate travel on snow and ice. Jo tried the door handle, and the vehicle was unlocked, a key fob sitting neatly in one of the cup holders. The keychain attached to the fob was a black rectangle with the words 'Seagram Industries ' stamped on it in silver letters. Jo assumed the truck had either been left there for them as a result of the deceptive text from dead Beverly or permanently lived there as a means for anyone from Seagram Industries to get from the dock to the hangar.

Jo removed her backpack and climbed in the driver's seat, holding her backpack in her lap. She pressed the brake with her right foot and then pressed the start button with her right forefinger. The truck started with some effort. She closed the door and adjusted the climate controls to get the heat started. Tanner got in the passenger seat, removing his backpack and tossing it to Jake, who had settled into the back seat. The truck's navigation system appeared on the screen, and Jo immediately saw how to get to the airfield, which was closer than she thought.

"Seatbelts, please," Jo said as she buckled her own. "Don't want to ruin this for stupid things." She laughed nervously as Jake and Tanner buckled their belts.

Jo reached the center console with her right hand and moved the shifter to drive. She tentatively pressed the gas pedal, and the truck moved forward slowly. They all remained silent as Jo competently drove them to the airfield and to the largest of the three hangars. During the short drive, Tanner thought about how beneficial it was to have someone like Jo, with her military background and intelligent disposition. He made a mental note to thank her for this once they were on the plane. If they got on the plane, that is.

Jo pulled up to the side of the hangar and placed it in park. She turned towards Jake and Tanner before turning off the truck. "We need to act like everything is normal. The pilot is expecting us, and we just need to continue as if Beverly sent us and everything is normal. Understand?" Both Tanner and Jake nodded in agreement.

She turned off the truck and opened the door, putting on her backpack, which had remained securely in her lap during the drive. Tanner opened his door and stood by the truck while he held his backpack by the top handle, letting it hang by his side. He waited for Jake to get out of the truck before he closed his own door. Each of them took deep breaths and walked to the door of the hangar. Tanner opened the door and stepped inside, followed by Jake and then Jo.

The inside of the hangar was warm. Beverly's plane sat in the middle of the large space. A small SUV was parked in the corner, presumably belonging to the pilot. The stairs to the aircraft had been lowered. As they walked towards the plane, the pilot appeared at the top of the stairs. He looked to be in his mid-fifties, fit, with salt and pepper hair peeking from under his cap. He was dressed in black pants and a white short-sleeve shirt typical of pilots. The epaulets on his shoulders had three bold lines in gold joined by an ornate letter 'S' that Tanner recognized as an obsolete logo of Seagram Industries.

"Hey there! I was wondering when you would show up." He said, smiling. "Let's get you on board and get going. Any bags?"

"Good evening!" Jo said cheerfully. "Nope, just our backpacks. It will be a short trip there and back. I think you're taking Ms. Seagram tomorrow?"

"Yes. There and back for me, and there again." The pilot laughed. "I'm Jake, by the way."

"Good to meet you, Jake. I'm Jo, and this is Tanner, and also Jake." She laughed as she motioned to Tanner and Jake, in turn.

The pilot laughed. "Two Jake's! I'm afraid it's just me on the flight today. The attendant couldn't get here due to the weather. But there's plenty of food and drinks. And it's a short flight."

They all entered the plane as they spoke, and the pilot showed them to the main cabin, pointing out the location of the galley and head as they moved. Jo sat on a long sofa-like seat along the left side of the cabin. Tanner and Jake sat opposite her on a similar, but shorter, seat.

"Buckle up, and we'll be on our way in about twenty minutes. I just need to call for a push and someone to open the hangar door. Oh, did you feel the small earthquake a couple of hours ago? We don't get many up here, but I felt a small rumble." Jake the pilot asked.

"Yes!" Tanner said. We didn't know what it was and assumed it was a small earthquake. We've never felt one up here before."

"It happens occasionally. Usually, no damage though." The pilot said. "Okay, buckle up, and I'll get us going."

They all fastened their lap belts and settled in, looking at each other with relief. They heard Jake, the pilot, talking on the radio with someone. A few minutes later, they all looked out the windows of the aircraft as the large door of the hangar slid open. Then the aircraft started slowly moving backwards. When it was fully out of the hangar, the tractor pushing the plane positioned it to face the runway. The pilot moved the airplane forward under its own power and taxied to the end of the single runway.

Tanner could feel the plane slip and skid as it barreled down the snowy runway, gaining speed before eventually lifting into the air. The climb was bumpy but soon calmed as they reached cruising altitude. The pilot's voice came over the intercom. "Might be a little bumpy, folks, but make yourselves comfortable. We'll be in Winnipeg in two hours and twenty minutes. Come see me if you need anything. The door to the cockpit is closed but unlocked."

"Anyone want something to eat or drink? I know I need something." Jo said, unbuckling her seatbelt and walking to the galley.

"I think a round of whiskey is deserved. And maybe some snacks." Tanner said. "Let us know what they have."

Jo disappeared into the cubby of the galley and returned a few moments later with a small tray containing three short glasses of amber-colored liquid surrounded by individual packs of snack crackers and cookies.

"Whiskey, neat." She said, placing the tray on the small table attached to the arm of the sofa, "And some snacks. There are sandwiches and other drinks, as well."

"This will do for now," Jake said, picking up a glass and raising it towards the others in a toast. Jo and Tanner picked up their glasses and raised them in a toast, clinking the glasses together before each took a sip.

"This is really good whiskey!" Jake said.

"You don't know Beverly like we do, but she would only have the best and most expensive stuff on board," Jo said.

"Then here's to Beverly and good taste," Jake said, raising his glass again.

Tanner and Jo returned the toast, remembering the importance of keeping up appearances until they had landed and departed the airport in Winnipeg. The remained of the flight was uneventful. They had sandwiches and sodas and chatted briefly about what to do after landing. Still worried about someone overhearing them, they talked in general terms about getting from the airport to the hotel and where they would meet Beverly tomorrow evening. Tanner ended the conversation by saying that they would talk about next steps once they had landed.

Jake, the pilot, came on the intercom and asked them to make sure their seatbelts were securely fastened and that they would be on the ground in ten minutes. True to his word, they landed ten minutes later, and it was a short taxi to the Seagram private hangar. When the plane had parked in the hangar and the doors had closed, Jake, the pilot, opened the door for them and lowered the steps.

"Thanks, folks, I called a car for you. Just let the driver know where you want to go. I'm going to say a quick goodbye to get the aircraft ready for this quick turn. I'll see you in a few days for the trip back." Jake, the pilot said.

They all thanked him and walked down the steps to the waiting black sedan. The driver, a young woman in her twenties, dressed in all black, her dark brown hair extending flatly from her brimmed cap, stepped out of the car and opened the doors for them. Jo took the passenger seat, placing her backpack on the floor between her legs.

"Where would you like to go?" the driver asked, looking to the side at Jo.

"We need to go to the main terminal to meet someone. If you can just drop us off at the arrivals area, please." Jo said, looking back at the others.

"Will do. Do you need me to wait?" The driver asked.

"No, thank you. We have other transportation arranged with the person we are meeting, who is arriving on a commercial flight." Jo responded quickly. Tanner was again thankful for Jo's ability to think on her feet.

The driver dropped them at the arrivals area, as requested, and the three exited the car and walked into the terminal. Once the driver had driven off, Jake turned to the other two.

"Now what?" he asked.

"I think we should get on the next flight to Albuquerque. We can talk about other things while we wait. We need to go over who might be left, who knows we were there. And what the possible fallout might be. I also think we should buy burner phones to keep in contact with one another." Jo suggested.

Tanner and Jake agreed. They waited in line at the ticket counter for a U.S. domestic airline and purchased tickets to Albuquerque, via Denver. Tanner used his bank card to purchase the tickets, and they had a moment of panic about identification at the counter until Jake realized that his wallet had remained in Tanner's backpack. Jo, of course, had kept her identification, along with some cash and other documents, in her backpack the entire time she had been at Rio House.

Once through the security checkpoint, they found a kiosk selling electronics where they purchased pay-as-you-go phones. Jo suggested they choose ones that allowed them to assign a U.S. phone number, rather than using a Canadian area code. The two hours before the flight boarded to Denver were spent setting up the phones and exchanging numbers.

The flight to Denver was smooth, and they settled into a quiet corner at the Denver airport to wait out the four hours until their flight to Albuquerque. Tanner used the internet browser on his new phone to search for news about any incidents reported in the Baker Lake area. He showed Jake and Jo the article that came up in the search.

BAKER LAKE, NU – *A large explosion has occurred at a private facility on a small island located in the eastern section of Baker Lake, Nunavut. The facility is rumoured to be owned by Seagram Industries. Aerial video taken by a helicopter tour company shows the complete devastation of the area known as Rio Island. If there were inhabitants, it is assumed there are no survivors. This is a developing story.*

The video accompanying the news brief showed a blackened island in the waters of Baker Lake. A large crater existed where Tanner recognized the institute building once stood. They all stared at the video, conflicting emotions running through them. They felt relief at the level of destruction. Pete had done his job and hopefully had escaped. They also felt the underlying worry of someone knowing they might have been there. And that they were no longer there.

"Who knows we were there?" Jo asked.

"Well, other than Pete, just the pilot. I don't think the driver would necessarily know that we were at the institute, just that we were at the airport." Tanner said. "The pilot will assume that Beverly was killed in the explosion. And Seagram Industries will most likely be looking for us, but I'm not sure how much they will care at this point, with Beverly presumed dead and her private project destroyed. They will be tied up in settling her estate for years. Beverly compartmentalized information about SISR. I know that she did not allow anyone on the board of Seagram Industries to discuss it. And they let her have it because it kept her out of their way. All that being said, I think we need to be cautious, but otherwise, I think we are safe. Everything that threatened us has been destroyed."

"I hope it's that simple, Tanner. I really do." Jo said softly.

"Me too," Jake said. "I think we should just get on with our lives. For you two, you can always say that Beverly fired you and sent you home. No one would know otherwise. And from what I've heard from you, it is not uncommon for her to discard people when she has no use for them."

"You have no idea," Tanner said, tears forming in his eyes as he thought of Connor.

"What? What did I say?" Jake asked, concerned that he had said something inappropriate.

"Nothing," Jo said. "Beverly didn't just fire people. She literally disposed of them. We both lost people close to us while working at SISR."

"Oh, I see. I'm sorry." Jake said.

"You wouldn't have known. And it's a conversation you and I will have later." Tanner said, putting his arm on Jake's shoulder in comfort.

The flight to Albuquerque was easy. Tanner and Jake decided that Jo would stay with them until she could figure out what she wanted to do and where she wanted to be. They took a car service from the airport to their house and were reminded of the struggle when they entered. Tanner started cleaning up, needing to get things back to normal. Jo settled in the guest room and started making a list of things she would need. Tanner suggested they go to dinner at a local place that was a favorite of his and Jake's. Over enchiladas and beer, they finally acknowledged the events of the past few weeks. The stories Jake heard were fantastically unbelievable.

Tanner recounted the history of the statue and the story of Beverly's great-grandfather and the bear. He talked about Beverly's disease and her monomaniacal quest for a cure. Jo told them the story of her recruitment, pointing out common features between Beverly's approach towards recruiting Tanner. Jake listened quietly, asking questions when he truly did not understand something.

"I hope you can forgive me for lying to you," Tanner said to Jake.

"I do forgive you, Tanner. After hearing your stories, I understand why you did what you did. Anyone would have done the same. You've endured a lot to be free from her." Jake reassured him. "I just want us to pick up where we left off. We just need to discuss what we want out of the rest of our lives and what that looks like." Jo smiled at them as they had this conversation in front of her.

"Thank you, Jake. You mean the world to me. I don't want to lose you." Tanner said, thinking of things he might or might not tell Jake. Like the phyconanobots that lived happily in their suspension liquid in a vial behind a section of wall that he had cut out in the closet of Jake's house. The bots that he had with him when they met. Did Jake really need to know about this? He wasn't sure. And for now, it wasn't important.

35

Pete's body slammed into the console of the boat. The shockwave from the blast pushed his face into the glass of the windshield, breaking his nose. Blood splattered on the controls and steering wheel, causing Pete to momentarily lose his grip. The boat careened wildly to the left, threatening to turn back towards the island. He pushed himself upright and regained a firm grip on the wheel, putting the boat back on course towards the western end of the lake. He thought he had gained enough distance to avoid damage, but the blast had been stronger than he had calculated.

Before pressing the buttons on the devices, he had decided what he would do if he lived. He was going to turn himself in to the Seagram board of directors. He repeated the story in his mind: Beverly had directed the research team to do something they did not want to do. He was not sure what it was since he did not understand the words they used. The research team argued with her, but in the end, she won. She always did. Beverly always got what she wanted. She had sent him on an errand to patrol the waters around Rio Island and the surrounding smaller islands. She was paranoid that a foreign government wanted her research. Pete had been on the boat when the explosion occurred. He turned back after the shockwave and circled the island. When he saw the damage, he immediately used the radio to call for help, but no one answered his calls. So, he headed for the airfield, thinking he would find someone there to help him.

Pete thought the story was both solid and believable. Anyone who knew Beverly would not doubt that she could strong-arm her workers into doing what she wanted. He would also tell them that all the researchers were still on the island when the explosion happened. This would solve the mystery of the ones that he had killed. The ones presumed missing. It would also help Jo, Tanner, and Jake live their lives without fear.

His biggest challenge would be hiding the bags containing the money. If he could get them to Winnipeg, he could hide them before going to the board. He would worry later about how to get the money into the U.S.

When Pete arrived at the airfield, he saw the ice sled moored to the dock. He prayed that the three people on it had made it safely to Winnipeg. He locked the bags in a compartment in the hold of the boat and walked in the dark to the airfield. He had accompanied Beverly on many trips from the airfield and had been responsible for her safety. His working knowledge of the area and the buildings was better than the people who worked there. His face was still bloody from hitting the windshield, so he cleaned it with snow as best he could on the walk. He entered the Seagram hangar and noticed that the plane was gone. Seeing the missing plane gave him hope that the others had escaped. There was a light coming from the window of the small office that was built into the corner of the hangar. The hangar was warm, and Pete walked slowly towards the office, allowing himself to warm up and not wanting to startle whoever might be in the office.

He knocked lightly on the office door. There was movement from the other side, and the door opened, revealing an older man in dirty coveralls, his shaggy gray hair sticking limply to his forehead. The man recognized Pete as Beverly's chief of security.

"Hi Joe," Pete said. "Sorry to bother you so late."

"Hi ya, Pete. No worries. What can I do ya for" Joe said in his Newfie accent. From previous interactions with Joe, Pete had learned that he had grown up in St. John's. Joe's personality reminded Pete of his own father.

"Well, Joe, I need to get to Winnipeg. I know Beverly's plane is taking a few of the scientists there, and then the plane is returning to take Beverly tomorrow. Is there another plane that can take me tonight?" Pete tried to sound desperate.

"I think there might be a guy with a smaller plane. Is it just you? Any cargo?" Joe asked.

"Just me. And two bags." Pete said.

Joe picked up the phone on the desk and dialed a number. He had a brief conversation with the person on the other end and hung up. "Toad'll take you. It's a small Cessna, but it'll get you there."

"Toad?" Pete asked.

"Yeah, always called him that. I think because he's always under something. Working on a plane, a car, or heavy equipment. He's not much of a talker, so don't try to chat him up. And he'll bill the Seagram account, but if you have any extra, he'd appreciate it." Joe continued.

"I can take care of that," Pete said. "Any suggestion on how much? 500? 1000?"

"Oh, 500'll do it. A thousand might be too much." Joe said. "Where are your bags?"

"On the boat. I'll get them." Pete said.

"Take my truck. It's out back." Joe tossed a set of keys at Pete. "I'll have him pull the plane into the hangar. He should be ready to go in about 30 minutes."

Pete took the keys and drove Joe's old Dodge truck to the dock. He retrieved the bags from the boat, threw the boat keys in the lake, and tossed the bags into the bed of the truck. By the time he got back to the hangar, Toad was waiting with his 1987 Cessna 182R Skylane. What a perfect choice, Pete thought. The 182R had an increased cargo load capacity, seating for four, and enhanced range. The aircraft looked brand new. Toad clearly took care of it. Toad walked around from behind the plane, extending his hand in greeting.

"Toad," Toad said.

"Pete," Pete said

"Winnipeg?" Toad asked.

"Yep," Pete said, extending his hand with five hundred dollars he had taken from his smaller bag. "For your troubles."

"Thanks, throw yer bags in the back and sit up front with me. We'll get in the air right away." Toad said.

Pete opened the small cargo door and tossed the two bags into the compartment. He walked around to the other side of the aircraft and got in the front seat next to Toad, who was ready to go. Toad handed him a headset.

"I'm not much for talkin, but if you have a question or need anything..." Toad said, letting his word drift off, indicating his preference not to talk.

Pete donned the headset, and Toad started the single-engine plane. They taxied quickly to the end of the dark runway and were in the air two minutes later. There was no visual reference during most of the flight. The dark of northern Canada with few towns between Baker Lake and Winnipeg felt like flying into the unknown, an analogy that was not lost on Pete. At some point, he fell asleep. He woke when Toad contacted the Winnipeg air traffic controllers.

"On the ground in five minutes," Toad said, turning his head and smiling at Pete.

Pete nodded and looked around him. The sun would soon rise, and there was an ethereal haze oozing from the horizon. The landing was smooth, proof that Toad had been flying this plane for a long time. It would not have surprised Pete if he had learned that Toad had bought the plane new, with money he had saved for many years. They taxied to the Seagram hangar and Toad parked the aircraft, exiting it with a nimbleness that surprised Pete, considering they had been sitting in the same position for three hours. Pete, however, was stiff, and it took him several minutes to stand upright after getting out of the tight quarters.

"Thanks, Toad. I owe you one." Pete said.

"Welcome, Pete. I'll fly you any time." Toad said, extending his hand for a shake.

Pete shook his hand and walked to the office in the hangar. The station master knew Pete on site and rushed out to greet him. Letting him know the car was ready to take him where he needed to go.

Pete got in the back seat of the car and noticed the female driver, who was unfamiliar to him.

"Did you drive for the others that arrived earlier?" He asked.

"Yes, I took them to the arrivals pick-up area. Said they were meeting someone there." She said, "Where would you like to go?"

"Car rental center, please," Pete said.

She dropped him off at the car rental center, where Pete rented a small car. He carefully placed his bags in the trunk and sat in the driver's seat. He pushed the button to start the vehicle and adjusted the heat to get warm. While the car warmed up, he looked on his phone for the nearest indoor storage facility. He put the address in the navigation and tried to go over his plan on the short drive. He would rent a small storage unit, place the bags there, and then contact Seagram Industries. When he arrived at the storage facility, he rented the smallest unit available and paid cash for a year in advance. As he was moving the bags to the storage, his phone rang. The caller ID said 'Unknown'. Pete decided to let them leave a voicemail. Very few people had his number, and the chance of it being a telemarketer was rare.

When he had secured the bags in the storage locker, making sure to take out some cash and the backpack he had shoved into the larger bag, he checked the voicemail. It was Seagram Industries. They were trying to locate any survivors from the explosion at the Seagram Institute for Scientific Research on Rio Island. They left a number for him to call that was different from the number that was called. Pete dialed the number.

"Tom Tidewell," the voice on the other end answered the call. Pete recognized the name. Tom was the chairman of the board for Seagram Industries.

"This is Pete Harris," Pete said.

"Hello, Pete. We need to talk. Were there any other survivors?" Tom asked.

"No. Just me. I'm safe. Just disoriented. I can be in Winnipeg tomorrow." Pete said.

"Perfect. My office. 4pm. You know the address?" Tom asked.

"Yes. I'll see you then." Pete said

Pete drove to a hotel downtown near the Seagram Industries building and got a room for three nights, thinking that he could extend it if he needed to, but planned on otherwise leaving after that. He checked into the room, ordered food, ate, and fell asleep. His sleep was deep, and he didn't wake up until midday on the day of his meeting with Tom. He walked the two blocks to the Seagram Industries building and took the elevator to the 31st floor. He entered the heavy wooden doors to the executive offices and told the receptionist who he was. She immediately escorted him to Tom's office.

The meeting with Tom was brief and to the point. Tom wanted to know what had happened. They had sent investigators to the island that morning and assumed that everyone was dead. Pete told his story, as he had practiced it. Tom seemed relieved that Beverly might be dead and tried to hide this from Pete. Pete remained stoic during the conversation, not wishing any additional attention on himself or the three survivors who had escaped. Pete also considered that no one knew Jake had been on the island. And he knew that Mateo-Tanner had no living relatives, and neither did Jo. So, who would they contact?

Tom thanked Pete and told him that the SISR initiative would thankfully be dissolved. And that he would be compensated for his dedication to Beverly and her cause. Pete asked about Beverly's estate. Tom told him that Beverly had assumed that she would one day have an heir but never did. So, the proceeds of her fortune would go to various charities and, of course, back into the company itself. Tom's comments indicated that the board had made sure that things were legally intact should anything ever happen to Beverly.

"We all know how Beverly can be. Could be, I mean. So, there's no point in pretending otherwise. Everyone who has ever worked for her ends up with the same understanding about her. The board knows this well." Tom said. "All we need from you, Pete, is a couple of signatures on the NDAs, then you're free to go on with your life as if you had never met Beverly Lynn Seagram. How does that sound?" Tom wanted to extend as much courtesy as possible.

"Sounds good. I'll gladly sign the non-disclosure agreements and never talk, or think, about SISR or Seagram Industries again." Pete said firmly.

Pete signed the NDAs and left the Seagram Industries building feeling good about his actions and the destruction of Rio House. He went back to the hotel and booked a plane ticket to Dallas. He would live there with a buddy of his until he could figure out what he wanted to do with his life, and more importantly, how to get the roughly three million dollars in cash to the U.S.

36

The two nuclear devices counted down to zero. The detonation that occurred was strengthened by sixteen canisters of lab gases, twenty-three fragmentation grenades, eighteen concussion grenades, seven blocks of C4 plastic explosive, and a small variety of experimental explosive devices that Pete had otherwise acquired. There was one crucial piece of information that no one currently alive knew about the construction of Rio House.

Beverly's father and grandfather had designed Rio House to withstand the harsh winters of northern Canada and to stand strong under any other disaster, including the threat of war. The solution - at the time of construction - had been to line the roof of the building with a five-inch layer of lead. The architect had told Jacob and James that the absurd amount of lead would not only protect the inside of the building from outside threats but would also protect the outside from any exceptional anomalies that might happen on the inside as a result of experiments being conducted there. They agreed with the extreme suggestion, withholding no cost to reach their goal. Support columns were redesigned and strengthened to accommodate the weight. The adjustments required engineering that seemed risky. Weighing in at 2.05 pounds per square inch, the roof of the building would exceed a total weight of just over six thousand tons. Defying the risk involved, the building had remained intact and protective of its purpose for decades.

The explosion that Pete had intended to blow UP the building blew it DOWN instead. When the enhanced explosion released its vast amount of energy, the lead shield forced the expanding reaction down and out, instead of up. The typical mushroom cloud occurred as a result of the explosion escaping the sides of the building, however, a full eighty percent of the force pushed the building, and everything that it contained into a deep crater that was neatly capped by a massive slab of molten lead that had melted into a misshaped subterranean dome over the debris of Rio House.

The dust that was launched into the air eventually settled on top of the dome of metal, giving the appearance of a scorched island, rather than a destroyed building. The aerial surveillance by Seagram Industries aircraft showed flattened trees on neighboring islands with only blackened dirt on Rio Island itself.

Beneath the mass of lead and layers of earth, Sednamaroq remained upright, a soft blue light emanating from it, permeating mere millimeters into the dirt that enclosed it. As the statue's blue glow intensified, the enemy of Sednamaroq awakened.

Called Adharc-Biastag by the Picts, the depiction of a worm with the head of a unicorn stood proudly and defiantly in Fingal's Cave on the isle of Staffa. The deep red glow from the body of the Stoor worm intensified as the light from Sednamaroq diminished. Sednamaroq decided to sleep, but not to die, and would wait until it was needed again.

Epilogue

Tanner sat on his knees in the closet of the bedroom that he shared with Jake. He cleared the items blocking the back wall of the closet and ran his fingers along the baseboard to feel a barely discernable seam in the sheetrock. He pressed firmly and broke the seal of the two-inch by four-inch panel that he had removed months ago to hide the small vial of phyconanobots. He reached into the tight space and removed the vial, looking at it thoughtfully. Jake would be home in an hour, and he needed to decide what to do.

Earlier that day, a parcel had been left on their front porch, and a knock on the door and the security camera alerted him of someone's presence. The camera showed a figure, dressed in black, with a ball cap pulled low to hide their face. The parcel was a black duffel bag. Pete opened the door, looked around, and dragged the bag inside. He cautiously examined the bag and noticed a note attached by a string to the two joined handles that rested on top. Tanner unfolded the note without detaching it and read it twice to make sure he understood its meaning.

Tanner — *I hope you and Jake are doing well. I am good. Use this to continue your research. For the good of mankind, not bad. I will be in touch when I can, I promise.* — **Pete**

Tanner opened the bag and revealed neatly arranged bundles of hundred-dollar bills. With a quick calculation, Tanner estimated the amount to be near one million dollars. What did this mean? And where did Pete get this kind of cash? How would he explain this to Jake without telling him about the bots he had stashed?

This is what brought him to his current dilemma. He would have to tell Jake. Jo had remained in Albuquerque and was working at a local private research lab. He was sure she would partner with him to start a lab of their own. When Jake arrived home, Tanner was sitting in a chair at the kitchen table, holding the green-glowing vial gently in his lap.

"What's that?" Jake asked.

"We need to talk," Tanner answered, hoping that this would be the beginning of many things, and not the end.

About Gray Taylor

Gray Taylor lives in Albuquerque, New Mexico, with his husband and their corgi. You might find him writing at local coffeehouse or running in the Bosque. If you see him, please compliment his kilt and his beard – he loves that. And don't forget to ask him what he's writing next.

An apology from the author:

A previous addition of this novel was published, in error, in an unedited format that contained errors. If you purchased one of these copies, please contact me through my website (provide verification of purchase, if possible) and I will send you an updated edition.

Sincerely, Gray

www.BooksByGray.com

Acknowledgements

As with any literary work, I have depended on the support of many in this endeavor — too many to name individually. For those that might feel left out, I apologize. Foremost, I am deeply grateful for the support of my husband, Shayne. He believed in this project when others thought that my focus should have been elsewhere. As he often reminds me, we are on this path together. Additionally, I would like to thank my dear friend Jason — you are always there to listen, provide honest feedback, and encouragement. I appreciate the time with you more than you will ever know.

To the folks at the Iceland Writers Retreat, my time with you all in 2025 kick-started this particular book. Each of you, in ways that you don't know, encouraged me to keep writing. I look forward to future retreats and to connecting both there and outside the IWR environment.

To those the fellow writers that met over coffee, flapjacks, and Welsh cakes at Hay Festival in 2025 — thank you. Much of this manuscript was written in a yurt, in a field, near Hay-on-Wye, as well as in the Hay Festival lounge. I love living in a world where thousands gather in a remote Welsh village to celebrate literature.

To other friends and family, thank you for tolerating my ramblings as I researched the various subtleties of organic nanobots, much of which influenced the story but never made it into the manuscript. My parents always allowed me to indulge my imagination and follow my dreams, and for that I am grateful.

And to my fans – those that say hello in coffee shops, compliment my beard, and ask about my kilts; those who carry copies of the Volywr books for me to sign at gatherings, and those who send me pictures of themselves reading the Gray Wilder books – Thank you for your support. Thank you for reading my books. Thank you for reaching out with questions and comments. Thank you for the connections.